THE GIFT OF THE MAGI

AND

OTHER STORIES

THE WORLD'S BEST READING

The Reader's Digest Association, Inc.
Pleasantville, N.Y. Montreal

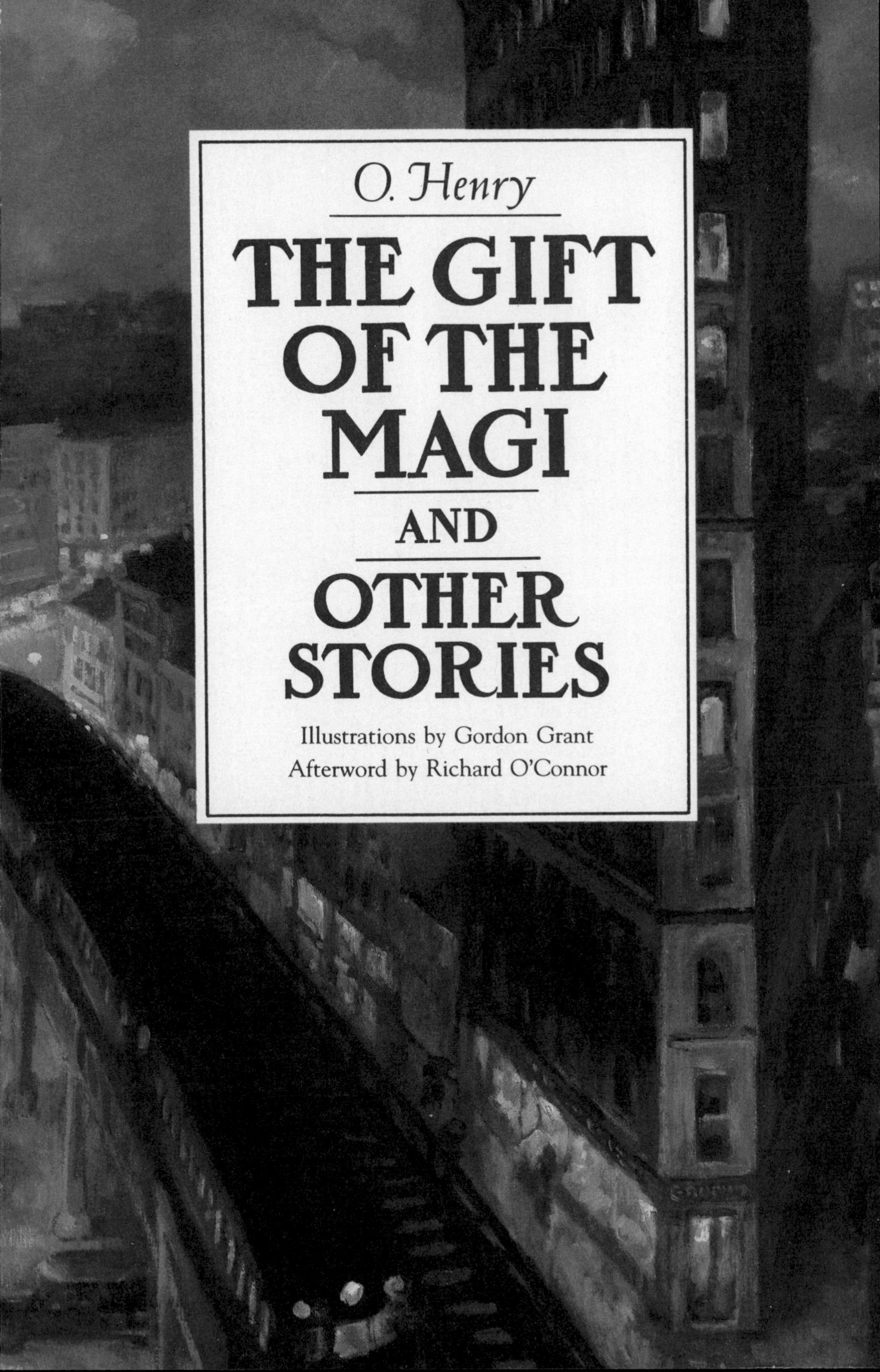

O. Henry

THE GIFT OF THE MAGI AND OTHER STORIES

Illustrations by Gordon Grant
Afterword by Richard O'Connor

The Gift of the Magi and Other Stories

Title page painting courtesy of The National Gallery of Art, Washington, D.C. Gift of Helen Farr Sloan.

Illustrations by Gordon Grant courtesy of Douglas Grant.

Library of Congress Catalog Card Number 87-60922
ISBN 0-89577-266-3

Printed in the United States of America

CONTENTS

ILLUSTRATIONS

THE GIFT OF THE MAGI

ONE dollar and eighty-seven cents. That was all. And sixty cents of it was in pennies. Pennies saved one and two at a time by bulldozing the grocer and the vegetable man and the butcher until one's cheeks burned with the silent imputation of parsimony that such close dealing implied. Three times Della counted it. One dollar and eighty-seven cents. And the next day would be Christmas.

There was clearly nothing to do but flop down on the shabby little couch and howl. So Della did it. Which instigates the moral reflection that life is made up of sobs, sniffles, and smiles, with sniffles predominating.

While the mistress of the home is gradually subsiding from the first stage to the second, take a look at the home. A furnished flat at eight dollars per week. It did not exactly beggar description, but it certainly had that word on the lookout for the mendicancy squad.

In the vestibule below was a letter-box into which no letter would go, and an electric button from which no mortal finger could coax a ring. Also appertaining thereunto was a card bearing the name "Mr. James Dillingham Young."

The "Dillingham" had been flung to the breeze during a former period of prosperity when its possessor was being paid thirty dollars per week. Now, when the income was shrunk to twenty dollars, the letters of "Dillingham" looked blurred, as though they were thinking seriously of contracting to a modest and unassuming D. But whenever Mr. James Dillingham Young came home and reached his flat above he was called "Jim" and greatly hugged by Mrs. James Dillingham Young, already introduced to you as Della. Which is all very good.

Della finished her cry and attended to her cheeks with the powder rag. She stood by the window and looked out dully at a gray cat walking a gray fence in a gray backyard. Tomorrow would be Christmas Day, and she had only $1.87 with which to buy Jim a present. She had been saving every penny she could for months, with this result. Twenty dollars a week doesn't go far. Expenses had been greater than she had calculated. They always are. Only $1.87 to buy a present for Jim. Her Jim. Many a happy hour she had spent planning for something nice for him. Something fine and rare and sterling—something just a little bit near to being worthy of the honor of being owned by Jim.

There was a pier-glass between the windows of the room. Perhaps you have seen a pier-glass in an eight-dollar flat. A very thin and very agile person may, by observing his reflection in a rapid sequence of longitudinal strips, obtain a fairly accurate conception of his looks. Della, being slender, had mastered the art.

Suddenly she whirled from the window and stood before the glass. Her eyes were shining brilliantly, but her face had lost its color within twenty seconds. Rapidly she pulled down her hair and let it fall to its full length.

Now, there were two possessions of the James Dillingham Youngs in which they both took a mighty pride. One was Jim's gold watch that had been his father's and his grandfather's. The other was Della's hair. Had the Queen of Sheba lived in the flat across the air-shaft, Della would have let her hair hang out the window some day to dry just to depreciate Her Majesty's jewels and gifts. Had King Solomon been the janitor, with all his treasures piled up in the basement, Jim would have pulled out his watch every time he passed, just to see him pluck at his beard from envy.

So now Della's beautiful hair fell about her, rippling and shining like a cascade of brown waters. It reached below her knee and made itself almost a garment for her. And then she did it up again nervously and quickly. Once she faltered for a minute and stood still while a tear or two splashed on the worn red carpet.

On went her old brown jacket; on went her old brown hat. With a whirl of skirts and with the brilliant sparkle still in her eyes, she fluttered out the door and down the stairs to the street.

Where she stopped the sign read: "Mme. Sofronie. Hair Goods of

All Kinds." One flight up Della ran, and collected herself, panting. Madame, large, too white, chilly, hardly looked the "Sofronie."

"Will you buy my hair?" asked Della.

"I buy hair," said Madame. "Take yer hat off and let's have a sight at the looks of it."

Down rippled the brown cascade.

"Twenty dollars," said Madame, lifting the mass with a practised hand.

"Give it to me quick," said Della.

Oh, and the next two hours tripped by on rosy wings. Forget the hashed metaphor. She was ransacking the stores for Jim's present.

She found it at last. It surely had been made for Jim and no one else. There was no other like it in any of the stores, and she had turned all of them inside out. It was a platinum fob chain simple and chaste in design, properly proclaiming its value by substance alone and not by meretricious ornamentation—as all good things should do. It was even worthy of The Watch. As soon as she saw it she knew that it must be Jim's. It was like him. Quietness and value—the description applied to both. Twenty-one dollars they took from her for it, and she hurried home with the eighty-seven cents. With that chain on his watch Jim might be properly anxious about the time in any company. Grand as the watch was, he sometimes looked at it on the sly on account of the old leather strap that he used in place of a chain.

When Della reached home her intoxication gave way a little to prudence and reason. She got out her curling irons and lighted the gas and went to work repairing the ravages made by generosity added to love. Which is always a tremendous task, dear friends—a mammoth task.

Within forty minutes her head was covered with tiny, close-lying curls that made her look wonderfully like a truant schoolboy. She looked at her reflection in the mirror long, carefully, and critically.

"If Jim doesn't kill me," she said to herself, "before he takes a second look at me, he'll say I look like a Coney Island chorus girl. But what could I do—oh! what could I do with a dollar and eighty-seven cents?"

At seven o'clock the coffee was made and the frying-pan was on the back of the stove, hot and ready to cook the chops.

Jim was never late. Della doubled the fob chain in her hand and sat on the corner of the table near the door that he always entered. Then she heard his step on the stair away down on the first flight, and she turned white for just a moment. She had a habit of saying little silent prayers about the simplest everyday things, and now she whispered: "Please God, make him think I am still pretty."

The door opened and Jim stepped in and closed it. He looked thin and very serious. Poor fellow, he was only twenty-two—and to be burdened with a family! He needed a new overcoat and he was without gloves.

Jim stopped inside the door, as immovable as a setter at the scent of quail. His eyes were fixed upon Della, and there was an expression in them that she could not read, and it terrified her. It was not anger, nor surprise, nor disapproval, nor horror, nor any of the sentiments that she had been prepared for. He simply stared at her fixedly with that peculiar expression on his face.

Della wriggled off the table and went for him.

"Jim, darling," she cried, "don't look at me that way. I had my hair cut off and sold it because I couldn't have lived through Christmas without giving you a present. It'll grow out again—you won't mind, will you? I just had to do it. My hair grows awfully fast. Say 'Merry Christmas!' Jim, and let's be happy. You don't know what a nice—what a beautiful, nice gift I've got for you."

"You've cut off your hair?" asked Jim, laboriously, as if he had not arrived at that patent fact yet even after the hardest mental labor.

"Cut it off and sold it," said Della. "Don't you like me just as well, anyhow? I'm me without my hair, ain't I?"

Jim looked about the room curiously.

"You say your hair is gone?" he said, with an air almost of idiocy.

"You needn't look for it," said Della. "It's sold, I tell you—sold and gone, too. It's Christmas Eve, boy. Be good to me, for it went for you. Maybe the hairs of my head were numbered," she went on with a sudden serious sweetness, "but nobody could ever count my love for you. Shall I put the chops on, Jim?"

Out of his trance Jim seemed quickly to wake. He enfolded his Della. For ten seconds let us regard with discreet scrutiny some inconsequential object in the other direction. Eight dollars a week or a million a year—what is the difference? A mathematician or a wit would give you the wrong answer. The magi brought valuable gifts, but that was not among them. This dark assertion will be illuminated later on.

Jim drew a package from his overcoat pocket and threw it upon the table.

"Don't make any mistake, Dell," he said, "about me. I don't think there's anything in the way of a haircut or a shave or a shampoo that could make me like my girl any less. But if you'll unwrap that package you may see why you had me going awhile at first."

White fingers and nimble tore at the string and paper. And then an ecstatic scream of joy; and then, alas! a quick feminine change to hysterical tears and wails, necessitating the immediate employment of all the comforting powers of the lord of the flat.

For there lay The Combs—the set of combs, side and back, that Della had worshipped for long in a Broadway window. Beautiful combs, pure tortoise shell, with jewelled rims—just the shade to wear in the beautiful vanished hair. They were expensive combs, she knew, and her heart had simply craved and yearned over them without the least hope of possession. And now, they were hers, but the tresses that should have adorned the coveted adornments were gone.

But she hugged them to her bosom, and at length she was able to look up with dim eyes and a smile and say: "My hair grows so fast, Jim!"

And then Della leaped up like a little singed cat and cried, "Oh, oh!"

Jim had not yet seen his beautiful present. She held it out to him eagerly upon her open palm. The dull precious metal seemed to flash with a reflection of her bright and ardent spirit.

"Isn't it a dandy, Jim? I hunted all over town to find it. You'll have to look at the time a hundred times a day now. Give me your watch. I want to see how it looks on it."

Instead of obeying, Jim tumbled down on the couch and put his hands under the back of his head and smiled.

"Dell," said he, "let's put our Christmas presents away and keep 'em awhile. They're too nice to use just at present. I sold the watch to get the money to buy your combs. And now suppose you put the chops on."

The magi, as you know, were wise men—wonderfully wise men—

who brought gifts to the Babe in the manger. They invented the art of giving Christmas presents. Being wise, their gifts were no doubt wise ones, possibly bearing the privilege of exchange in case of duplication. And here I have lamely related to you the uneventful chronicle of two foolish children in a flat who most unwisely sacrificed for each other the greatest treasures of their house. But in a last word to the wise of these days let it be said that of all who give gifts these two were the wisest. Of all who give and receive gifts, such as they are wisest. Everywhere they are wisest. They are the magi.

A RETRIEVED REFORMATION

A GUARD came to the prison shoe-shop, where Jimmy Valentine was assiduously stitching uppers, and escorted him to the front office. There the warden handed Jimmy his pardon, which had been signed that morning by the governor. Jimmy took it in a tired kind of way. He had served nearly ten months of a four-year sentence. He had expected to stay only about three months, at the longest. When a man with as many friends on the outside as Jimmy Valentine had is received in the "stir" it is hardly worth while to cut his hair.

"Now, Valentine," said the warden, "you'll go out in the morning. Brace up, and make a man of yourself. You're not a bad fellow at heart. Stop cracking safes, and live straight."

"Me?" said Jimmy, in surprise. "Why, I never cracked a safe in my life."

"Oh, no," laughed the warden. "Of course not. Let's see, now. How was it you happened to get sent up on that Springfield job? Was it because you wouldn't prove an alibi for fear of compromising somebody in extremely high-toned society? Or was it simply a case of a mean old jury that had it in for you? It's always one or the other with you innocent victims."

"Me?" said Jimmy, still blankly virtuous. "Why, warden, I never was in Springfield in my life!"

"Take him back, Cronin," smiled the warden, "and fix him up with outgoing clothes. Unlock him at seven in the morning, and let him come to the bull-pen. Better think over my advice, Valentine."

At a quarter past seven on the next morning Jimmy stood in the warden's outer office. He had on a suit of the villainously fitting, ready-made clothes and a pair of the stiff, squeaky shoes that the state furnishes to its discharged compulsory guests.

The clerk handed him a railroad ticket and the five-dollar bill with which the law expected him to rehabilitate himself into good citizenship and prosperity. The warden gave him a cigar, and shook hands. Valentine, 9762, was chronicled on the books "Pardoned by Governor," and Mr. James Valentine walked out into the sunshine.

Disregarding the song of the birds, the waving green trees, and the smell of the flowers, Jimmy headed straight for a restaurant. There he tasted the first sweet joys of liberty in the shape of a broiled chicken and a bottle of white wine—followed by a cigar a grade better than the one the warden had given him. From there he proceeded leisurely to the depot. He tossed a quarter into the hat of a blind man sitting by the door, and boarded his train. Three hours set him down in a little town near the state line. He went to the café of one Mike Dolan and shook hands with Mike, who was alone behind the bar.

"Sorry we couldn't make it sooner, Jimmy, me boy," said Mike. "But we had that protest from Springfield to buck against, and the governor nearly balked. Feeling all right?"

"Fine," said Jimmy. "Got my key?"

He got his key and went upstairs, unlocking the door of a room at the rear. Everything was just as he had left it. There on the floor was still Ben Price's collar-button that had been torn from that eminent detective's shirt-band when they had overpowered Jimmy to arrest him.

Pulling out from the wall a folding-bed, Jimmy slid back a panel in the wall and dragged out a dust-covered suit-case. He opened this and gazed fondly at the finest set of burglar's tools in the East. It was a complete set, made of specially tempered steel, the latest designs in drills, punches, braces and bits, jimmies, clamps, and augers, with two or three novelties, invented by Jimmy himself, in which he took pride. Over nine hundred dollars they had cost him to have made at ——, a place where they make such things for the profession.

In half an hour Jimmy went downstairs and through the café. He was now dressed in tasteful and well-fitting clothes, and carried his dusted and cleaned suit-case in his hand.

"Got anything on?" asked Mike Dolan, genially.

"Me?" said Jimmy, in a puzzled tone. "I don't understand. I'm representing the New York Amalgamated Short Snap Biscuit Cracker and Frazzled Wheat Company."

This statement delighted Mike to such an extent that Jimmy had to take a seltzer-and-milk on the spot. He never touched "hard" drinks.

A week after the release of Valentine, 9762, there was a neat job of safe-burglary done in Richmond, Indiana, with no clue to the author. A scant eight hundred dollars was all that was secured. Two weeks after that a patented, improved, burglar-proof safe in Logansport was opened like a cheese to the tune of fifteen hundred dollars, currency; securities and silver untouched. That began to interest the rogue-catchers. Then an old-fashioned bank-safe in Jefferson City became active and threw out of its crater an eruption of bank-notes amounting to five thousand dollars. The losses were now high enough to bring the matter up into Ben Price's class of work. By comparing notes, a remarkable similarity in the methods of the burglaries was noticed. Ben Price investigated the scenes of the robberies, and was heard to remark:

"That's Dandy Jim Valentine's autograph. He's resumed business. Look at that combination knob—jerked out as easy as pulling up a radish in wet weather. He's got the only clamps that can do it. And look how clean those tumblers were punched out! Jimmy never has to drill but one hole. Yes, I guess I want Mr. Valentine. He'll do his bit next time without any short-time or clemency foolishness."

Ben Price knew Jimmy's habits. He had learned them while working up the Springfield case. Long jumps, quick get-aways, no confederates, and a taste for good society—these ways had helped Mr. Valentine to become noted as a successful dodger of retribution. It was given out that Ben Price had taken up the trail of the elusive cracksman, and other people with burglar-proof safes felt more at ease.

One afternoon Jimmy Valentine and his suit-case climbed out of the mail-hack in Elmore, a little town five miles off the railroad down in the black-jack country of Arkansas. Jimmy, looking like an athletic young senior just home from college, went down the board sidewalk toward the hotel.

A young lady crossed the street, passed him at the corner and entered a door over which was the sign "The Elmore Bank." Jimmy Valentine looked into her eyes, forgot what he was, and became another man. She lowered her eyes and colored slightly. Young men of Jimmy's style and looks were scarce in Elmore.

Jimmy collared a boy that was loafing on the steps of the bank as if he were one of the stockholders, and began to ask him questions about the town, feeding him dimes at intervals. By and by the young lady came out, looking royally unconscious of the young man with the suit-case, and went her way.

"Isn't that young lady Miss Polly Simpson?" asked Jimmy, with specious guile.

"Naw," said the boy. "She's Annabel Adams. Her pa owns this bank. What'd you come to Elmore for? Is that a gold watch-chain? I'm going to get a bulldog. Got any more dimes?"

Jimmy went to the Planters' Hotel, registered as Ralph D. Spencer, and engaged a room. He leaned on the desk and declared his platform to the clerk. He said he had come to Elmore to look for a location to go into business. How was the shoe business, now, in the town? He had thought of the shoe business. Was there an opening?

The clerk was impressed by the clothes and manner of Jimmy. He, himself, was something of a pattern of fashion to the thinly gilded youth of Elmore, but he now perceived his shortcomings. While trying to figure out Jimmy's manner of tying his four-in-hand he cordially gave information.

Yes, there ought to be a good opening in the shoe line. There wasn't an exclusive shoe-store in the place. The dry-goods and general stores handled them. Business in all lines was fairly good. Hoped Mr. Spencer would decide to locate in Elmore. He would find it a pleasant town to live in, and the people very sociable.

Mr. Spencer thought he would stop over in the town a few days and look over the situation. No, the clerk needn't call the boy. He would carry up his suit-case, himself; it was rather heavy.

Mr. Ralph Spencer, the phoenix that arose from Jimmy Valentine's ashes—ashes left by the flame of a sudden and alterative attack of love—remained in Elmore, and prospered. He opened a shoe-store and secured a good run of trade.

Socially he was also a success, and made many friends. And he accomplished the wish of his heart. He met Miss Annabel Adams, and became more and more captivated by her charms.

At the end of a year the situation of Mr. Ralph Spencer was this: he had won the respect of the community, his shoe-store was flourishing, and he and Annabel were engaged to be married in two weeks. Mr. Adams, the typical, plodding, country banker, approved of Spencer. Annabel's pride in him almost equalled her affection. He was as much at home in the family of Mr. Adams and that of Annabel's married sister as if he were already a member.

One day Jimmy sat down in his room and wrote this letter, which he mailed to the safe address of one of his old friends in St. Louis:

DEAR OLD PAL:

I want you to be at Sullivan's place, in Little Rock, next Wednesday night, at nine o'clock. I want you to wind up some little matters for me. And, also, I want to make you a present of my kit of tools. I know you'll be glad to get them—you couldn't duplicate the lot for a thousand dollars. Say, Billy, I've quit the old business—a year ago. I've got a nice store. I'm making an honest living, and I'm going to marry the finest girl on earth two weeks from now. It's the only life, Billy—the straight one. I wouldn't touch a dollar of another man's money now for a million. After I get married I'm going to sell out and go West, where there won't be so much danger of having old scores brought up against me. I tell you, Billy, she's an angel. She believes in me; and I wouldn't do another crooked thing for the whole world. Be sure to be at Sully's, for I must see you. I'll bring along the tools with me.

Your old friend,
JIMMY.

On the Monday night after Jimmy wrote this letter, Ben Price jogged unobtrusively into Elmore in a livery buggy. He lounged about town in his quiet way until he found out what he wanted to know. From the drug-store across the street from Spencer's shoe-store he got a good look at Ralph D. Spencer.

"Going to marry the banker's daughter are you, Jimmy?" said Ben to himself, softly. "Well, I don't know!"

The next morning Jimmy took breakfast at the Adamses. He was going to Little Rock that day to order his wedding-suit and buy something nice for Annabel. That would be the first time he had left town since he came to Elmore. It had been more than a year now since those last professional "jobs," and he thought he could safely venture out.

After breakfast quite a family party went downtown together—Mr. Adams, Annabel, Jimmy, and Annabel's married sister with her two little girls, aged five and nine. They came by the hotel where Jimmy still boarded, and he ran up to his room and brought along his suit-case. Then they went on to the bank. There stood Jimmy's horse and buggy and Dolph Gibson, who was going to drive him over to the railroad station.

All went inside the high, carved oak railings into the banking-room—Jimmy included, for Mr. Adams's future son-in-law was welcome anywhere. The clerks were pleased to be greeted by the good-looking, agreeable young man who was going to marry Miss Annabel. Jimmy set his suit-case down. Annabel, whose heart was bubbling with happiness and lively youth, put on Jimmy's hat, and picked up the suit-case. "Wouldn't I make a nice drummer?" said Annabel. "My! Ralph, how heavy it is. Feels like it was full of gold bricks."

"Lot of nickel-plated shoe-horns in there," said Jimmy, coolly, "that I'm going to return. Thought I'd save express charges by taking them up. I'm getting awfully economical."

The Elmore Bank had just put in a new safe and vault. Mr. Adams was very proud of it, and insisted on an inspection by everyone. The vault was a small one, but it had a new, patented door. It fastened with three solid steel bolts thrown simultaneously with a single handle, and had a time-lock. Mr. Adams beamingly explained its workings to Mr. Spencer, who showed a courteous but not too intelligent interest. The two children, May and Agatha, were delighted by the shining metal and funny clock and knobs.

While they were thus engaged Ben Price sauntered in and leaned on his elbow, looking casually inside between the railings. He told the teller that he didn't want anything; he was just waiting for a man he knew.

Suddenly there was a scream or two from the women, and a commotion. Unperceived by the elders, May, the nine-year-old girl, in a spirit of play, had shut Agatha in the vault. She had then shot the bolts and turned the knob of the combination as she had seen Mr. Adams do.

The old banker sprang to the handle and tugged at it for a moment.

"The door can't be opened," he groaned. "The clock hasn't been wound nor the combination set."

Agatha's mother screamed again, hysterically.

"Hush!" said Mr. Adams, raising his trembling hand. "All be quiet for a moment. Agatha!" he called as loudly as he could. "Listen to me." During the following silence they could just hear the faint sound of the child wildly shrieking in the dark vault in a panic of terror.

"My precious darling!" wailed the mother. "She will die of fright! Open the door! Oh, break it open! Can't you men do something?"

"There isn't a man nearer than Little Rock who can open that door," said Mr. Adams, in a shaky voice. "My God! Spencer, what shall we do? That child—she can't stand it long in there. There isn't enough air, and, besides, she'll go into convulsions from fright."

Agatha's mother, frantic now, beat the door of the vault with her hands. Somebody wildly suggested dynamite. Annabel turned to Jimmy, her large eyes full of anguish, but not yet despairing. To a woman nothing seems quite impossible to the powers of the man she worships.

"Can't you do something, Ralph—*try*, won't you?"

He looked at her with a queer, soft smile on his lips and in his keen eyes.

"Annabel," he said, "give me that rose you are wearing, will you?"

Hardly believing that she heard him aright, she unpinned the bud from the bosom of her dress, and placed it in his hand. Jimmy stuffed it into his vest-pocket, threw off his coat and pulled up his shirt-sleeves. With that act Ralph D. Spencer passed away and Jimmy Valentine took his place.

"Get away from the door, all of you," he commanded, shortly.

He set his suit-case on the table, and opened it out flat. From that time on he seemed to be unconscious of the presence of anyone else. He laid out the shining, queer implements swiftly and orderly, whistling softly to himself as he always did when at work. In a deep silence and immovable, the others watched him as if under a spell.

In a minute Jimmy's pet drill was biting smoothly into the steel door. In ten minutes—breaking his own burglarious record—he threw back the bolts and opened the door.

Agatha, almost collapsed, but safe, was gathered into her mother's arms.

Jimmy Valentine put on his coat, and walked outside the railings toward the front door. As he went he thought he heard a far-away voice that he once knew call "Ralph!" But he never hesitated.

At the door a big man stood somewhat in his way.

"Hello, Ben!" said Jimmy, still with his strange smile. "Got around at last, have you? Well, let's go. I don't know that it makes much difference, now."

And then Ben Price acted rather strangely.

"Guess you're mistaken, Mr. Spencer," he said. "Don't believe I recognize you. Your buggy's waiting for you, ain't it?"

And Ben Price turned and strolled down the street.

ONE THOUSAND DOLLARS

"ONE thousand dollars," repeated Lawyer Tolman, solemnly and severely, "and here is the money."

Young Gillian gave a decidedly amused laugh as he fingered the thin package of new fifty-dollar notes.

"It's such a confoundedly awkward amount," he explained, genially, to the lawyer. "If it had been ten thousand a fellow might wind up with a lot of fireworks and do himself credit. Even fifty dollars would have been less trouble."

"You heard the reading of your uncle's will," continued Lawyer Tolman, professionally dry in his tones. "I do not know if you paid much attention to its details. I must remind you of one. You are required to render to us an account of the manner of expenditure of this one thousand dollars as soon as you have disposed of it. The will stipulates that. I trust that you will so far comply with the late Mr. Gillian's wishes."

"You may depend upon it," said the young man, politely, "in spite of the extra expense it will entail. I may have to engage a secretary. I was never good at accounts."

Gillian went to his club. There he hunted out one whom he called Old Bryson.

Old Bryson was calm and forty and sequestered. He was in a corner reading a book, and when he saw Gillian approaching he sighed, laid down his book, and took off his glasses.

"Old Bryson, wake up," said Gillian. "I've a funny story to tell you."

"I wish you would tell it to someone in the billiard room," said Old Bryson. "You know how I hate your stories."

"This is a better one than usual," said Gillian, rolling a cigarette;

"and I'm glad to tell it to you. It's too sad and funny to go with the rattling of billiard balls. I've just come from my late uncle's firm of legal corsairs. He leaves me an even thousand dollars. Now, what can a man possibly do with a thousand dollars?"

"I thought," said Old Bryson, showing as much interest as a bee shows in a vinegar cruet, "that the late Septimus Gillian was worth something like half a million."

"He was," assented Gillian, joyously, "and that's where the joke comes in. He's left his whole cargo of doubloons to a microbe. That is, part of it goes to the man who invents a new bacillus and the rest to establish a hospital for doing away with it again. There are one or two trifling bequests on the side. The butler and the housekeeper get a seal ring and ten dollars each. His nephew gets one thousand dollars."

"You've always had plenty of money to spend," observed Old Bryson.

"Tons," said Gillian. "Uncle was the fairy godmother as far as an allowance was concerned."

"Any other heirs?" asked Old Bryson.

"None." Gillian frowned at his cigarette and kicked the upholstered leather of a divan uneasily. "There is a Miss Hayden, a ward of my uncle, who lived in his house. She's a quiet thing—musical—the daughter of somebody who was unlucky enough to be his friend. I forgot to say that she was in on the seal ring and ten-dollar joke, too. I wish I had been. Then I could have had two bottles of brut, tipped the waiter with the ring, and had the whole business off my hands. Don't be superior and insulting, Old Bryson—tell me what a fellow can do with a thousand dollars."

Old Bryson rubbed his glasses and smiled. And when Old Bryson smiled, Gillian knew that he intended to be more offensive than ever.

"A thousand dollars," he said, "means much or little. One man may buy a happy home with it and laugh at Rockefeller. Another could send his wife South with it and save her life. A thousand dollars would buy pure milk for one hundred babies during June, July, and August and save fifty of their lives. You could count upon a half hour's diversion with it at faro in one of the fortified art galleries. It would furnish an education to an ambitious boy. I am told that a genuine Corot was secured for that amount in an auction room yesterday. You could move to a New Hampshire town and live respectably two years on it. You could rent Madison Square Garden for one evening with it, and lecture your audience, if you should have one, on the precariousness of the profession of heir presumptive."

"People might like you, Old Bryson," said Gillian, always unruffled, "if you wouldn't moralize. I asked you to tell me what I could do with a thousand dollars."

"You?" said Bryson, with a gentle laugh. "Why, Bobby Gillian, there's only one logical thing you could do. You can go buy Miss Lotta Lauriere a diamond pendant with the money, and then take yourself off to Idaho and inflict your presence upon a ranch. I advise a sheep ranch, as I have a particular dislike for sheep."

"Thanks," said Gillian, rising. "I thought I could depend upon you, Old Bryson. You've hit on the very scheme. I wanted to chuck the money in a lump, for I've got to turn in an account for it, and I hate itemizing."

Gillian phoned for a cab and said to the driver:

"The stage entrance of the Columbine Theatre."

Miss Lotta Lauriere was assisting nature with a powder puff, almost ready for her call at a crowded matinée, when her dresser mentioned the name of Mr. Gillian.

"Let it in," said Miss Lauriere. "Now, what is it, Bobby? I'm going on in two minutes."

"Rabbit-foot your right ear a little," suggested Gillian, critically. "That's better. It won't take two minutes for me. What do you say to a little thing in the pendant line? I can stand three ciphers with a figure one in front of 'em."

"Oh, just as you say," carolled Miss Lauriere. "My right glove, Adams. Say, Bobby, did you see that necklace Della Stacey had on the other night? Twenty-two hundred dollars it cost at Tiffany's. But, of course—pull my sash a little to the left, Adams."

"Miss Lauriere for the opening chorus!" cried the call boy without.

Gillian strolled out to where his cab was waiting.

"What would you do with a thousand dollars if you had it?" he asked the driver.

"Open a s'loon," said the cabby, promptly and huskily. "I know a place I could take money in with both hands. It's a four-story brick on a corner. I've got it figured out. Second story—Chinks and chop suey; third floor—manicures and foreign missions; fourth floor—poolroom. If you was thinking of putting up the cap—"

"Oh, no," said Gillian, "I merely asked from curiosity. I take you by the hour. Drive till I tell you to stop."

Eight blocks down Broadway Gillian poked up the trap with his cane and got out. A blind man sat upon a stool on the sidewalk selling pencils. Gillian went out and stood before him.

"Excuse me," he said, "but would you mind telling me what you would do if you had a thousand dollars?"

"You got out of that cab that just drove up, didn't you?" asked the blind man.

"I did," said Gillian.

"I guess you are all right," said the pencil dealer, "to ride in a cab by daylight. Take a look at that, if you like."

He drew a small book from his coat pocket and held it out. Gillian opened it and saw that it was a bank deposit book. It showed a balance of $1,785 to the blind man's credit.

Gillian returned the book and got into the cab.

"I forgot something," he said. "You may drive to the law offices of Tolman and Sharp, at —— Broadway."

Lawyer Tolman looked at him hostilely and inquiringly through his gold-rimmed glasses.

"I beg your pardon," said Gillian, cheerfully, "but may I ask you a question? It is not an impertinent one, I hope. Was Miss Hayden left anything by my uncle's will besides the ring and the ten dollars?"

"Nothing," said Mr. Tolman.

"I thank you very much, sir," said Gillian, and out he went to his cab. He gave the driver the address of his late uncle's home.

Miss Hayden was writing letters in the library. She was small and slender and clothed in black. But you would have noticed her eyes. Gillian drifted in with his air of regarding the world as inconsequent.

"I've just come from Old Tolman's," he explained. "They've been going over the papers down there. They found a"—Gillian searched

I AM
BLIND
GORDON GRANT

his memory for a legal term—"they found an amendment or a postscript or something to the will. It seemed that the old boy loosened up a little on second thoughts and willed you a thousand dollars. I was driving up this way and Tolman asked me to bring you the money. Here it is. You'd better count it to see if it's right." Gillian laid the money beside her hand on the desk.

Miss Hayden turned white. "Oh!" she said, and again "Oh!"

Gillian half turned and looked out the window.

"I suppose, of course," he said, in a low voice, "that you know I love you."

"I am sorry," said Miss Hayden, taking up her money.

"There is no use?" asked Gillian, almost light-heartedly.

"I am sorry," she said again.

"May I write a note?" asked Gillian, with a smile. He seated himself at the big library table. She supplied him with paper and pen, and then went back to her secrétaire.

Gillian made out his account of his expenditure of the thousand dollars in these words:

"Paid by the black sheep, Robert Gillian, $1,000 on account of the eternal happiness, owed by Heaven to the best and dearest woman on earth."

Gillian slipped his writing into an envelope, bowed and went his way.

His cab stopped again at the offices of Tolman & Sharp.

"I have expended the thousand dollars," he said, cheerily, to Tolman of the gold glasses, "and I have come to render account of it, as I agreed. There is quite a feeling of summer in the air—do you not think so, Mr. Tolman?" He tossed a white envelope on the lawyer's table. "You will find there a memorandum, sir, of the *modus operandi* of the vanishing of the dollars."

Without touching the envelope, Mr. Tolman went to a door and called his partner, Sharp. Together they explored the caverns of an immense safe. Forth they dragged as trophy of their search a big envelope sealed with wax. This they forcibly invaded, and wagged their venerable heads together over its contents. Then Tolman became spokesman.

"Mr. Gillian," he said, formally, "there was a codicil to your uncle's will. It was intrusted to us privately, with instructions that it not be opened until you had furnished us with a full account of your handling of the one-thousand-dollar bequest in the will. As you have fulfilled the conditions, my partner and I have read the codicil. I do not wish to encumber your understanding with its legal phraseology, but I will acquaint you with the spirit of its contents.

"In the event that your disposition of the one thousand dollars demonstrates that you possess any of the qualifications that deserve reward, much benefit will accrue to you. Mr. Sharp and I are named as the judges, and I assure you that we will do our duty strictly according to justice—with liberality. We are not at all unfavorably disposed toward you, Mr. Gillian. But let us return to the letter of the codicil. If your disposal of the money in question has been prudent, wise, or unselfish, it is in our power to hand you over bonds to the value of fifty thousand dollars, which have been placed in our hands for that purpose. But if—as our client, the late Mr. Gillian, explicitly provides—you have used this money as you have used money in the past—I quote the late Mr. Gillian—in reprehensible dissipation among disreputable associates—the fifty thousand dollars is to be paid to Miriam Hayden, ward of the late Mr. Gillian, without delay. Now, Mr. Gillian, Mr. Sharp and I will examine your account in regard to the one thousand dollars. You submit it in writing, I believe. I hope you will repose confidence in our decision."

Mr. Tolman reached for the envelope. Gillian was a little the quicker in taking it up. He tore the account and its cover leisurely into strips and dropped them into his pocket.

"It's all right," he said, smilingly. "There isn't a bit of need to bother you with this. I don't suppose you'd understand these itemized bets, anyway. I lost the thousand dollars on the races. Good-day to you, gentlemen."

Tolman & Sharp shook their heads mournfully at each other when Gillian left, for they heard him whistling gaily in the hallway as he waited for the elevator.

AN ADJUSTMENT OF NATURE

IN AN art exhibition the other day I saw a painting that had been sold for five thousand dollars. The painter was a young scrub out of the West named Kraft, who had a favorite food and a pet theory. His pabulum was an unquenchable belief in the Unerring Artistic Adjustment of Nature. His theory was fixed around corned-beef hash with poached egg. There was a story behind the picture, so I went home and let it drip out of a fountain pen. The idea of Kraft—but that is not the beginning of the story.

Three years ago Kraft, Bill Judkins (a poet), and I took our meals at Cypher's, on Eighth Avenue. I say "took." When we had money, Cypher got it "off of" us, as he expressed it. We had no credit; we went in, called for food and ate it. We paid or we did not pay. We had confidence in Cypher's sullenness and smouldering ferocity. Deep down in his sunless soul he was either a prince, a fool, or an artist. He sat at a worm-eaten desk, covered with files of waiters' checks so old that I was sure the bottomest one was for clams that Hendrik Hudson had eaten and paid for. Cypher had the power, in common with Napoleon III and the goggle-eyed perch, of throwing a film over his eyes, rendering opaque the windows of his soul. Once when we left him unpaid, with egregious excuses, I looked back and saw him shaking with inaudible laughter behind his film. Now and then we paid up back scores.

But the chief thing at Cypher's was Milly. Milly was a waitress. She was a grand example of Kraft's theory of the artistic adjustment of nature. She belonged, largely, to waiting, as Minerva did to the art of scrapping, or Venus to the science of serious flirtation. Pedestalled and in bronze she might have stood with the noblest of her heroic sisters as

"Liver-and-Bacon Enlivening the World." She belonged to Cypher's. You expected to see her colossal figure loom through that reeking blue cloud of smoke from frying fat just as you expect the Palisades to appear through a drifting Hudson River fog. There amid the steam of vegetables and the vapors of acres of "ham and," the crash of crockery, the clatter of steel, the screaming of "short orders," the cries of the hungering and all the horrid tumult of feeding man, surrounded by swarms of the buzzing winged beasts bequeathed us by Pharaoh, Milly steered her magnificent way like some great liner cleaving among the canoes of howling savages.

Our Goddess of Grub was built on lines so majestic that they could be followed only with awe. Her sleeves were always rolled above her elbows. She could have taken us three musketeers in her two hands and dropped us out of the window. She had seen fewer years than any of us, but she was of such superb Evehood and simplicity that she mothered us from the beginning. Cypher's store of eatables she poured out upon us with royal indifference to price and quantity, as from a cornucopia that knew no exhaustion. Her voice rang like a great silver bell; her smile was many-toothed and frequent; she seemed like a yellow sunrise on mountaintops. I never saw her but I thought of the Yosemite. And yet, somehow, I could never think of her as existing outside of Cypher's. There nature had placed her, and she had taken root and grown mightily. She seemed happy, and took her few poor dollars on Saturday nights with the flushed pleasure of a child that receives an unexpected donation.

It was Kraft who first voiced the fear that each of us must have held latently. It came up apropos, of course, of certain questions of art at which we were hammering. One of us compared the harmony existing between a Haydn symphony and pistache ice cream to the exquisite congruity between Milly and Cypher's.

"There is a certain fate hanging over Milly," said Kraft, "and if it overtakes her she is lost to Cypher's and to us."

"She will grow fat?" asked Judkins, fearsomely.

"She will go to night school and become refined?" I ventured anxiously.

"It is this," said Kraft, punctuating in a puddle of spilled coffee with a stiff forefinger. "Caesar had his Brutus—the cotton has its bollworm, the chorus girl has her Pittsburger, the summer boarder has his poison ivy, the hero has his Carnegie medal, art has its Morgan, the rose has its—"

"Speak," I interrupted, much perturbed. "You do not think that Milly will begin to lace?"

"One day," concluded Kraft, solemnly, "there will come to Cypher's for a plate of beans a millionaire lumberman from Wisconsin, and he will marry Milly."

"Never!" exclaimed Judkins and I, in horror.

"A lumberman," repeated Kraft, hoarsely.

"And a millionaire lumberman!" I sighed, despairingly.

"From Wisconsin!" groaned Judkins.

We agreed that the awful fate seemed to menace her. Few things were less improbable. Milly, like some vast virgin stretch of pine woods, was made to catch the lumberman's eye. And well we knew the habits of the Badgers, once fortune smiled upon them. Straight to New York they hie, and lay their goods at the feet of the girl who serves them beans in a beanery. Why, the alphabet itself connives. The Sunday newspaper's headliner's work is cut for him.

"Winsome Waitress Wins Wealthy Wisconsin Woodsman."

For a while we felt that Milly was on the verge of being lost to us.

It was our love of the Unerring Artistic Adjustment of Nature that inspired us. We could not give her over to a lumberman, doubly accursed by wealth and provincialism. We shuddered to think of Milly, with her voice modulated and her elbows covered, pouring tea in the marble teepee of a tree murderer. No! In Cypher's she belonged—in the bacon smoke, the cabbage perfume, the grand, Wagnerian chorus of hurled ironstone china and rattling casters.

Our fears must have been prophetic, for on that same evening the wildwood discharged upon us Milly's preordained confiscator—our fee to adjustment and order. But Alaska and not Wisconsin bore the burden of the visitation.

We were at our supper of beef stew and dried apples when he trotted in as if on the heels of a dog team, and made one of the mess at our table. With the freedom of the camps he assaulted our ears and claimed the fellowship of men lost in the wilds of a hash house. We embraced him as a specimen, and in three minutes we had all but died for one another as friends.

He was rugged and bearded and wind-dried. He had just come off the "trail," he said, at one of the North River ferries. I fancied I could see the snow dust of Chilcoot yet powdering his shoulders. And then he strewed the table with the nuggets, stuffed ptarmigans, bead work, and seal pelts of the returned Klondiker, and began to prate to us of his millions.

"Bank drafts for two millions," was his summing up, "and a thousand a day piling up from my claims. And now I want some beef stew and canned peaches. I never got off the train since I mushed out of Seattle, and I'm hungry. You gentlemen order what you want."

And then Milly loomed up with a thousand dishes on her bare arm—loomed up big and white and pink and awful as Mount Saint Elias—with a smile like day breaking in a gulch. And the Klondiker threw down his pelts and nuggets as dross, and let his jaw fall halfway, and stared at her. You could almost see the diamond tiaras on Milly's brow and the hand-embroidered silk Paris gowns that he meant to buy for her.

At last the bollworm had attacked the cotton—the poison ivy was reaching out its tendrils to entwine the summer boarder—the millionaire lumberman, thinly disguised as the Alaskan miner, was about to engulf our Milly and upset Nature's adjustment.

Kraft was the first to act. He leaped up and pounded the Klondiker's back. "Come out and drink," he shouted. "Drink first and eat afterward." Judkins seized one arm and I the other. Gaily, roaringly, irresistibly, in jolly-good-fellow style, we dragged him from the restaurant to a café, stuffing his pockets with his embalmed birds and indigestible nuggets.

There he rumbled a roughly good-humored protest. "That's the girl for my money," he declared. "She can eat out of my skillet the rest of her life. Why, I never see such a fine girl. I'm going back there and ask her to marry me. I guess she won't want to sling hash anymore when she sees the pile of dust I've got."

"You'll take another whiskey and milk now," Kraft persuaded, with Satan's smile. "I thought you up-country fellows were better sports."

Kraft spent his puny store of coin at the bar and then gave Judkins and me such an appealing look that we went down to the last dime we had in toasting our guest.

Then, when our ammunition was gone and the Klondiker, still somewhat sober, began to babble again of Milly, Kraft whispered into his ear such a polite, barbed insult relating to people who were miserly with their funds, that the miner crashed down handful after handful of silver and notes, calling for all the fluids in the world to drown the imputation.

Thus the work was accomplished. With his own guns we drove him from the field. And then we had him carted to a distant small hotel and put to bed with his nuggets and baby sealskins stuffed around him.

"He will never find Cypher's again," said Kraft. "He will propose to the first white apron he sees in a dairy restaurant tomorrow. And Milly—I mean the Natural Adjustment—is saved!"

And back to Cypher's went we three, and, finding customers scarce, we joined hands and did an Indian dance with Milly in the center.

This, I say, happened three years ago. And about that time a little luck descended upon us three, and we were enabled to buy costlier and less wholesome food than Cypher's. Our paths separated, and I saw Kraft no more and Judkins seldom.

But, as I said, I saw a painting the other day that was sold for five thousand dollars. The title was "Boadicea," and the figure seemed to fill all out-of-doors. But of all the picture's admirers who stood before it, I believe I was the only one who longed for Boadicea to stalk from her frame, bringing me corned-beef hash with poached egg.

I hurried away to see Kraft. His satanic eyes were the same, his hair was worse tangled, but his clothes had been made by a tailor.

"I didn't know," I said to him.

"We've bought a cottage in the Bronx with the money," said he. "Any evening at seven."

"Then," said I, "when you led us against the lumberman—the—Klondiker—it wasn't altogether on account of the Unerring Artistic Adjustment of Nature?"

"Well, not altogether," said Kraft, with a grin.

THE HALBERDIER OF THE LITTLE RHEINSCHLOSS

I GO sometimes into the *Bierhalle* and restaurant called Old Munich. Not long ago it was a resort of interesting Bohemians, but now only artists and musicians and literary folk frequent it. But the Pilsner is yet good, and I take some diversion from the conversation of Waiter No. 18.

For many years the customers of Old Munich have accepted the place as a faithful copy from the ancient German town. The big hall with its smoky rafters, rows of imported steins, portrait of Goethe, and verses painted on the walls—translated into German from the original of the Cincinnati poets—seems atmospherically correct when viewed through the bottom of a glass.

But not long ago the proprietors added the room above, called it the Little Rheinschloss, and built in a stairway. Up there was an imitation stone parapet, ivy-covered, and the walls were painted to represent depth and distance, with the Rhine winding at the base of the vine-yarded slopes, and the castle of Ehrenbreitstein looming directly opposite the entrance. Of course there were tables and chairs; and you could have beer and food brought you, as you naturally would on the top of a castle on the Rhine.

I went into Old Munich one afternoon when there were few customers, and sat at my usual table near the stairway. I was shocked and almost displeased to perceive that the glass cigar-case by the orchestra stand had been smashed to smithereens. I did not like things to happen in Old Munich. Nothing had ever happened there before.

Waiter No. 18 came and breathed on my neck. I was his by right of discovery. Eighteen's brain was built like a corral. It was full of ideas which, when he opened the gate, came huddling out like a flock of sheep that might get together afterward or might not. I did not shine as a shepherd. As a type Eighteen fitted nowhere. I did not find out if he had a nationality, family, creed, grievance, hobby, soul, preference, home, or vote. He only came always to my table and, as long as his leisure would permit, let words flutter from him like swallows leaving a barn at daylight.

"How did the cigar-case come to be broken, Eighteen?" I asked, with a certain feeling of personal grievance.

"I can tell you about that, sir," said he, resting his foot on the chair next to mine. "Did you ever have anybody hand you a double handful of good luck while both your hands was full of bad luck, and stop to notice how your fingers behaved?"

"No riddles, Eighteen," said I. "Leave out palmistry and manicuring."

"You remember," said Eighteen, "the guy in the hammered brass Prince Albert and the oroide gold pants and the amalgamated copper hat, that carried the combination meat-axe, ice-pick, and liberty-pole, and used to stand on the first landing as you go up to the Little Rindslosh?"

"Why, yes," said I. "The halberdier. I never noticed him particularly. I remember I thought he was only a suit of armor. He had a perfect poise."

"He had more than that," said Eighteen. "He was me friend. He was an advertisement. The boss hired him to stand on the stairs for a kind of scenery to show there was something doing in the has-been line upstairs. What did you call him—a what kind of a beer?"

"A halberdier," said I. "That was an ancient man-at-arms of many hundred years ago."

"Some mistake," said Eighteen. "This one wasn't that old. He wasn't over twenty-three or four.

"It was the boss's idea, rigging a man up in an ante-bellum suit of tinware and standing him on the landing of the slosh. He bought the goods at a Fourth Avenue antique store, and hung a sign out: 'Able-bodied hal—halberdier wanted. Costume furnished.'

"The same morning a young man with wrecked good clothes and a hungry look comes in, bringing the sign with him. I was filling the mustard-pots at my station.

" 'I'm it,' says he, 'whatever it is. But I never halberdiered in a restaurant. Put me on. Is it a masquerade?'

" 'I hear talk in the kitchen of a fishball,' says I.

" 'Bully for you, Eighteen,' says he. 'You and I'll get on. Show me the boss's desk.'

"Well, the boss tries the Harveyized pajamas on him, and they fitted him like the scales on a baked redsnapper, and he gets the job. You've seen what it is—he stood straight up in the corner of the first landing with his halberd to his shoulder, looking right ahead and guarding the Portugals of the castle. The boss is nutty about having the true Old-World flavor to his joint. 'Halberdiers goes with Rindsloshes,' says he, 'just as rats goes with rathskellers and white cotton stockings with Tyrolean villages.' The boss is a kind of a antiologist, and is all posted up on data and such information.

"From eight P.M. to two in the morning was the halberdier's hours. He got two meals with us help and a dollar a night. I eat with him at the table. He liked me. He never told his name. He was travelling impromptu, like kings, I guess. The first time at supper I says to him: 'Have some more of the spuds, Mr. Frelinghuysen.' 'Oh, don't be so formal and offish, Eighteen,' says he. 'Call me Hal—that's short for halberdier.' 'Oh, don't think I wanted to pry for names,' says I. 'I know all about the dizzy fall from wealth and greatness. We've got a count washing dishes in the kitchen; and the third bartender used to be a Pullman conductor. And they *work,* Sir Percival,' says I, sarcastic.

" 'Eighteen,' says he, 'as a friendly devil in a cabbage-scented hell, would you mind cutting up this piece of steak for me? I don't say that it's got more muscle than I have, but—' And then he shows me the insides of his hands. They was blistered and cut and corned and swelled up till they looked like a couple of flank steaks criss-crossed with a knife—the kind the butchers hide and take home, knowing what is the best.

" 'Shovelling coal,' says he, 'and piling bricks and loading drays. But they gave out, and I had to resign. I was born for a halberdier, and I've been educated for twenty-four years to fill the position. Now, quit knocking my profession, and pass along a lot more of that ham. I'm holding the closing exercises,' says he, 'of a forty-eight-hour fast.'

"The second night he was on the job he walks down from his corner to the cigar-case and calls for cigarettes. The customers at the tables all snicker out loud to show their acquaintance with history. The boss is on.

" 'An'—let's see—oh, yes—'An anarchism,' says the boss. 'Cigarettes was not made at the time when halberdiers was invented.'

" 'The ones you sell was,' says Sir Percival. 'Caporal wins from chronology by the length of a cork tip.' So he gets 'em and lights one, and puts the box in his brass helmet, and goes back to patrolling the Rindslosh.

"He made a big hit, 'specially with the ladies. Some of 'em would poke him with their fingers to see if he was real or only a kind of a stuffed figure like they burn in elegy. And when he'd move they'd squeak, and make eyes at him as they went up to the slosh. He looked fine in his halber-dashery. He slept at two dollars a week in a hall-room on Third Avenue. He invited me up there one night. He had a little book on the washstand that he read instead of shopping in the saloons after hours. 'I'm on to that,' says I, 'from reading about it in novels. All the heroes on the bum carry the little book. It's either Tantalus or Liver or Horace, and it's printed in Latin, and you're a college man. And I wouldn't be surprised,' says I, 'if you wasn't educated, too.' But it was only the batting averages of the League for the last ten years.

"One night, about half-past eleven, there comes in a party of these high-rollers that are always hunting up new places to eat in and poke fun at. There was a swell girl in a forty H.-P. auto tan coat and veil, and a fat old man with white side-whiskers, and a young chap that couldn't keep his feet off the tail of the girl's coat, and an oldish lady that looked upon life as immoral and unnecessary. 'How perfectly delightful,' they says, 'to sup in a slosh.' Up the stairs they go; and in half a minute back down comes the girl, her skirts swishing like the waves on the beach. She stops on the landing and looks our halberdier in the eye.

" 'You!' she says, with a smile that reminded me of lemon sherbet. I was waiting upstairs in the slosh, then, and I was right down here by the door, putting some vinegar and cayenne into an empty bottle of Tabasco, and I heard all they said.

" 'It,' says Sir Percival, without moving. 'I'm only local color. Are my hauberk, helmet, and halberd on straight?"

" 'Is there an explanation to this?' says she. 'Is it a practical joke such as men play in those Griddle-cake and Lamb Clubs? I'm afraid I don't see the point. I heard, vaguely, that you were away. For three months I—we have not seen you or heard from you.'

" 'I'm halberdiering for my living,' says the statue. 'I'm working,' says he. 'I don't suppose you know what work means.'

" 'Have you—have you lost your money?' she asks.

"Sir Percival studies a minute.

" 'I am poorer,' says he, 'than the poorest sandwich man on the streets—if I don't earn my living.'

" 'You call this work?' says she. 'I thought a man worked with his hands or his head instead of becoming a mountebank.'

" 'The calling of a halberdier,' says he, 'is an ancient and honorable one. Sometimes,' says he, 'the man-at-arms at the door has saved the castle while the plumed knights were cake-walking in the banquet-halls above.'

" 'I see you're not ashamed,' says she, 'of your peculiar tastes. I wonder, though, that the manhood I used to think I saw in you didn't prompt you to draw water or hew wood instead of publicly flaunting your ignominy in this disgraceful masquerade.'

"Sir Percival kind of rattles his armor and says: 'Helen, will you suspend sentence in this matter for just a little while? You don't understand,' says he. 'I've got to hold this job down a bit longer.'

" 'You like being a harlequin—or halberdier, as you call it?' says she.

" 'I wouldn't get thrown out of the job just now,' says he, with a grin, 'to be appointed Minister to the Court of St. James's.'

"And then the forty H.-P. girl's eyes sparkled as hard as diamonds.

" 'Very well,' says she. 'You shall have full run of your serving-man's tastes this night.' And she swims over to the boss's desk and gives him a smile that knocks the specks off his nose.

" 'I think your Rindslosh,' says she, 'is as beautiful as a dream. It is a little slice of the Old World set down in New York. We shall have a nice supper up there; but if you will grant us one favor the illusion will be perfect—give us your halberdier to wait on our table.'

"That hit the boss's antiology hobby just right. 'Sure,' says he, 'dot vill be fine. Und der orchestra shall blay "Die Wacht am Rhein" all der time.' And he goes over and tells the halberdier to go upstairs and hustle the grub at the swells' table.

" 'I'm on the job,' says Sir Percival, taking off his helmet and hanging it on his halberd and leaning 'em in the corner. The girl goes up and takes her seat and I see her jaw squared tight under her smile. 'We're going to be waited on by a real halberdier,' says she, 'one who is proud of his profession. Isn't it sweet?'

" 'Ripping,' says the swell young man. 'Much prefer a waiter,' says the fat old gent. 'I hope he doesn't come from a cheap museum,' says the old lady; 'he might have microbes in his costume.'

"Before he goes to the table, Sir Percival takes me by the arm. 'Eighteen,' says he, 'I've got to pull off this job without a blunder. You coach me straight or I'll take that halberd and make hash out of you.' And then he goes up to the table with his coat of mail on and a napkin over his arm and waits for the order.

" 'Why, it's Deering!' says the young swell. 'Hello, old man. What the—'

" 'Beg pardon, sir,' interrupts the halberdier, 'I'm waiting on the table.'

"The old man looks at him grim, like a Boston bull. 'So, Deering,' he says, 'you're at work yet.'

" 'Yes, sir,' says Sir Percival, quiet and gentlemanly as I could have been myself, 'for almost three months, now.' 'You haven't been discharged during the time?' asks the old man. 'Not once, sir,' says he, 'though I've had to change my work several times.'

" 'Waiter,' orders the girl, short and sharp, 'another napkin.' He brings her one, respectful.

"I never saw more devil, if I may say it, stirred up in a lady. There was two bright red spots on her cheeks, and her eyes looked exactly like a wildcat's I'd seen in the zoo. Her foot kept slapping the floor all the time.

" 'Waiter,' she orders, 'bring me filtered water without ice. Bring me a footstool. Take away this empty salt-cellar.' She kept him on the jump. She was sure giving the halberdier his.

"There wasn't but a few customers up in the slosh at that time, so I hung out near the door so I could help Sir Percival serve.

"He got along fine with the olives and celery and the bluepoints. They was easy. And then the consommé came up the dumb-waiter all in one big silver tureen. Instead of serving it from the side-table he picks it up between his hands and starts to the dining-table with it. When nearly there he drops the tureen smash on the floor, and the soup soaks all the lower part of that girl's swell silk dress.

" 'Stupid—incompetent,' says she, giving him a look. 'Standing in a corner with a halberd seems to be your mission in life.'

" 'Pardon me, lady,' says he. 'It was just a little bit hotter than blazes. I couldn't help it.'

"The old man pulls out a memorandum book and hunts in it. 'The twenty-fifth of April, Deering,' says he. 'I know it,' says Sir Percival. 'And ten minutes to twelve o'clock,' says the old man. 'By Jupiter! you haven't won yet.' And he pounds the table with his fist and yells to me: 'Waiter, call the manager at once—tell him to hurry here as fast as he can.' I go after the boss, and old Brockmann hikes up to the slosh on the jump.

" 'I want this man discharged at once,' roars the old guy. 'Look what he's done. Ruined my daughter's dress. It cost at least six hundred dollars. Discharge this awkward lout at once or I'll sue you for the price of it.'

" 'Dis is bad pizness,' says the boss. 'Six hundred dollars is much. I reckon I vill haf to—'

" 'Wait a minute, Herr Brockmann,' says Sir Percival, easy and smiling. But he was worked up under his tin suitings; I could see that. And then he made the finest, neatest little speech I ever listened to. I can't give you the words, of course. He give the millionaires a lovely roast in a sarcastic way, describing their automobiles and opera-boxes and diamonds; and then he got around to the working-classes and the kind of grub they eat and the long hours they work—and all that sort of stuff—bunkum, of course. 'The restless rich,' says he, 'never content with their luxuries, always prowling among the haunts of the poor and humble, amusing themselves with the imperfections and misfortunes of their fellow men and women. And even here, Herr Brockmann,' he says, 'in this beautiful Rindslosh, a grand and enlightening reproduction of Old-World history and architecture, they come to disturb its symmetry and picturesqueness by demanding in their arrogance that the halberdier of the castle wait upon their table! I have faithfully and conscientiously,' says he, 'performed my duties as a halberdier. I know nothing of a waiter's duties. It was the insolent whim of these transient, pampered aristocrats that I should be detailed to serve them food. Must I be blamed—must I be deprived of the means of a livelihood,' he goes on, 'on account of an accident that was the result of their own presumption and haughtiness? But what hurts me more than all,' says Sir Percival, 'is the desecration that has been done to this splendid Rindslosh—the confiscation of its halberdier to serve menially at the banquet board.'

"Even I could see that this stuff was piffle; but it caught the boss.

" 'Mein Gott,' says he, 'you vas right. Ein halberdier have not got der right to dish up soup. Him I vill not discharge. Have anoder waiter if you like, und let mein halberdier go back und stand mit his halberd. But, gentlemen,' he says, pointing to the old man, 'you go ahead and sue mit der dress. Sue me for six hundred dollars or six thousand dollars. I stand der suit.' And the boss puffs off down-stairs. Old Brockmann was an all-right Dutchman.

"Just then the clock strikes twelve, and the old guy laughs loud. 'You win, Deering,' says he. 'Let me explain to all,' he goes on. 'Some time ago Mr. Deering asked me for something that I did not want to give him.' (I looks at the girl, and she turns as red as a pickled beet.) 'I told him,' says the old guy, 'if he would earn his own living for three months without once being discharged for incompetence, I would give him what he wanted. It seems that the time was up at twelve o'clock tonight. I came near fetching you, though, Deering, on that soup question,' says the old boy, standing up and grabbing Sir Percival's hand.

"The halberdier lets out a yell and jumps three feet high.

" 'Look out for those hands,' says he, and he holds 'em up. You never saw such hands except on a laborer in a limestone quarry.

" 'Heavens, boy!' says old side-whiskers, 'what have you been doing to 'em?'

" 'Oh,' says Sir Percival, 'little chores like hauling coal and excavating rock till they went back on me. And when I couldn't hold a pick or a whip I took up halberdiering to give 'em a rest. Tureens full of hot soup don't seem to be a particularly soothing treatment.'

"I would have bet on that girl. That high-tempered kind always go as far the other way, according to my experience. She whizzes round the table like a cyclone and catches both his hands in hers. 'Poor hands—dear hands,' she sings out, and sheds tears on 'em and holds 'em close to her bosom. Well, sir, with all that Rindslosh scenery it was just like a play. And the halberdier sits down at the table at the girl's side, and I served the rest of the supper. And that was about all, except that when they left he shed his hardware store and went with 'em."

I dislike to be side-tracked from an original proposition.

"But you haven't told me, Eighteen," said I, "how the cigar-case came to be broken."

"Oh, that was last night," said Eighteen. "Sir Percival and the girl drove up in a cream-colored motor-car, and had dinner in the Rindslosh. 'The same table, Billy,' I heard her say as they went up. I waited on 'em. We've got a new halberdier now, a bow-legged guy with a face like a sheep. As they came down-stairs Sir Percival passes him a ten-case note. The new halberdier drops his halberd, and it falls on the cigar-case. That's how that happened."

MAMMON AND THE ARCHER

OLD Anthony Rockwall, retired manufacturer and proprietor of Rockwall's Eureka Soap, looked out the library window of his Fifth Avenue mansion and grinned. His neighbor to the right—the aristocratic clubman, G. Van Schuylight Suffolk-Jones—came out to his waiting motor-car, wrinkling a contumelious nostril, as usual, at the Italian Renaissance sculpture of the soap palace's front elevation.

"Stuck-up old statuette of nothing doing!" commented the ex-Soap King. "The Eden Musee'll get that old frozen Nesselrode yet if he don't watch out. I'll have his house painted red, white, and blue next summer and see if that'll make his Dutch nose turn up any higher."

And then Anthony Rockwall, who never cared for bells, went to the door of his library and shouted "Mike!" in the same voice that had once chipped off pieces of the welkin on the Kansas prairies.

"Tell my son," said Anthony to the answering menial, "to come in here before he leaves the house."

When young Rockwall entered the library the old man laid aside his newspaper, looked at him with a kindly grimness on his big, smooth, ruddy countenance, rumpled his mop of white hair with one hand, and rattled the keys in his pocket with the other.

"Richard," said Anthony Rockwall, "what do you pay for the soap that you use?"

Richard, only six months home from college, was startled a little. He had not yet taken the measure of this sire of his, who was as full of unexpectednesses as a girl at her first party.

"Six dollars a dozen, I think, Dad."

"And your clothes?"

"I suppose about sixty dollars, as a rule."

"You're a gentleman," said Anthony, decidedly. "I've heard of these young bloods spending twenty-four dollars a dozen for soap, and going over the hundred mark for clothes. You've got as much money to waste as any of 'em, and yet you stick to what's decent and moderate. Now I use the old Eureka—not only for sentiment, but it's the purest soap made. Whenever you pay more than ten cents a cake for soap you buy bad perfumes and labels. But fifty cents is doing very well for a young man in your generation, position, and condition. As I said, you're a gentleman. They say it takes three generations to make one. They're off. Money'll do it as slick as soap grease. It's made you one. By hokey—it's almost made one of me. I'm nearly as impolite and disagreeable and ill-mannered as these two old Knickerbocker gents on each side of me that can't sleep of nights because I bought in between 'em."

"There are some things that money can't accomplish," remarked young Rockwall, rather gloomily.

"Now, don't say that," said old Anthony, shocked. "I bet my money on money every time. I've been through the encyclopedia down to Y looking for something you can't buy with it; and I expect to have to take up the appendix next week. I'm for money against the field. Tell me something money won't buy."

"For one thing," answered Richard, rankling a little, "it won't buy one into the exclusive circles of society."

"Oho! won't it?" thundered the champion of the root of evil. "You tell me where your exclusive circles would be if the first Astor hadn't had the money to pay for his steerage passage over?"

Richard sighed.

"And that's what I was coming to," said the old man, less boisterously. "That's why I asked you to come in. There's something going wrong with you, boy. I've been noticing it for two weeks. Out with it. I guess I could lay my hands on eleven millions within twenty-four hours, besides the real estate. If it's your liver, there's the *Rambler* down in the bay, coaled, and ready to steam down to the Bahamas in two days."

"Not a bad guess, Dad; you haven't missed it far."

"Ah," said Anthony, keenly; "what's her name?"

Richard began to walk up and down the library floor. There was enough comradeship and sympathy in this crude old father of his to draw his confidence.

"Why don't you ask her?" demanded old Anthony. "She'll jump at you. You've got the money and the looks, and you're a decent boy. Your hands are clean. You've got no Eureka soap on 'em. You've been to college, but she'll overlook that."

"I haven't had a chance," said Richard.

"Make one," said Anthony. "Take her for a walk in the park, or a straw ride, or walk home with her from church. Chance! Pshaw!"

"You don't know the social mill, Dad. She's part of the stream that turns it. Every hour and minute of her time is arranged for days in advance. I must have that girl, Dad, or this town is a black-jack swamp forevermore. And I can't write it—I can't do that."

"Tut!" said the old man. "Do you mean to tell me that with all the money I've got you can't get an hour or two of a girl's time for yourself?"

"I've put it off too late. She's going to sail for Europe at noon day after tomorrow for a two years' stay. I'm to see her alone tomorrow evening for a few minutes. She's at Larchmont now at her aunt's. I can't go there. But I'm allowed to meet her with a cab at the Grand Central Station tomorrow evening at the eight-thirty train. We drive down Broadway to Wallack's at a gallop, where her mother and a box party will be waiting for us in the lobby. Do you think she would listen to a declaration from me during that six or eight minutes under those circumstances? No. And what chance would I have in the theatre or afterward? None. No, Dad, this is one tangle that your money can't unravel. We can't buy one minute of time with cash; if we could, rich people would live longer. There's no hope of getting a talk with Miss Lantry before she sails."

"All right, Richard, my boy," said old Anthony, cheerfully. "You may run along down to your club now. I'm glad it ain't your liver. But don't forget to burn a few punk sticks in the joss house to the great god Mazuma from time to time. You say money won't buy time? Well, of course, you can't order eternity wrapped up and delivered at your residence for a price, but I've seen Father Time get pretty bad stone bruises on his heels when he walked through the gold diggings."

That night came Aunt Ellen, gentle, sentimental, wrinkled, sighing, oppressed by wealth, in to Brother Anthony at his evening paper, and began discourse on the subject of lovers' woes.

"He told me all about it," said Brother Anthony, yawning. "I told him my bank account was at his service. And then he began to knock money. Said money couldn't help. Said the rules of society couldn't be bucked for a yard by a team of ten-millionaires."

"Oh, Anthony," sighed Aunt Ellen, "I wish you would not think so much of money. Wealth is nothing where a true affection is concerned. Love is all-powerful. If he only had spoken earlier! She could not have refused our Richard. But now I fear it is too late. He will have no opportunity to address her. All your gold cannot bring happiness to your son."

At eight o'clock the next evening Aunt Ellen took a quaint old gold ring from a moth-eaten case and gave it to Richard.

"Wear it tonight, nephew," she begged. "Your mother gave it to me. Good luck in love she said it brought. She asked me to give it to you when you had found the one you loved."

Young Rockwall took the ring reverently and tried it on his smallest finger. It slipped as far as the second joint and stopped. He took it off and stuffed it into his vest pocket, after the manner of man. And then he phoned for his cab.

At the station he captured Miss Lantry out of the gadding mob at 8:32.

"We mustn't keep Mamma and the others waiting," said she.

"To Wallack's Theatre as fast as you can drive!" said Richard loyally.

They whirled up Forty-second to Broadway, and then down the white-starred lane that leads from the soft meadows of sunset to the rocky hills of morning.

At Thirty-fourth Street young Richard quickly thrust up the trap and ordered the cabman to stop.

"I've dropped a ring," he apologized, as he climbed out. "It was my mother's, and I'd hate to lose it. I won't detain you a minute—I saw where it fell."

In less than a minute he was back in the cab with the ring.

But within that minute a crosstown car had stopped directly in front of the cab. The cabman tried to pass to the left, but a heavy express wagon cut him off. He tried the right, and had to back away from a furniture van that had no business to be there. He tried to back out, but dropped his reins and swore dutifully. He was blockaded in a tangled mess of vehicles and horses.

One of those street blockades had occurred that sometimes tie up commerce and movement quite suddenly in the big city.

"Why don't you drive on?" said Miss Lantry, impatiently. "We'll be late."

Richard stood up in the cab and looked around. He saw a congested flood of wagons, trucks, cabs, vans, and street cars filling the vast space where Broadway, Sixth Avenue, and Thirty-fourth Street cross one another as a twenty-six-inch maiden fills her twenty-two-inch girdle. And still from all the cross streets they were hurrying and rattling toward the converging point at full speed, and hurling themselves into the struggling mass, locking wheels and adding their drivers' imprecations to the clamor. The entire traffic of Manhattan seemed to have jammed itself around them. The oldest New Yorker among the thousands of spectators that lined the sidewalks had not witnessed a street blockade of the proportions of this one.

"I'm very sorry," said Richard, as he resumed his seat, "but it looks as if we are stuck. They won't get this jumble loosened up in an hour. It was my fault. If I hadn't dropped the ring we—"

"Let me see the ring," said Miss Lantry. "Now that it can't be helped, I don't care. I think theatres are stupid, anyway."

At eleven o'clock that night somebody tapped lightly on Anthony Rockwall's door.

"Come in," shouted Anthony, who was in a red dressing-gown, reading a book of piratical adventures.

Somebody was Aunt Ellen, looking like a gray-haired angel that had been left on earth by mistake.

"They're engaged, Anthony," she said, softly. "She has promised to marry our Richard. On their way to the theatre there was a street blockade, and it was two hours before their cab could get out of it.

"And oh, Brother Anthony, don't ever boast of the power of money again. A little emblem of true love—a little ring that symbolized unending and unmercenary affection—was the cause of our Richard finding his happiness. He dropped it in the street, and got out to recover it. And before they could continue the blockade occurred. He spoke to his love and won her there while the cab was hemmed in. Money is dross compared with true love, Anthony."

"All right," said old Anthony. "I'm glad the boy has got what he wanted. I told him I wouldn't spare any expense in the matter if—"

"But, Brother Anthony, what good could your money have done?"

"Sister," said Anthony Rockwall, "I've got my pirate in a devil of a scrape. His ship has just been scuttled, and he's too good a judge of the value of money to let drown. I wish you would let me go on with this chapter."

The story should end here. I wish it would as heartily as you who read it wish it did. But we must go to the bottom of the well for truth.

The next day a person with red hands and a blue polka-dot necktie, who called himself Kelly, called at Anthony Rockwall's house, and was at once received in the library.

"Well," said Anthony, reaching for his check-book, "it was a good bilin' of soap. Let's see—you had five thousand dollars in cash."

"I paid out three hundred more of my own," said Kelly. "I had to go a little above the estimate. I got the express wagons and cabs mostly for five dollars; but the trucks and two-horse teams mostly raised me to ten dollars. The motormen wanted ten dollars, and some of the loaded teams twenty dollars. The cops struck me hardest—fifty dollars I paid two, and the rest twenty dollars and twenty-five dollars. But didn't it work beautiful, Mr. Rockwall? I'm glad William A. Brady wasn't onto that little outdoor vehicle mob scene. I wouldn't want William to break his heart with jealousy. And never a rehearsal, either! The boys was on time to the fraction of a second. It was two hours before a snake could get below Greeley's statue."

"Thirteen hundred—there you are, Kelly," said Anthony, tearing off a check. "Your thousand, and the three hundred you were out. You don't despise money, do you, Kelly?"

"Me?" said Kelly. "I can lick the man that invented poverty."

Anthony called Kelly when he was at the door.

"You didn't notice," said he, "anywhere in the tie-up, a kind of a fat boy without any clothes on shooting arrows around with a bow, did you?"

"Why, no," said Kelly, mystified. "I didn't. If he was like you say, maybe the cops pinched him before I got there."

"I thought the little rascal wouldn't be on hand," chuckled Anthony. "Good-bye, Kelly."

AFTER TWENTY YEARS

THE policeman on the beat moved up the avenue impressively. The impressiveness was habitual and not for show, for spectators were few. The time was barely ten o'clock, at night, but chilly gusts of wind with a taste of rain in them had well nigh depeopled the streets.

Trying doors as he went, twirling his club with many intricate and artful movements, turning now and then to cast his watchful eye adown the pacific thoroughfare, the officer, with his stalwart form and slight swagger, made a fine picture of a guardian of the peace. The vicinity was one that kept early hours. Now and then you might see the lights of a cigar store or of an all-night lunch counter; but the majority of the doors belonged to business places that had long since been closed.

When about midway of a certain block the policeman suddenly slowed his walk. In the doorway of a darkened hardware store a man leaned, with an unlighted cigar in his mouth. As the policeman walked up to him the man spoke up quickly.

"It's all right, officer," he said, reassuringly. "I'm just waiting for a friend. It's an appointment made twenty years ago. Sounds a little funny to you, doesn't it? Well, I'll explain if you'd like to make certain it's all straight. About that long ago there used to be a restaurant where this store stands—'Big Joe' Brady's restaurant."

"Until five years ago," said the policeman. "It was torn down then."

The man in the doorway struck a match and lit his cigar. The light showed a pale, square-jawed face with keen eyes, and a little white scar near his right eyebrow. His scarfpin was a large diamond, oddly set.

"Twenty years ago tonight," said the man, "I dined here at 'Big Joe' Brady's with Jimmy Wells, my best chum, and the finest chap in the world. He and I were raised here in New York, just like two brothers, together. I was eighteen and Jimmy was twenty. The next morning I was to start for the West to make my fortune. You couldn't have dragged Jimmy out of New York; he thought it was the only place on earth. Well, we agreed that night that we would meet here again exactly twenty years from that date and time, no matter what our conditions might be or from what distance we might have to come. We figured that in twenty years each of us ought to have our destiny worked out and our fortunes made, whatever they were going to be."

"It sounds pretty interesting," said the policeman. "Rather a long time between meets, though, it seems to me. Haven't you heard from your friend since you left?"

"Well, yes, for a time we corresponded," said the other. "But after a year or two we lost track of each other. You see, the West is a pretty big proposition, and I kept hustling around over it pretty lively. But I know Jimmy will meet me here if he's alive, for he always was the truest, stanchest old chap in the world. He'll never forget. I came a thousand miles to stand in this door tonight, and it's worth it if my old partner turns up."

The waiting man pulled out a handsome watch, the lids of it set with small diamonds.

"Three minutes to ten," he announced. "It was exactly ten o'clock when we parted here at the restaurant door."

"Did pretty well out West, didn't you?" asked the policeman.

"You bet! I hope Jimmy has done half as well. He was a kind of plodder, though, good fellow as he was. I've had to compete with some of the sharpest wits going to get my pile. A man gets in a groove in New York. It takes the West to put a razor-edge on him."

The policeman twirled his club and took a step or two.

"I'll be on my way. Hope your friend comes around all right. Going to call time on him sharp?"

"I should say not!" said the other. "I'll give him half an hour at least. If Jimmy is alive on earth he'll be here by that time. So long, officer."

"Good-night, sir," said the policeman, passing on along his beat, trying doors as he went.

There was now a fine, cold drizzle falling, and the wind had risen from its uncertain puffs into a steady blow. The few foot passengers astir in that quarter hurried dismally and silently along with coat collars turned high and pocketed hands. And in the door of the hardware store the man who had come a thousand miles to fill an appointment, uncertain almost to absurdity, with the friend of his youth, smoked his cigar and waited.

About twenty minutes he waited, and then a tall man in a long overcoat, with collar turned up to his ears, hurried across from the opposite side of the street. He went directly to the waiting man.

"Is that you, Bob?" he asked, doubtfully.

"Is that you, Jimmy Wells?" cried the man in the door.

"Bless my heart!" exclaimed the new arrival, grasping both the other's hands with his own. "It's Bob, sure as fate. I was certain I'd find you here if you were still in existence. Well, well, well!—twenty years is a long time. The old restaurant's gone, Bob; I wish it had lasted, so we could have had another dinner there. How has the West treated you, old man?"

"Bully; it has given me everything I asked it for. You've changed lots, Jimmy. I never thought you were so tall by two or three inches."

"Oh, I grew a bit after I was twenty."

"Doing well in New York, Jimmy?"

"Moderately. I have a position in one of the city departments. Come on, Bob; we'll go around to a place I know of, and have a good long talk about old times."

The two men started up the street, arm in arm. The man from the West, his egotism enlarged by success, was beginning to outline the history of his career. The other, submerged in his overcoat, listened with interest.

At the corner stood a drug store, brilliant with electric lights. When they came into this glare each of them turned simultaneously to gaze upon the other's face.

The man from the West stopped suddenly and released his arm.

"You're not Jimmy Wells," he snapped. "Twenty years is a long time, but not long enough to change a man's nose from a Roman to a pug."

"It sometimes changes a good man into a bad one," said the tall

GORDON GRANT

man. "You've been under arrest for ten minutes, 'Silky' Bob. Chicago thinks you may have dropped over our way and wires us she wants to have a chat with you. Going quietly, are you? That's sensible. Now, before we go on to the station here's a note I was asked to hand you. You may read it here at the window. It's from Patrolman Wells."

The man from the West unfolded the little piece of paper handed him. His hand was steady when he began to read, but it trembled a little by the time he had finished. The note was rather short.

BOB: I was at the appointed place on time. When you struck the match to light your cigar I saw it was the face of the man wanted in Chicago. Somehow I couldn't do it myself, so I went around and got a plainclothes-man to do the job.

JIMMY.

SCHOOLS AND SCHOOLS

I

OLD Jerome Warren lived in a hundred-thousand-dollar house at 35 East Fifty-Soforth Street. He was a downtown broker, so rich that he could afford to walk—for his health—a few blocks in the direction of his office every morning, and then call a cab.

He had an adopted son, the son of an old friend named Gilbert—Cyril Scott could play him nicely—who was becoming a successful painter as fast as he could squeeze the paint out of his tubes. Another member of the household was Barbara Ross, a stepniece. Man is born to trouble; so, as old Jerome had no family of his own, he took up the burdens of others.

Gilbert and Barbara got along swimmingly. There was a tacit and tactical understanding all round that the two would stand up under a floral bell some high noon, and promise the minister to keep old Jerome's money in a state of high commotion. But at this point complications must be introduced.

Thirty years before, when old Jerome was young Jerome, there was a brother of his named Dick. Dick went West to seek his or somebody else's fortune. Nothing was heard of him until one day old Jerome had a letter from his brother. It was badly written on ruled paper that smelled of salt bacon and coffee-grounds. The writing was asthmatic and the spelling St. Vitusy.

It appeared that instead of Dick having forced Fortune to stand and deliver, he had been held up himself, and made to give hostages to the enemy. That is, as his letter disclosed, he was on the point of pegging out with a complication of disorders that even whiskey had failed to check. All that his thirty years of prospecting had netted him was one daughter, nineteen years old, as per invoice, whom he was shipping East, charges prepaid, for Jerome to clothe, feed, educate, comfort, and cherish for the rest of her natural life or until matrimony should them part.

Old Jerome was a board-walk. Everybody knows that the world is supported by the shoulders of Atlas; and that Atlas stands on a rail-fence; and that the rail-fence is built on a turtle's back. Now, the turtle has to stand on something; and that is a board-walk made of men like old Jerome.

I do not know whether immortality shall accrue to man; but if not so, I would like to know when men like old Jerome get what is due them.

They met Nevada Warren at the station. She was a little girl, deeply sunburned and wholesomely good-looking, with a manner that was frankly unsophisticated, yet one that not even a cigar-drummer would intrude upon without thinking twice. Looking at her, somehow you would expect to see her in a short skirt and leather leggings, shooting glass balls or taming mustangs. But in her plain white waist and black skirt she sent you guessing again. With an easy exhibition of strength she swung along a heavy valise, which the uniformed porters tried in vain to wrest from her.

"I am sure we shall be the best of friends," said Barbara, pecking at the firm, sunburned cheek.

"I hope so," said Nevada.

"Dear little niece," said old Jerome, "you are as welcome to my home as if it were your father's own."

"Thanks," said Nevada.

"And I am going to call you 'cousin,' " said Gilbert, with his charming smile.

"Take the valise, please," said Nevada. "It weighs a million pounds. It's got samples from six of Dad's old mines in it," she explained to Barbara. "I calculate they'd assay about nine cents to the thousand tons, but I promised him to bring them along."

II

It is a common custom to refer to the usual complication between one man and two ladies, or one lady and two men, or a lady and a man and a nobleman, or—well, any of those problems—as the triangle. But they are never unqualified triangles. They are always isosceles—never equilateral. So, upon the coming of Nevada Warren, she and Gilbert and Barbara Ross lined up into such a figurative triangle; and of that triangle Barbara formed the hypotenuse.

One morning old Jerome was lingering long after breakfast over the dullest morning paper in the city before setting forth to his downtown fly-trap. He had become quite fond of Nevada, finding in her much of his dead brother's quiet independence and unsuspicious frankness.

A maid brought in a note for Miss Nevada Warren.

"A messenger-boy delivered it at the door, please," she said. "He's waiting for an answer."

Nevada, who was whistling a Spanish waltz between her teeth, and watching the carriages and autos roll by in the street, took the envelope. She knew it was from Gilbert, before she opened it, by the little gold palette in the upper left-hand corner.

After tearing it open she pored over the contents for a while, absorbedly. Then, with a serious face, she went and stood at her uncle's elbow.

"Uncle Jerome, Gilbert is a nice boy, isn't he?"

"Why, bless the child!" said old Jerome, crackling his paper loudly; "of course he is. I raised him myself."

"He wouldn't write anything to anybody that wasn't exactly—I mean that everybody couldn't know and read, would he?"

"I'd just like to see him try it," said Uncle, tearing a handful from his newspaper. "Why, what—"

"Read this note he just sent me, Uncle, and see if you think it's all right and proper. You see, I don't know much about city people and their ways."

Old Jerome threw his paper down and set both his feet upon it. He took Gilbert's note and fiercely perused it twice, and then a third time.

"Why, child," said he, "you had me almost excited, although I was sure of that boy. He's a duplicate of his father, and he was a gilt-edged diamond. He only asks if you and Barbara will be ready at four o'clock this afternoon for an automobile drive over to Long Island. I don't see anything to criticize in it except the stationery. I always did hate that shade of blue."

"Would it be all right to go?" asked Nevada, eagerly.

"Yes, yes, yes, child; of course. Why not? Still, it pleases me to see you so careful and candid. Go, by all means."

"I didn't know," said Nevada, demurely. "I thought I'd ask you. Couldn't you go with us, Uncle?"

"I? No, no, no, no! I've ridden once in a car that boy was driving. Never again! But it's entirely proper for you and Barbara to go. Yes, yes. But I will not. No, no, no, no!"

Nevada flew to the door, and said to the maid:

"You bet we'll go. I'll answer for Miss Barbara. Tell the boy to say to Mr. Warren, 'You bet we'll go.' "

"Nevada," called old Jerome, "pardon me, my dear, but wouldn't it be as well to send him a note in reply? Just a line would do."

"No, I won't bother about that," said Nevada, gaily. "Gilbert will understand—he always does. I never rode in an automobile in my life; but I've paddled a canoe down Little Devil River through the Lost Horse Cañon, and if it's any livelier than that I'd like to know!"

III

Two months are supposed to have elapsed.

Barbara sat in the study of the hundred-thousand-dollar house. It was a good place for her. Many places are provided in the world where men and women may repair for the purpose of extricating themselves from divers difficulties. There are cloisters, wailing-places, watering-places, confessionals, hermitages, lawyers' offices, beauty-parlors, air-ships, and studies; and the greatest of these are studies.

It usually takes a hypotenuse a long time to discover that it is the longest side of a triangle. But it's a long line that has no turning.

Barbara was alone. Uncle Jerome and Nevada had gone to the theatre. Barbara had not cared to go. She wanted to stay at home and study in the study. If you, miss, were a stunning New York girl, and saw every day that a brown, ingenuous Western witch was getting hobbles and a lasso on the young man you wanted for yourself, you, too, would lose taste for the oxidized-silver setting of a musical comedy.

Barbara sat by the quartered-oak library table. Her right arm rested upon the table, and her dextral fingers nervously manipulated a sealed letter. The letter was addressed to Nevada Warren; and in the upper left-hand corner of the envelope was Gilbert's little gold palette. It had been delivered at nine o'clock, after Nevada had left.

Barbara would have given her pearl necklace to know what the letter contained; but she could not open and read it by the aid of steam, or a pen-handle, or a hairpin, or any of the generally approved methods, because her position in society forbade such an act. She had tried to read some of the lines of the letter by holding the envelope up to a strong light and pressing it hard against the paper, but Gilbert had too good a taste in stationery to make that possible.

At eleven-thirty the theatre-goers returned. It was a delicious winter night. Even so far as from the cab to the door they were powdered thickly with the big flakes downpouring diagonally from the east. Old Jerome growled good-naturedly about villainous cab service and blockaded streets. Nevada, colored like a rose, with sapphire eyes, babbled of the stormy nights in the mountains around Dad's cabin. During all these wintry apostrophes, Barbara, cold at heart, sawed wood—the only appropriate thing she could think of to do.

Old Jerome went immediately upstairs to hot-water-bottles and quinine. Nevada fluttered into the study, the only cheerfully lighted room, subsided into an armchair, and, while at the interminable task of unbuttoning her elbow gloves, gave oral testimony as to the demerits of the "show."

"Yes, I think Mr. Fields is really amusing—sometimes," said Barbara. "Here is a letter for you, dear, that came by special delivery just after you had gone."

"Who is it from?" asked Nevada, tugging at a button.

"Well, really," said Barbara, with a smile, "I can only guess. The envelope has that queer little thing in one corner that Gilbert calls a palette, but which looks to me rather like a gilt heart on a schoolgirl's valentine."

"I wonder what he's writing to me about," remarked Nevada, listlessly.

"We're all alike," said Barbara; "all women. We try to find out what is in a letter by studying the postmark. As a last resort we use scissors, and read it from the bottom upward. Here it is."

She made a motion as if to toss the letter across the table to Nevada.

"Great catamounts!" exclaimed Nevada. "These center-fire buttons are a nuisance. I'd rather wear buckskins. Oh, Barbara, please shuck the hide off that letter and read it. It'll be midnight before I get these gloves off!"

"Why, dear, you don't want me to open Gilbert's letter to you? It's for you, and you wouldn't wish anyone else to read it, of course!"

Nevada raised her steady, calm, sapphire eyes from her gloves.

"Nobody writes me anything that everybody mightn't read," she said. "Go on, Barbara. Maybe Gilbert wants us to go out in his car again tomorrow."

Curiosity can do more things than kill a cat; and if emotions, well recognized as feminine, are inimical to feline life, then jealousy would soon leave the whole world catless. Barbara opened the letter, with an indulgent, slightly bored air.

"Well, dear," said she, "I'll read it if you want me to."

She slit the envelope, and read the missive with swift-travelling eyes; read it again, and cast a quick, shrewd glance at Nevada, who, for the time, seemed to consider gloves as the world of her interest, and letters from rising artists as no more than messages from Mars.

For a quarter of a minute Barbara looked at Nevada with a strange steadfastness; and then a smile so small that it widened her mouth only the sixteenth part of an inch, and narrowed her eyes no more than a twentieth, flashed like an inspired thought across her face.

Since the beginning no woman has been a mystery to another woman. Swift as light travels, each penetrates the heart and mind of another, sifts her sister's words of their cunningest disguises, reads her most hidden desires, and plucks the sophistry from her wiliest talk like hairs from a comb, twiddling them sardonically between her thumb and fingers before letting them float away on the breezes of fundamental doubt. Long ago Eve's son rang the door-bell of the family residence in Paradise Park, bearing a strange lady on his arm, whom he introduced.

Eve took her daughter-in-law aside and lifted a classic eyebrow.

"The Land of Nod," said the bride, languidly flirting the leaf of a palm. "I suppose you've been there, of course?"

"Not lately," said Eve, absolutely unstaggered. "Don't you think the apple-sauce they serve over there is execrable? I rather like that mulberry-leaf tunic effect, dear; but, of course, the real fig goods are not to be had over there. Come over behind this lilac-bush while the gentlemen split a celery tonic. I think the caterpillar-holes have made your dress open a little in the back."

So, then and there—according to the records—was the alliance formed by the only two who's-who ladies in the world. Then it was agreed that woman should forever remain as clear as a pane of glass—though glass was yet to be discovered—to other women, and that she should palm herself off on man as a mystery.

Barbara seemed to hesitate.

"Really, Nevada," she said; with a little show of embarrassment, "you shouldn't have insisted on my opening this. I—I'm sure it wasn't meant for anyone else to know."

Nevada forgot her gloves for a moment.

"Then read it aloud," she said. "Since you've already read it, what's the difference? If Mr. Warren has written to me something that anyone else oughtn't to know, that is all the more reason why everybody should know it."

"Well," said Barbara, "this is what it says: 'Dearest Nevada—Come to my studio at twelve o'clock tonight. Do not fail.' " Barbara rose and dropped the note in Nevada's lap. "I'm awfully sorry," she said, "that I knew. It isn't like Gilbert. There must be some mistake. Just consider that I am ignorant of it, will you, dear? I must go upstairs now, I have such a headache. I'm sure I don't understand the note. Perhaps Gilbert has been dining too well, and will explain. Good-night!"

IV

Nevada tiptoed to the hall, and heard Barbara's door close upstairs. The bronze clock in the study told the hour of twelve was fifteen minutes away. She ran swiftly to the front door, and let herself out into the snowstorm. Gilbert Warren's studio was six squares away.

By aerial ferry the white, silent forces of the storm attacked the city from beyond the sullen East River. Already the snow lay a foot deep on the pavements, the drifts heaping themselves like scaling-ladders against the walls of the besieged town. The Avenue was as quiet as a street in Pompeii. Cabs now and then skimmed past like white-winged gulls over a moonlit ocean; and less frequent motor-cars—sustaining the comparison—hissed through the foaming waves like submarine boats on their jocund, perilous journeys.

Nevada plunged like a wind-driven storm-petrel on her way. She looked up at the ragged sierras of cloud-capped buildings that rose above the streets, shaded by the night lights and the congealed vapors to gray, drab, ashen, lavender, dun, and cerulean tints. They were so like the wintry mountains of her Western home that she felt a satisfaction such as the hundred-thousand-dollar house had seldom brought her.

A policeman caused her to waver on a corner, just by his eye and weight.

"Hello, Mabel!" said he. "Kind of late for you to be out, ain't it?"

"I—I am just going to the drug store," said Nevada, hurrying past him.

The excuse serves as a passport for the most sophisticated. Does it prove that woman never progresses, or that she sprang from Adam's rib, full-fledged in intellect and wiles?

Turning eastward, the direct blast cut down Nevada's speed one-half. She made zigzag tracks in the snow; but she was as tough as a piñon sapling, and bowed to it as gracefully. Suddenly the studio-building loomed before her, a familiar landmark, like a cliff above some well-remembered cañon. The haunt of business and its hostile neighbor, art, was darkened and silent. The elevator stopped at ten.

Up eight flights of Stygian stairs Nevada climbed, and rapped firmly at the door numbered "89." She had been there many times before, with Barbara and Uncle Jerome.

Gilbert opened the door. He had a crayon pencil in one hand, a green shade over his eyes, and a pipe in his mouth. The pipe dropped to the floor.

"Am I late?" asked Nevada. "I came as quick as I could. Uncle and me were at the theatre this evening. Here I am, Gilbert!"

Gilbert did a Pygmalion-and-Galatea act. He changed from a statue of stupefaction to a young man with a problem to tackle. He admitted Nevada, got a whisk-broom, and began to brush the snow from her clothes. A great lamp, with a green shade, hung over an easel, where the artist had been sketching in crayon.

"You wanted me," said Nevada simply, "and I came. You said so in your letter. What did you send for me for?"

"You read my letter?" inquired Gilbert, sparring for wind.

"Barbara read it to me. I saw it afterward. It said: 'Come to my studio at twelve tonight, and do not fail.' I thought you were sick, of course, but you don't seem to be."

"Aha!" said Gilbert irrelevantly. "I'll tell you why I asked you to come, Nevada. I want you to marry me immediately—tonight. What's a little snowstorm? Will you do it?"

"You might have noticed that I would, long ago," said Nevada. "And I'm rather stuck on the snowstorm idea, myself. I surely would hate one of these flowery church noon-weddings. Gilbert, I didn't know you had grit enough to propose it this way. Let's shock 'em—it's our funeral, ain't it?"

"You bet!" said Gilbert. "Where did I hear that expression?" he added to himself. "Wait a minute, Nevada; I want to do a little phoning."

He shut himself in a little dressing-room, and called upon the lightnings of the heavens—condensed into unromantic numbers and districts.

"That you, Jack? You confounded sleepy-head! Yes, wake up; this is me—or I—oh, bother the difference in grammar! I'm going to be married right away. Yes! Wake up your sister—don't answer me back; bring her along, too—you *must*. Remind Agnes of the time I saved her from drowning in Lake Ronkonkoma—I know it's caddish to refer to it, but she *must* come with you. Yes! Nevada is here, waiting. We've been engaged quite a while. Some opposition among the relatives, you know, and we have to pull it off this way. We're waiting here for you. Don't let Agnes out-talk you—bring her! You will? Good old boy! I'll order a carriage to call for you, double-quick time. Confound you, Jack, you're all right!"

Gilbert returned to the room where Nevada waited.

"My old friend, Jack Peyton, and his sister were to have been here at a quarter to twelve," he explained; "but Jack is so confoundedly slow. I've just phoned them to hurry. They'll be here in a few minutes. I'm the happiest man in the world, Nevada! What did you do with the letter I sent you today?"

"I've got it cinched here," said Nevada, pulling it out from beneath her opera-cloak.

Gilbert drew the letter from the envelope and looked it over carefully. Then he looked at Nevada thoughtfully.

"Didn't you think it rather queer that I should ask you to come to my studio at midnight?" he asked.

"Why, no," said Nevada, rounding her eyes. "Not if you needed me. Out West, when a pal sends you a hurry call—ain't that what you say here?—we get there first and talk about it after the row is over. And it's usually snowing there, too, when things happen. So I didn't mind."

Gilbert rushed into another room, and came back burdened with overcoats warranted to turn wind, rain, or snow.

"Put this raincoat on," he said, holding it for her. "We have a quarter of a mile to go. Old Jack and his sister will be here in a few minutes." He began to struggle into a heavy coat. "Oh, Nevada," he said, "just look at the headlines on the front page of that evening paper on the table, will you? It's about your section of the West, and I know it will interest you."

He waited a full minute, pretending to find trouble in the getting on of his overcoat, and then turned. Nevada had not moved. She was looking at him with strange and pensive directness. Her cheeks had a flush on them beyond the color that had been contributed by the wind and snow; but her eyes were steady.

"I was going to tell you," she said, "anyhow, before you—before we—before—well, before anything. Dad never gave me a day of schooling. I never learned to read or write a darned word. Now if—"

Pounding their uncertain way upstairs, the feet of Jack, the somnolent, and Agnes, the grateful, were heard.

V

When Mr. and Mrs. Gilbert Warren were spinning softly homeward in a closed carriage, after the ceremony, Gilbert said:

"Nevada, would you really like to know what I wrote you in the letter that you received tonight?"

"Fire away!" said his bride.

"Word for word," said Gilbert, "it was this: 'My dear Miss Warren—You were right about the flower. It was a hydrangea, and not a lilac.' "

"All right," said Nevada. "But let's forget it. The joke's on Barbara, anyway!"

THE DEFEAT OF THE CITY

ROBERT WALMSLEY'S descent upon the city resulted in a Kilkenny struggle. He came out of the fight victor by a fortune and a reputation. On the other hand, he was swallowed up by the city. The city gave him what he demanded and then branded him with its brand. It remodelled, cut, trimmed, and stamped him to the pattern it approves. It opened its social gates to him and shut him in on a close-cropped, formal lawn with the select herd of ruminants. In dress, habits, manners, provincialism, routine, and narrowness he acquired that charming insolence, that irritating completeness, that sophisticated crassness, that overbalanced poise that makes the Manhattan gentleman so delightfully small in his greatness.

One of the up-state rural counties pointed with pride to the successful young metropolitan lawyer as a product of its soil. Six years earlier this county had removed the wheat straw from between its huckleberry-stained teeth and emitted a derisive and bucolic laugh as old man Walmsley's freckle-faced "Bob" abandoned the certain three-per-diem meals of the one-horse farm for the discontinuous quick lunch counters of the three-ringed metropolis. At the end of the six years no murder trial, coaching party, automobile accident, or cotillion was complete in which the name of Robert Walmsley did not figure. Tailors waylaid him in the street to get a new wrinkle from the cut of his unwrinkled trousers. Hyphenated fellows in the clubs and members of the oldest subpoenaed families were glad to clap him on the back and allow him three letters of his name.

But the Matterhorn of Robert Walmsley's success was not scaled until he married Alicia Van Der Pool. I cite the Matterhorn, for just so high and cool and white and inaccessible was this daughter of the old burghers. The social Alps that ranged about her—over whose bleak passes a thousand climbers struggled—reached only to her knees. She towered in her own atmosphere, serene, chaste, prideful, wading in no fountains, dining no monkeys, breeding no dogs for bench shows. She was a Van Der Pool. Fountains were made to play for her; monkeys were made for other people's ancestors; dogs, she understood, were created to be companions of blind persons and objectionable characters who smoked pipes.

This was the Matterhorn that Robert Walmsley accomplished. If he found, with the good poet with the game foot and artificially curled hair, that he who ascends to mountaintops will find the loftiest peaks most wrapped in clouds and snow, he concealed his chilblains beneath a brave and smiling exterior. He was a lucky man and knew it, even though he were imitating the Spartan boy with an ice-cream freezer beneath his doublet frappéeing the region of his heart.

After a brief wedding tour abroad, the couple returned to create a decided ripple in the calm cistern (so placid and cool and sunless it is) of the best society. They entertained at their red-brick mausoleum of ancient greatness in an old square that is a cemetery of crumbled glory. And Robert Walmsley was proud of his wife; although while one of his hands shook his guests' the other held tightly to his alpenstock and thermometer.

One day Alicia found a letter written to Robert by his mother. It was an unerudite letter, full of crops and motherly love and farm notes. It chronicled the health of the pig and the recent red calf, and asked concerning Robert's in return. It was a letter direct from the soil, straight from home, full of biographies of bees, tales of turnips, paeans of new-laid eggs, neglected parents, and the slump in dried apples.

"Why have I not been shown your mother's letters?" asked Alicia. There was always something in her voice that made you think of lorgnettes, of accounts at Tiffany's, of sledges smoothly gliding on the trail from Dawson to Forty Mile, of the tinkling of pendant prisms on your grandmothers' chandeliers, of snow lying on a convent roof, of a police sergeant refusing bail. "Your mother," continued Alicia, "invites us to make a visit to the farm. I have never seen a farm. We will go there for a week or two, Robert."

"We will," said Robert, with the grand air of an associate Supreme Justice concurring in an opinion. "I did not lay the invitation before you because I thought you would not care to go. I am much pleased at your decision."

"I will write to her myself," answered Alicia, with a faint foreshadowing of enthusiasm. "Félice shall pack my trunks at once. Seven, I think, will be enough. I do not suppose that your mother entertains a great deal. Does she give many house parties?"

Robert arose, and as attorney for rural places filed a demurrer against six of the seven trunks. He endeavored to define, picture, elucidate, set forth, and describe a farm. His own words sounded strange in his ears. He had not realized how thoroughly urbsidized he had become.

A week passed and found them landed at the little country station five hours out from the city. A grinning, stentorian, sarcastic youth driving a mule to a spring wagon hailed Robert savagely.

"Hallo, Mr. Walmsley. Found your way back at last, have you? Sorry I couldn't bring in the automobile for you, but Dad's bull-tonguing the ten-acre clover patch with it today. Guess you'll excuse my not wearing a dress suit over to meet you—it ain't six o'clock yet, you know."

"I'm glad to see you, Tom," said Robert, grasping his brother's hand. "Yes, I've found my way at last. You've a right to say 'at last.' It's been over two years since the last time. But it will be oftener after this, my boy."

Alicia, cool in the summer heat as an Arctic wraith, white as a Norse snow maiden in her flimsy muslin and fluttering lace parasol, came round the corner of the station; and Tom was stripped of his assurance. He became chiefly eyesight clothed in blue jeans, and on the homeward drive to the mule alone did he confide in language the inwardness of his thoughts.

They drove homeward. The low sun dropped a spendthrift flood of gold upon the fortunate fields of wheat. The cities were far away. The road lay curling around wood and dale and hill like a ribbon lost from the robe of careless summer. The wind followed like a whinnying colt in the track of Phoebus's steeds.

By and by the farmhouse peeped gray out of its faithful grove; they saw the long lane with its convoy of walnut trees running from the road to the house; they smelled the wild rose and the breath of cool, damp willows in the creek's bed. And then in unison all the voices of the soil began a chant addressed to the soul of Robert Walmsley. Out of the tilted aisles of the dim wood they came hollowly; they chirped and buzzed from the parched grass; they trilled from the ripples of the creek ford; they floated up in clear Pan's pipe notes from the dimming meadows; the whippoorwills joined in as they pursued midges in the upper air; slow-going cow-bells struck out a homely accompaniment—and this was what each one said: "You've found your way back at last, have you?"

The old voices of the soil spoke to him. Leaf and bud and blossom conversed with him in the old vocabulary of his careless youth—the inanimate things, the familiar stones and rails, the gates and furrows and roofs and turns of the road had an eloquence, too, and a power in the transformation. The country had smiled and he had felt the breath of it, and his heart was drawn as if in a moment back to his old love. The city was far away.

This rural atavism, then, seized Robert Walmsley and possessed him. A queer thing he noticed in connection with it was that Alicia, sitting at his side, suddenly seemed to him a stranger. She did not belong to this recurrent phase. Never before had she seemed so remote, so colorless and high—so intangible and unreal. And yet he had never admired her more than when she sat there by him in the rickety spring wagon, chiming no more with his mood and with her environment than the Matterhorn chimes with a peasant's cabbage garden.

That night when the greetings and the supper were over, the entire family, including Buff, the yellow dog, bestrewed itself upon the front porch. Alicia, not haughty but silent, sat in the shadow dressed in an exquisite pale-gray tea gown. Robert's mother discoursed to her happily concerning marmalade and lumbago. Tom sat on the top step; Sisters Millie and Pam on the lowest step to catch the lightning bugs. Mother had the willow rocker. Father sat in the big armchair with one of its arms gone. Buff sprawled in the middle of the porch in everybody's way. The twilight pixies and pucks stole forth unseen and plunged other poignant shafts of memory into the heart of Robert. A rural madness entered his soul. The city was far away.

Father sat without his pipe, writhing in his heavy boots, a sacrifice to rigid courtesy. Robert shouted: "No, you don't!" He fetched the pipe and lit it; he seized the old gentleman's boots and tore them off. The last one slipped suddenly, and Mr. Robert Walmsley, of Washington Square, tumbled off the porch backward with Buff on top of him, howling fearfully. Tom laughed sarcastically.

Robert tore off his coat and vest and hurled them into a lilac bush.

"Come out here, you landlubber," he cried to Tom, "and I'll put grass seed on your back. I think you called me a 'dude' a while ago. Come along and cut your capers."

Tom understood the invitation and accepted it with delight. Three times they wrestled on the grass, "side holds," even as the giants of the mat. And twice was Tom forced to bite grass at the hands of the distinguished lawyer. Dishevelled, panting, each still boasting of his own prowess, they stumbled back to the porch. Millie cast a pert reflection upon the qualities of a city brother. In an instant Robert had secured a horrid katydid in his fingers and bore down upon her. Screaming wildly, she fled up the lane, pursued by the avenging glass of form. A quarter of a mile and they returned, she full of apology to the victorious "dude." The rustic mania possessed him unabatedly.

"I can do up a cowpenful of you slow hayseeds," he proclaimed, vaingloriously. "Bring on your bulldogs, your hired men and your log-rollers."

He turned handsprings on the grass that prodded Tom to envious sarcasm. And then, with a whoop, he clattered to the rear and brought back Uncle Ike, a battered colored retainer of the family, with his banjo, and strewed sand on the porch and danced "Chicken in the Bread Tray" and did buck-and-wing wonders for half an hour longer. Incredibly wild and boisterous things he did. He sang, he told stories that set all but one shrieking, he played the yokel, the humorous clodhopper; he was mad, mad with the revival of the old life in his blood.

He became so extravagant that once his mother sought gently to reprove him. Then Alicia moved as though she were about to speak, but she did not. Through it all she sat immovable, a slim, white spirit in the dusk that no man might question or read.

By and by she asked permission to ascend to her room, saying that she was tired. On her way she passed Robert. He was standing in the door, the figure of vulgar comedy, with ruffled hair, reddened face, and unpardonable confusion of attire—no trace there of the immaculate Robert Walmsley, the courted clubman and ornament of select circles. He was doing a conjuring trick with some household utensils, and the family, now won over to him without exception, was beholding him with worshipful admiration.

As Alicia passed in Robert started suddenly. He had forgotten for the moment that she was present. Without a glance at him she went on upstairs.

After that the fun grew quiet. An hour passed in talk, and then Robert went up himself.

She was standing by the window when he entered their room. She was still clothed as when they were on the porch. Outside and crowding against the window was a giant apple tree, full blossomed.

Robert sighed and went near the window. He was ready to meet his fate. A confessed vulgarian, he foresaw the verdict of justice in the shape of that still, white-clad form. He knew the rigid lines that a Van Der Pool would draw. He was a peasant gambolling indecorously in the valley, and the pure, cold, white, unthawed summit of the Matterhorn could not but frown on him. He had been unmasked by his own actions. All the polish, the poise, the form that the city had given him, had fallen from him like an ill-fitting mantle at the first breath of a country breeze. Dully he awaited the approaching condemnation.

"Robert," said the calm, cool voice of his judge, "I thought I married a gentleman."

Yes, it was coming. And yet, in the face of it, Robert Walmsley was eagerly regarding a certain branch of the apple tree upon which he used to climb out of that very window. He believed he could do it now. He wondered how many blossoms there were on the tree—ten millions? But here was someone speaking again:

"I thought I married a gentleman," the voice went on, "but—"

Why had she come and was standing so close by his side?

"But I find that I have married"—was this Alicia talking?—"something better—a man—Bob, dear, kiss me, won't you?"

The city was far away.

A SERVICE OF LOVE

WHEN one loves one's Art no service seems too hard.

That is our premise. This story shall draw a conclusion from it, and show at the same time that the premise is incorrect. That will be a new thing in logic, and a feat in story-telling somewhat older than the great wall of China.

Joe Larrabee came out of the post-oak flats of the Middle West pulsing with a genius for pictorial art. At six he drew a picture of the town pump with a prominent citizen passing it hastily. This effort was framed and hung in the drug store window by the side of the ear of corn with an uneven number of rows. At twenty he left for New York with a flowing necktie and a capital tied up somewhat closer.

Delia Caruthers did things in six octaves so promisingly in a pine-tree village in the South that her relatives chipped in enough in her chip hat for her to go "North" and "finish." They could not see her f— but that is our story.

Joe and Delia met in an atelier where a number of art and music students had gathered to discuss chiaroscuro, Wagner, music, Rembrandt's works, pictures, Waldenteufel, wall paper, Chopin, and Oolong.

Joe and Delia became enamored one of the other, or each of the other, as you please, and in a short time were married—for (see above), when one loves one's Art no service seems too hard.

Mr. and Mrs. Larrabee began housekeeping in a flat. It was a lonesome flat—something like the A sharp way down at the left-hand end of the keyboard. And they were happy; for they had their Art, and they had each other. And my advice to the rich young man would be—sell all thou hast, and give it to the poor—janitor for the privilege of living in a flat with your Art and your Delia.

Flat-dwellers shall indorse my dictum that theirs is the only true happiness. If a home is happy it cannot fit too close—let the dresser collapse and become a billiard table; let the mantel turn to a rowing machine, the escritoire to a spare bedchamber, the washstand to an upright piano; let the four walls come together, if they will, so you and your Delia are between. But if home be the other kind, let it be wide and long—enter you at the Golden Gate, hang your hat on Hatteras, your cape on Cape Horn, and go out by the Labrador.

Joe was painting in the class of the great Magister—you know his fame. His fees are high; his lessons are light—his high-lights have brought him renown. Delia was studying under Rosenstock—you know his repute as a disturber of the piano keys.

They were mighty happy as long as their money lasted. So is every—but I will not be cynical. Their aims were very clear and defined. Joe was to become capable very soon of turning out pictures that old gentlemen with thin side-whiskers and thick pocketbooks would sand-bag one another in his studio for the privilege of buying. Delia was to become familiar and then contemptuous with Music, so that when she saw the orchestra seats and boxes unsold she could have sore throat and lobster in a private dining-room and refuse to go on the stage.

But the best, in my opinion, was the home life in the little flat—the ardent, voluble chats after the day's study; the cozy dinners and fresh, light breakfasts; the interchange of ambitions—ambitions interwoven each with the other's or else inconsiderable—the mutual help and inspiration; and—overlook my artlessness—stuffed olives and cheese sandwiches at eleven P.M.

But after a while Art flagged. It sometimes does, even if some switchman doesn't flag it. Everything going out and nothing coming in, as the vulgarians say. Money was lacking to pay Mr. Magister and Herr Rosenstock their prices. When one loves one's Art no service seems too hard. So, Delia said she must give music lessons to keep the chafing dish bubbling.

For two or three days she went out canvassing for pupils. One evening she came home elated.

"Joe dear," she said, gleefully, "I've a pupil. And, oh, the loveliest people! General—General A. B. Pinkney's daughter—on Seventy-first Street. Such a splendid house, Joe—you ought to see the front door! Byzantine I think you would call it. And inside! Oh, Joe, I never saw anything like it before.

"My pupil is his daughter Clementina. I dearly love her already. She's a delicate thing—dresses always in white; and the sweetest, simplest manners! Only eighteen years old. I'm to give three lessons a week; and, just think, Joe! five dollars a lesson. I don't mind it a bit; for when I get two or three more pupils I can resume my lessons with Herr Rosenstock. Now, smooth out that wrinkle between your brows, dear, and let's have a nice supper."

"That's all right for you, Dele," said Joe, attacking a can of peas with a carving knife and hatchet, "but how about me? Do you think I'm going to let you hustle for wages while I philander in the regions of high art? Not by the bones of Benvenuto Cellini! I guess I can sell papers or lay cobblestones, and bring in a dollar or two."

Delia came and hung about his neck.

"Joe, dear, you are silly. You must keep on at your studies. It is not as if I had quit my music and gone to work at something else. While I teach I learn. I am always with my music. And we can live as happily as millionaires on fifteen dollars a week. You mustn't think of leaving Mr. Magister."

"All right," said Joe, reaching for the blue scalloped vegetable dish. "But I hate for you to be giving lessons. It isn't Art. But you're a trump and a dear to do it."

"When one loves one's Art no service seems too hard," said Delia.

"Magister praised the sky in that sketch I made in the park," said Joe. "And Tinkle gave me permission to hang two of them in his window. I may sell one if the right kind of a moneyed idiot sees them."

"I'm sure you will," said Delia, sweetly. "And now let's be thankful for General Pinkney and this veal roast."

During all of the next week the Larrabees had an early breakfast. Joe was enthusiastic about some morning-effect sketches he was doing in Central Park, and Delia packed him off breakfasted, coddled, praised, and kissed at seven o'clock. Art is an engaging mistress. It was most times seven o'clock when he returned in the evening.

At the end of the week, Delia, sweetly proud but languid, triumphantly tossed three five-dollar bills on the 8 x 10 (inches) center table of the 8 x 10 (feet) flat parlor.

"Sometimes," she said, a little wearily, "Clementina tries me. I'm afraid she doesn't practise enough, and I have to tell her the same things so often. And then she always dresses entirely in white, and that does get monotonous. But General Pinkney is the dearest old man! I wish you could know him, Joe. He comes in sometimes when I am with Clementina at the piano—he is a widower, you know—and stands there pulling his white goatee. 'And how are the semiquavers and the demisemiquavers progressing?' he always asks.

"I wish you could see the wainscoting in that drawing-room, Joe! And those Astrakhan rug portières. And Clementina has such a funny little cough. I hope she is stronger than she looks. Oh, I really am getting attached to her, she is so gentle and high bred. General Pinkney's brother was once Minister to Bolivia."

And then Joe, with the air of a Monte Cristo, drew forth a ten, a five, a two, and a one—all legal tender notes—and laid them beside Delia's earnings.

"Sold that watercolor of the obelisk to a man from Peoria," he announced overwhelmingly.

"Don't joke with me," said Delia—"not from Peoria!"

"All the way. I wish you could see him, Dele. Fat man with a woollen muffler and a quill toothpick. He saw the sketch in Tinkle's window and thought it was a windmill at first. He was game, though, and bought it anyhow. He ordered another—an oil sketch of the Lackawanna freight depot—to take back with him. Music lessons! Oh, I guess Art is still in it."

"I'm so glad you've kept on," said Delia, heartily. "You're bound to win, dear. Thirty-three dollars! We never had so much to spend before. We'll have oysters tonight."

"And filet mignon with champignons," said Joe. "Where is the olive fork?"

On the next Saturday evening Joe reached home first. He spread his eighteen dollars on the parlor table and washed what seemed to be a great deal of dark paint from his hands.

Half an hour later Delia arrived, her right hand tied up in a shapeless bundle of wraps and bandages.

"How is this?" asked Joe after the usual greetings. Delia laughed, but not very joyously.

"Clementina," she explained, "insisted upon a Welsh rabbit after her lesson. She is such a queer girl. Welsh rabbits at *five* in the afternoon. The General was there. You should have seen him run for the chafing dish, Joe, just as if there wasn't a servant in the house. I know Clementina isn't in good health; she is so nervous. In serving the rabbit she spilled a great lot of it, boiling hot, over my hand and wrist. It hurt awfully, Joe. And the dear girl was so sorry! But General Pinkney!—Joe, that old man nearly went distracted. He rushed downstairs and sent somebody—they said the furnace man or somebody in the basement—out to a drug store for some oil and things to bind it up with. It doesn't hurt so much now."

"What's this?" asked Joe, taking the hand tenderly and pulling at some white strands beneath the bandages.

"It's something soft," said Delia, "that had oil on it. Oh, Joe, did you sell another sketch?" She had seen the money on the table.

"Did I?" said Joe; "just ask the man from Peoria. He got his depot today, and he isn't sure but he thinks he wants another parkscape and a view on the Hudson. What time this afternoon did you burn your hand, Dele?"

"Five o'clock, I think," said Dele plaintively. "The iron—I mean the rabbit came off the fire about that time. You ought to have seen General Pinkney, Joe, when—"

"Sit down here a moment, Dele," said Joe. He drew her to the couch, sat beside her, and put his arm across her shoulders.

"What have you been doing for the last two weeks, Dele?" he asked.

She braved it for a moment or two with an eye full of love and stubbornness, and murmured a phrase or two vaguely of General Pinkney; but at length down went her head and out came the truth and tears.

"I couldn't get any pupils," she confessed. "And I couldn't bear to have you give up your lessons; and I got a place ironing shirts in that big Twenty-fourth Street laundry. And I think I did very well to make up both General Pinkney and Clementina, don't you, Joe? And when a girl in the laundry set down a hot iron on my hand this afternoon I was all the way home making up that story about the Welsh rabbit. You're not angry, are you, Joe? And if I hadn't got the work you mightn't have sold your sketches to that man from Peoria."

"He wasn't from Peoria," said Joe, slowly.

"Well, it doesn't matter where he was from. How clever you are, Joe—and—kiss me, Joe—and what made you ever suspect that I wasn't giving music lessons to Clementina?"

"I didn't," said Joe, "until to-night. And I wouldn't have then, only I sent up this cotton waste and oil from the engine-room this afternoon for a girl upstairs who had her hand burned with a smoothing-iron. I've been firing the engine in that laundry for the last two weeks."

"And then you didn't—"

"My purchaser from Peoria," said Joe, "and General Pinkney are both creations of the same art—but you wouldn't call it either painting or music."

And then they both laughed, and Joe began:

"When one loves one's Art no service seems—"

But Delia stopped him with her hand on his lips. "No," she said—"just 'When one loves.' "

THE COP AND THE ANTHEM

ON HIS bench in Madison Square Soapy moved uneasily. When wild geese honk high of nights, and when women without sealskin coats grow kind to their husbands, and when Soapy moves uneasily on his bench in the park, you may know that winter is near at hand.

A dead leaf fell in Soapy's lap. That was Jack Frost's card. Jack is kind to the regular denizens of Madison Square, and gives fair warning of his annual call. At the corners of four streets he hands his pasteboard to the North Wind, footman of the mansion of All Outdoors, so that the inhabitants thereof may make ready.

Soapy's mind became cognizant of the fact that the time had come for him to resolve himself into a singular Committee of Ways and Means to provide against the coming rigor. And therefore he moved uneasily on his bench.

The hibernatorial ambitions of Soapy were not of the highest. In them there were no considerations of Mediterranean cruises, of soporific Southern skies or drifting in the Vesuvian Bay. Three months on the Island was what his soul craved. Three months of assured board and bed and congenial company, safe from Boreas and bluecoats, seemed to Soapy the essence of things desirable.

For years the hospitable Blackwell's had been his winter quarters. Just as his more fortunate fellow New Yorkers had bought their tickets to Palm Beach and the Riviera each winter, so Soapy had made his humble arrangements for his annual hegira to the Island. And now the time was come. On the previous night three Sabbath newspapers, distributed beneath his coat, about his ankles, and over his lap, had failed to repulse the cold as he slept on his bench near the spurting fountain in the ancient square. So the Island loomed big and timely in Soapy's mind. He scorned the provisions made in the name of charity for the city's dependents. In Soapy's opinion the Law was more benign than Philanthropy. There was an endless round of institutions, municipal and eleemosynary, on which he might set out and receive lodging and food accordant with the simple life. But to one of Soapy's proud spirit the gifts of charity are encumbered. If not in coin you must pay in humiliation of spirit for every benefit received at the hands of philanthropy. As Caesar had his Brutus, every bed of charity must have its toll of a bath, every loaf of bread its compensation of a private and personal inquisition. Wherefore it is better to be a guest of the law, which, though conducted by rules, does not meddle unduly with a gentleman's private affairs.

Soapy, having decided to go to the Island, at once set about accomplishing his desire. There were many easy ways of doing this. The pleasantest was to dine luxuriously at some expensive restaurant; and then, after declaring insolvency, be handed over quietly and without uproar to a policeman. An accommodating magistrate would do the rest.

Soapy left his bench and strolled out of the square and across the level sea of asphalt, where Broadway and Fifth Avenue flow together. Up Broadway he turned, and halted at a glittering café, where are gathered together nightly the choicest products of the grape, the silkworm, and the protoplasm.

Soapy had confidence in himself from the lowest button of his vest upward. He was shaven, and his coat was decent and his neat black, ready-tied four-in-hand had been presented to him by a lady missionary on Thanksgiving Day. If he could reach a table in the restaurant unsuspected success would be his. The portion of him that would show above the table would raise no doubt in the waiter's mind. A roasted mallard duck, thought Soapy, would be about the thing—with a bottle of Chablis, and then Camembert, a demi-tasse and a cigar. One dollar for the cigar would be enough. The total would not be so high as to call forth any supreme manifestation of revenge from the café management; and yet the meat would leave him filled and happy for the journey to his winter refuge.

But as Soapy set foot inside the restaurant door the head waiter's eye fell upon his frayed trousers and decadent shoes. Strong and ready hands turned him about and conveyed him in silence and haste to the sidewalk and averted the ignoble fate of the menaced mallard.

Soapy turned off Broadway. It seemed that his route to the coveted Island was not to be an epicurean one. Some other way of entering limbo must be thought of.

At a corner of Sixth Avenue electric lights and cunningly displayed wares behind plate-glass made a shop window conspicuous. Soapy took a cobblestone and dashed it through the glass. People came running around the corner, a policeman in the lead. Soapy stood still, with his hands in his pockets, and smiled at the sight of brass buttons.

"Where's the man that done that?" inquired the officer excitedly.

"Don't you figure out that I might have had something to do with it?" said Soapy, not without sarcasm, but friendly, as one greets good fortune.

The policeman's mind refused to accept Soapy even as a clue. Men who smash windows do not remain to parley with the law's minions. They take to their heels. The policeman saw a man halfway down the block running to catch a car. With drawn club he joined in the pursuit. Soapy, with disgust in his heart, loafed along, twice unsuccessful.

On the opposite side of the street was a restaurant of no great pretensions. It catered to large appetites and modest purses. Its crockery and atmosphere were thick; its soup and napery thin. Into this place Soapy took his accusive shoes and telltale trousers without challenge. At a table he sat and consumed beefsteak, flapjacks, doughnuts, and pie. And then to the waiter he betrayed the fact that the minutest coin and himself were strangers.

"Now, get busy and call a cop," said Soapy. "And don't keep a gentleman waiting."

"No cop for youse," said the waiter, with a voice like butter cakes and an eye like the cherry in a Manhattan cocktail. "Hey, Con!"

Neatly upon his left ear on the callous pavement two waiters pitched Soapy. He arose, joint by joint, as a carpenter's rule opens, and beat the dust from his clothes. Arrest seemed but a rosy dream. The Island seemed very far away. A policeman who stood before a drug store two doors away laughed and walked down the street.

Five blocks Soapy travelled before his courage permitted him to woo capture again. This time the opportunity presented what he fatuously termed to himself a "cinch." A young woman of a modest and pleasing guise was standing before a show window gazing with sprightly interest at its display of shaving mugs and inkstands, and two yards from the window a large policeman of severe demeanor leaned against a water plug.

It was Soapy's design to assume the role of the despicable and execrated "masher." The refined and elegant appearance of his victim and the contiguity of the conscientious cop encouraged him to believe that he would soon feel the pleasant official clutch upon his arm that would insure his winter quarters on the right little, tight little isle.

Soapy straightened the lady missionary's ready-made tie, dragged his shrinking cuffs into the open, set his hat at a killing cant and sidled toward the young woman. He made eyes at her, was taken with sudden coughs and "hems," smiled, smirked, and went brazenly through the impudent and contemptible litany of the "masher." With half an eye Soapy saw that the policeman was watching him fixedly. The young woman moved away a few steps, and again bestowed her absorbed attention upon the shaving mugs. Soapy followed, boldly stepping to her side, raised his hat and said:

"Ah there, Bedelia! Don't you want to come and play in my yard?"

The policeman was still looking. The persecuted young woman had but to beckon a finger and Soapy would be practically en route for his insular haven. Already he imagined he could feel the cozy warmth of the station-house. The young woman faced him and, stretching out a hand, caught Soapy's coat sleeve.

"Sure, Mike," she said joyfully, "if you'll blow me to a pail of suds. I'd have spoke to you sooner, but the cop was watching."

With the young woman playing the clinging ivy to his oak Soapy walked past the policeman overcome with gloom. He seemed doomed to liberty.

At the next corner he shook off his companion and ran. He halted in the district where by night are found the lightest streets, hearts, vows, and librettos. Women in furs and men in greatcoats moved gaily in the wintry air. A sudden fear seized Soapy that some dreadful enchantment had rendered him immune to arrest. The thought brought a little of panic upon it, and when he came upon another policeman lounging grandly in front of a transplendent theatre he caught at the immediate straw of "disorderly conduct."

On the sidewalk Soapy began to yell drunken gibberish at the top of his harsh voice. He danced, howled, raved, and otherwise disturbed the welkin.

The policeman twirled his club, turned his back to Soapy, and remarked to a citizen:

" 'Tis one of them Yale lads celebratin' the goose egg they give to the Hartford College. Noisy; but no harm. We've instructions to lave them be."

Disconsolate, Soapy ceased his unavailing racket. Would never a policeman lay hands on him? In his fancy the Island seemed an unattainable Arcadia. He buttoned his thin coat against the chilling wind.

In a cigar store he saw a well-dressed man lighting a cigar at a swinging light. His silk umbrella he had set by the door on entering. Soapy stepped inside, secured the umbrella, and sauntered off with it slowly. The man at the cigar light followed hastily.

"My umbrella," he said, sternly.

"Oh, is it?" sneered Soapy, adding insult to petit larceny. "Well, why don't you call a policeman? I took it. Your umbrella! Why don't you call a cop? There stands one on the corner."

The umbrella owner slowed his steps. Soapy did likewise, with a presentiment that luck would again run against him. The policeman looked at the two curiously.

"Of course," said the umbrella man—"that is—well, you know how these mistakes occur—I—if it's your umbrella I hope you'll excuse me—I picked it up this morning in a restaurant—if you recognize it as yours, why—I hope you'll—"

"Of course it's mine," said Soapy, viciously.

The ex-umbrella man retreated. The policeman hurried to assist a tall blonde in an opera cloak across the street in front of a street car that was approaching two blocks away.

Soapy walked eastward through a street damaged by improvements. He hurled the umbrella wrathfully into an excavation. He muttered against the men who wear helmets and carry clubs. Because he wanted to fall into their clutches, they seemed to regard him as a king who could do no wrong.

At length Soapy reached one of the avenues to the east where the glitter and turmoil was but faint. He set his face down this toward Madison Square, for the homing instinct survives even when the home is a park bench.

But on an unusually quiet corner Soapy came to a standstill. Here was an old church, quaint and rambling and gabled. Through one violet-stained window a soft light glowed, where, no doubt, the organist loitered over the keys, making sure of his mastery of the coming Sabbath anthem. For there drifted out to Soapy's ears sweet music that caught and held him transfixed against the convolutions of the iron fence.

The moon was above, lustrous and serene; vehicles and pedestrians were few; sparrows twittered sleepily in the eaves—for a little while the scene might have been a country churchyard. And the anthem that the organist played cemented Soapy to the iron fence, for he had known it well in the days when his life contained such things as mothers and roses and ambitions and friends and immaculate thoughts and collars.

The conjunction of Soapy's receptive state of mind and the influences about the old church wrought a sudden and wonderful change in his soul. He viewed with swift horror the pit into which he had tumbled, the degraded days, unworthy desires, dead hopes, wrecked faculties, and base motives that made up his existence.

And also in a moment his heart responded thrillingly to this novel mood. An instantaneous and strong impulse moved him to battle with his desperate fate. He would pull himself out of the mire; he would make a man of himself again; he would conquer the evil that had taken possession of him. There was time; he was comparatively young yet; he would resurrect his old eager ambitions and pursue them without faltering. Those solemn but sweet organ notes had set up a revolution in him. Tomorrow he would go into the roaring downtown district and find work. A fur importer had once offered him a place as driver. He would find him tomorrow and ask for the position. He would be somebody in the world. He would—

Soapy felt a hand laid on his arm. He looked quickly around into the broad face of a policeman.

"What are you doin' here?" asked the officer.

"Nothin'," said Soapy.

"Then come along," said the policeman.

"Three months on the Island," said the Magistrate in the Police Court the next morning.

THE ENCHANTED KISS

BUT a clerk in the Cut-rate Drug Store was Samuel Tansey, yet his slender frame was a pad that enfolded the passion of Romeo, the gloom of Lara, the romance of D'Artagnan, and the desperate inspiration of Melnotte. Pity, then, that he had been denied expression, that he was doomed to the burden of utter timidity and diffidence, that Fate had set him tongue-tied and scarlet before the muslin-clad angels whom he adored and vainly longed to rescue, clasp, comfort, and subdue.

The clock's hands were pointing close upon the hour of ten while Tansey was playing billiards with a number of his friends. On alternate evenings he was released from duty at the store after seven o'clock. Even among his fellow-men Tansey was timorous and constrained. In his imagination he had done valiant deeds and performed acts of distinguished gallantry; but in fact he was a sallow youth of twenty-three, with an over-modest demeanor and scant vocabulary.

When the clock struck ten, Tansey hastily laid down his cue and struck sharply upon the show-case with a coin for the attendant to come and receive the pay for his score.

"What's your hurry, Tansey?" called one. "Got another engagement?"

"Tansey got an engagement!" echoed another. "Not on your life. Tansey's got to get home at ten by Mother Peek's orders."

"It's no such thing," chimed in a pale youth, taking a large cigar from his mouth; "Tansey's afraid to be late because Miss Katie might come downstairs to unlock the door, and kiss him in the hall."

This last delicate piece of raillery sent a fiery tingle into Tansey's blood, for the indictment was true—barring the kiss. That was a thing to dream of; to wildly hope for; but too remote and sacred a thing to think of lightly.

Casting a cold and contemptuous look at the speaker—a punishment commensurate with his own diffident spirit—Tansey left the room, descending the stairs into the street.

For two years he had silently adored Miss Peek, worshipping her from a spiritual distance through which her attractions took on stellar brightness and mystery. Mrs. Peek kept a few choice boarders, among whom was Tansey. The other young men romped with Katie, chased her with crickets in their fingers, and "jollied" her with an irreverent freedom that turned Tansey's heart into cold lead in his bosom. The signs of his adoration were few—a tremulous "Good-morning," stealthy glances at her during meals, and occasionally (Oh, rapture!) a blushing, delirious game of cribbage with her in the parlor on some rare evening when a miraculous lack of engagement kept her at home. Kiss him in the hall! Aye, he feared it, but it was an ecstatic fear such as Elijah must have felt when the chariot lifted him into the unknown.

But tonight the gibes of his associates had stung him to a feeling of forward, lawless mutiny; a defiant, challenging, atavistic recklessness. Spirit of corsair, adventurer, lover, poet, bohemian, possessed him. The stars he saw above him seemed no more unattainable, no less high, than the favor of Miss Peek or the fearsome sweetness of her delectable lips. His fate seemed to him strangely dramatic and pathetic, and to call for a solace consonant with its extremity. A saloon was nearby, and to this he flitted, calling for absinthe—beyond doubt the drink most adequate to his mood—the tipple of the roué, the abandoned, the vainly sighing lover.

Once he drank of it, and again, and then again until he felt a strange, exalted sense of non-participation in worldly affairs pervade him. Tansey was no drinker; his consumption of three absinthe anisettes within almost as few minutes proclaimed his unproficiency in the art; Tansey was merely flooding with unproven liquor his sorrows; which record and tradition alleged to be drownable.

Coming out upon the sidewalk, he snapped his fingers defiantly in the direction of the Peek homestead, turned the other way, and voyaged, Columbus-like into the wilds of an enchanted street. Nor is the figure exorbitant, for, beyond his store the foot of Tansey had scarcely been set for years—store and boarding-house; between these ports he was chartered to run, and contrary currents had rarely deflected his prow.

Tansey aimlessly protracted his walk, and, whether it was his unfamiliarity with the district, his recent accession of audacious errantry, or the sophistical whisper of a certain green-eyed fairy, he came at last to tread a shuttered, blank, and echoing thoroughfare, dark and unpeopled. And, suddenly, this way came to an end (as many streets do in the Spanish-built, archaic town of San Antone), butting its head against an imminent, high, brick wall. No—the street still lived! To the right and to the left it breathed through slender tubes of exit—narrow, somnolent ravines, cobble paved and unlighted. Accommodating a rise in the street to the right was reared a phantom flight of five luminous steps of limestone, flanked by a wall of the same height and of the same material.

Upon one of these steps Tansey seated himself and bethought him of his love, and how she might never know she was his love. And of Mother Peek, fat, vigilant and kind; not unpleased, Tansey thought, that he and Katie should play cribbage in the parlor together. For the Cut-rate had not cut his salary, which, sordidly speaking, ranked him star boarder at the Peeks'. And he thought of Captain Peek, Katie's father, a man he dreaded and abhorred; a genteel loafer and spendthrift, battening upon the labour of his women-folk; a very queer fish, and, according to repute, not of the freshest.

The night had turned chill and foggy. The heart of the town, with its noises, was left behind. Reflected from the high vapors, its distant lights were manifest in quivering, cone-shaped streamers, in questionable blushes of unnamed colors, in unstable, ghostly waves of far, electric flashes. Now that the darkness was become more friendly, the wall against which the street splintered developed a stone coping topped with an armature of spikes. Beyond it loomed what appeared to be the acute angles of mountain peaks, pierced here and there by little lambent parallelograms. Considering this vista, Tansey at length persuaded himself that the seeming mountains were, in fact, the convent of Santa Mercedes, with which ancient and bulky pile he was better familiar from different coigns of view. A pleasant noise of singing in his ears re-enforced his opinion. High, sweet, holy carolling, far and harmonious and uprising, as of sanctified nuns at their responses. At what hour did the Sisters sing? He tried to think—was it six, eight, twelve? Tansey leaned his back against the limestone wall and wondered. Strange things followed. The air was full of white, fluttering pigeons that circled about, and settled upon the convent wall. The wall blossomed with a quantity of shining green eyes that blinked and peered at him from the solid masonry. A pink, classic nymph came from an excavation in the cavernous road and danced, barefoot and airy, upon the ragged flints. The sky was traversed by a company of beribboned cats, marching in stupendous, aerial procession. The noise of singing grew louder; an illumination of unseasonable fireflies danced past, and strange whispers came out of the dark without meaning or excuse.

Without amazement Tansey took note of these phenomena. He was on some new plane of understanding, though his mind seemed to him clear and, indeed, happily tranquil.

A desire for movement and exploration seized him: he rose and turned into the black gash of street to his right. For a time the high wall formed one of its boundaries; but further on, two rows of black-windowed houses closed it in.

Here was the city's quarter once given over to the Spaniard. Here were still his forbidding abodes of concrete and adobe, standing cold and indomitable against the century. From the murky fissure, the eye saw, flung against the sky, the tangled filigree of his Moorish balconies. Through stone archways breaths of dead, vault-chilled air coughed upon him; his feet struck jingling iron rings in staples stone-buried for half a cycle. Along these paltry avenues had swaggered the arrogant Don, had caracoled and serenaded and blustered while the tomahawk and the pioneer's rifle were already uplifted to expel him from a continent. And Tansey, stumbling through this old-world dust, looked up, dark as it was, and saw Andalusian beauties glimmering on the balconies. Some of them were laughing and listening to the goblin music that still followed; others harked fearfully through the night, trying to catch the hoofbeats of caballeros whose last echoes from those stones had died away a century ago. Those women were silent, but Tansey heard the jangle of horseless bridle-bits, the whirr of riderless rowels, and, now and then, a muttered malediction in a foreign tongue. But he was not frightened. Shadows, nor shadows of sounds, could daunt him.

Afraid? No. Afraid of Mother Peek? Afraid to face the girl of his heart? Afraid of tipsy Captain Peek? Nay! nor of these apparitions, nor of that spectral singing that always pursued him. Singing! He would show them! He lifted up a strong and untuneful voice:

"When you hear them bells go tingalingling,"

serving notice upon those mysterious agencies that if it should come to a face-to-face encounter

"There'll be a hot time
In the old town
To-night!"

How long Tansey consumed in treading this haunted byway was not clear to him, but in time he emerged into a more commodious avenue. When within a few yards of the corner he perceived, through a window, that a small confectionery of mean appearance was set in the angle. His same glance that estimated its meagre equipment, its cheap soda-water fountain and stock of tobacco and sweets, took cognizance of Captain Peek within lighting a cigar at a swinging gaslight.

As Tansey rounded the corner Captain Peek came out, and they met *vis-à-vis*. An exultant joy filled Tansey when he found himself sustaining the encounter with implicit courage. Peek, indeed! He raised his hand, and snapped his fingers loudly.

It was Peek himself who quailed guiltily before the valiant mien of the drug clerk. Sharp surprise and a palpable fear bourgeoned upon the Captain's face. And, verily, that face was one to rather call up such expressions upon the faces of others. The face of a libidinous heathen idol, small eyed, with carven folds in the heavy jowls, and a consuming, pagan license in its expression. In the gutter just beyond the store Tansey saw a closed carriage standing with its back toward him and a motionless driver perched in his place.

"Why, it's Tansey!" exclaimed Captain Peek. "How are you, Tansey? H-have a cigar, Tansey?"

"Why, it's Peek!" cried Tansey, jubilant at his own temerity. "What deviltry are you up to now, Peek? Back streets and a closed carriage! Fie! Peek!"

"There's no one in the carriage," said the Captain, smoothly.

"Everybody out of it is in luck," continued Tansey, aggressively. "I'd love for you to know, Peek, that I'm not stuck on you. You're a bottle-nosed scoundrel."

"Why, the little rat's drunk!" cried the Captain, joyfully; "only drunk, and I thought he was on! Go home, Tansey, and quit bothering grown persons on the street."

But just then a white-clad figure sprang out of the carriage, and a shrill voice—Katie's voice—sliced the air: "Sam! Sam!—help me, Sam!"

Tansey sprang toward her, but Captain Peek interposed his bulky form. Wonder of wonders! the whilom spiritless youth struck out with his right, and the hulking Captain went over in a swearing heap. Tansey flew to Katie, and took her in his arms like a conquering knight. She raised her face, and he kissed her—violets! electricity! caramels! champagne! Here was the attainment of a dream that brought no disenchantment.

"Oh, Sam," cried Katie, when she could, "I knew you would come to rescue me. What do you suppose the mean things were going to do with me?"

"Have your picture taken," said Tansey, wondering at the foolishness of his remark.

"No, they were going to eat me. I heard them talking about it."

"Eat you!" said Tansey, after pondering a moment. "That can't be; there's no plates."

But a sudden noise warned him to turn. Down upon him were bearing the Captain and a monstrous long-bearded dwarf in a spangled cloak and red trunk-hose. The dwarf leaped twenty feet and clutched him. The Captain seized Katie and hurled her, shrieking, back into the carriage, himself followed, and the vehicle dashed away. The dwarf lifted Tansey high above his head and ran with him into the store. Holding him with one hand, he raised the lid of an enormous chest half filled with cakes of ice, flung Tansey inside, and closed down the cover.

The force of the fall must have been great, for Tansey lost consciousness. When his faculties revived his first sensation was one of severe cold along his back and limbs. Opening his eyes, he found himself to be seated upon the limestone steps still facing the wall and convent of Santa Mercedes. His first thought was of the ecstatic kiss from Katie. The outrageous villainy of Captain Peek, the unnatural mystery of the situation, his preposterous conflict with the improbable dwarf—these things roused and angered him, but left no impression of the unreal.

"I'll go back there tomorrow," he grumbled aloud, "and knock the head off that comic-opera squab. Running out and picking up perfect strangers, and shoving them into cold storage!"

But the kiss remained uppermost in his mind. "I might have done that long ago," he mused. "She liked it, too. She called me 'Sam' four times. I'll not go up that street again. Too much scrapping. Guess I'll move down the other way. Wonder what she meant by saying they were going to eat her!"

Tansey began to feel sleepy, but after a while he decided to move along again. This time he ventured into the street to his left. It ran level for a distance, and then dipped gently downward, opening into a vast, dim, barren space—the old Military Plaza. To his left, some hundred yards distant, he saw a cluster of flickering lights along the Plaza's border. He knew the locality at once.

Huddled within narrow confines were the remnants of the once-famous purveyors of the celebrated Mexican national cookery. A few years before, their nightly encampments upon the historic Alamo Plaza, in the heart of the city, had been a carnival, a saturnalia that was renowned throughout the land. Then the caterers numbered hundreds; the patrons thousands. Drawn by the coquettish *señoritas,* the music of the weird Spanish minstrels, and the strange piquant Mexican dishes served at a hundred competing tables, crowds thronged the Alamo Plaza all night. Travellers, rancheros, family parties, gay gasconading rounders, sightseers and prowlers of polyglot, owlish San Antone mingled there at the center of the city's fun and frolic. The popping of corks, pistols, and questions; the glitter of eyes, jewels, and daggers; the ring of laughter and coin—these were the order of the night.

But now no longer. To some half-dozen tents, fires, and tables had dwindled the picturesque festival, and these had been relegated to an ancient disused plaza.

Often had Tansey strolled down to these stands at night to partake of the delectable *chili-con-carne,* a dish evolved by the genius of Mexico, composed of delicate meats minced with aromatic herbs and the poignant *chili colorado*—a compound full of singular savor and a fiery zest delightful to the Southron's palate.

The titillating odor of this concoction came now, on the breeze, to the nostrils of Tansey, awakening in him hunger for it. As he turned in that direction he saw a carriage dash up to the Mexicans' tents out of the gloom of the Plaza. Some figures moved back and forward in the uncertain light of the lanterns, and then the carriage was driven swiftly away.

Tansey approached, and sat at one of the tables covered with gaudy oil-cloth. Traffic was dull at the moment. A few half-grown boys noisily fared at another table; the Mexicans hung listless and phlegmatic about their wares. And it was still. The night hum of the city crowded to the wall of dark buildings surrounding the Plaza, and subsided to an indefinite buzz through which sharply perforated the crackle of the languid fires and the rattle of fork and spoon. A sedative wind blew from the southeast. The starless firmament pressed down upon the earth like a leaden cover.

In all that quiet Tansey turned his head suddenly, and saw, without disquietude, a troop of spectral horsemen deploy into the Plaza and charge a luminous line of infantry that advanced to sustain the shock. He saw the fierce flame of cannon and small arms, but heard no sound. The careless victuallers lounged vacantly, not deigning to view the conflict. Tansey mildly wondered to what nations these mute combatants might belong; turned his back to them and ordered his chili and coffee from the Mexican woman who advanced to serve him. This woman was old and careworn; her face was lined like the rind of a cantaloupe. She fetched the viands from a vessel set by the smouldering fire, and then retired to a tent, dark within, that stood nearby.

Presently Tansey heard a turmoil in the tent; a wailing, brokenhearted pleading in the harmonious Spanish tongue, and then two figures tumbled out into the light of the lanterns. One was the old woman; the other was a man clothed with a sumptuous and flashing splendor. The woman seemed to clutch and beseech from him something against his will. The man broke from her and struck her brutally back into the tent, where she lay, whimpering and invisible. Observing

Tansey, he walked rapidly to the table where he sat. Tansey recognized him to be Ramon Torres, a Mexican, the proprietor of the stand he was patronizing.

Torres was a handsome, nearly full-blooded descendant of the Spanish, seemingly about thirty years of age, and of a haughty, but extremely courteous demeanor. Tonight he was dressed with signal magnificence. His costume was that of a triumphant *matador,* made of purple velvet almost hidden by jewelled embroidery. Diamonds of enormous size flashed upon his garb and his hands. He reached for a chair, and, seating himself at the opposite side of the table, began to roll a finical cigarette.

"Ah, Meester Tansee," he said, with a sultry fire in his silky, black eyes, "I give myself pleasure to see you this evening. Meester Tansee, you have many times come to eat at my table. I theenk you a safe man—a verree good friend. How much would it please you to leeve forever?"

"Not come back any more?" inquired Tansey.

"No; not leave—*leeve;* the not-to-die."

"I would call that," said Tansey, "a snap."

Torres leaned his elbows upon the table, swallowed a mouthful of smoke, and spake—each word being projected in a little puff of gray.

"How old do you theenk I am, Meester Tansee?"

"Oh, twenty-eight or thirty."

"Thees day," said the Mexican, "ees my birthday. I am four hundred and three years of old today."

"Another proof," said Tansey, airily, "of the healthfulness of our climate."

"Eet is not the air. I am to relate to you a secret of verree fine value. Listen me, Meester Tansee. At the age of twenty-three I arrive in Mexico from Spain. When? In the year fifteen hundred nineteen, with the *soldados* of Hernando Cortez. I come to thees country seventeen fifteen. I saw your Alamo reduced. It was like yesterday to me. Three hundred ninety-six year ago I learn the secret always to leeve. Look at these clothes I wear—at these *diamantes*. Do you theenk I buy them with the money I make with selling the *chili-con-carne,* Meester Tansee?"

"I should think not," said Tansey, promptly. Torres laughed loudly.

"*Valgame Dios!* but I do. But it not the kind you eating now. I make a deeferent kind, the eating of which makes men to always leeve. What do you think! One thousand people I supply—*diez pesos* each one pays me the month. You see! ten thousand *pesos* everee month! *Que diable!* how not I wear the fine *ropa*! You see that old woman try to hold me back a little while ago? That ees my wife. When I marry her she is young—seventeen year—*bonita*. Like the rest she ees become old and—what you say!—tough? I am the same—young all the time. Tonight I resolve to dress myself and find another wife befitting my age. This old woman try to scr-r-ratch my face. Ha! ha! Meester Tansee—same way they do *entre los Americanos*."

"And this health-food you spoke of?" said Tansey.

"Hear me," said Torres, leaning over the table until he lay flat upon it; "eet is the *chili-con-carne* made not from the beef or the chicken, but from the flesh of the *señorita*—young and tender. That ees the secret. Everee month you must eat of it, having care to do so before the moon is full, and you will not die any times. See how I trust you, friend Tansee! Tonight I have bought one young ladee—verree pretty—so *fina, gorda, blandita*! Tomorrow the *chili* will be ready. *Ahora si!* One thousand dollars I pay for thees young ladee. From an *Americano* I have bought—a verree tip-top man—*el Capitan Peek—que es, Señor?*"

For Tansey had sprung to his feet, upsetting the chair. The words of Katie reverberated in his ears: "They're going to eat me, Sam." This, then, was the monstrous fate to which she had been delivered by her unnatural parent. The carriage he had seen drive up from the Plaza was Captain Peek's. Where was Katie? Perhaps already—

Before he could decide what to do a loud scream came from the tent. The old Mexican woman ran out, a flashing knife in her hand. "I have released her," she cried. "You shall kill no more. They will hang you—*ingrato—encantador!*"

Torres, with a hissing exclamation, sprang at her.

"Ramoncito!" she shrieked; "once you loved me."

The Mexican's arm raised and descended. "You are old," he cried; and she fell and lay motionless.

Another scream; the flaps of the tent were flung aside, and there stood Katie, white with fear, her wrists still bound with a cruel cord.

"Sam!" she cried, "save me again!"

Tansey rounded the table, and flung himself, with superb nerve, upon the Mexican. Just then a clangor began; the clocks of the city were tolling the midnight hour. Tansey clutched at Torres, and, for a moment, felt in his grasp the crunch of velvet and the cold facets of the glittering gems. The next instant, the bedecked caballero turned in his hands to a shrunken, leather-visaged, white-bearded, old, old, screaming mummy, sandalled, ragged, and four hundred and three. The Mexican woman was crawling to her feet, and laughing. She shook her brown hand in the face of the whining *viejo*.

"Go, now," she cried, "and seek your *señorita.* It was I, Ramoncito, who brought you to this. Within each moon you eat of the life-giving *chili.* It was I that kept the wrong time for you. You should have eaten *yesterday* instead of *tomorrow*. It is too late. Off with you, *hombre!* You are too old for me!"

"This," decided Tansey, releasing his hold of the graybeard, "is a private family matter concerning age, and no business of mine."

With one of the table knives he hastened to saw asunder the fetters of the fair captive; and then, for the second time that night he kissed Katie Peek—tasted again the sweetness, the wonder, the thrill of it, attained once more the maximum of his incessant dreams.

The next instant an icy blade was driven deep between his shoulders; he felt his blood slowly congeal; heard the senile cackle of the perennial Spaniard; saw the Plaza rise and reel till the zenith crashed into the horizon—and knew no more.

When Tansey opened his eyes again he was sitting upon those selfsame steps gazing upon the dark bulk of the sleeping convent. In the middle of his back was still the acute, chilling pain. How had he been conveyed back there again? He got stiffly to his feet and stretched his cramped limbs. Supporting himself against the stonework he revolved in his mind the extravagant adventures that had befallen him each time he had strayed from the steps that night. In reviewing them certain features strained his credulity. Had he really met Captain Peek or Katie or the unparalleled Mexican in his wanderings—had he really encountered them under commonplace conditions and his over-stimulated brain had supplied the incongruities? However that might be, a sudden, elating thought caused him an intense joy. Nearly all of us have, at some point in our lives—either to excuse our own stupidity or placate our consciences—promulgated some theory of fatalism. We have set up an intelligent Fate that works by codes and signals. Tansey had done likewise; and now he read, through the night's incidents, the finger-prints of destiny. Each excursion that he had made had led to the one paramount finale—to Katie and that kiss, which survived and grew strong and intoxicating in his memory. Clearly, Fate was holding up to him the mirror that night, calling him to observe what awaited him at the end of whichever road he might take. He immediately turned, and hurried homeward.

Clothed in an elaborate, pale blue wrapper, cut to fit, Miss Katie Peek reclined in an armchair before a waning fire in her room. Her little, bare feet were thrust into house-shoes rimmed with swan's down. By the light of a small lamp she was attacking the society news of the latest Sunday paper. Some happy substance, seemingly indestructible, was being rhythmically crushed between her small white teeth. Miss Katie read of functions and furbelows, but she kept a vigilant ear for outside sounds and a frequent eye upon the clock over the mantel. At every footstep upon the asphalt sidewalk her smooth, round chin would cease for a moment its regular rise and fall, and a frown of listening would pucker her pretty brows.

At last she heard the latch of the iron gate click. She sprang up, tripped swiftly to the mirror, where she made a few of those feminine, flickering passes at her front hair and throat which are warranted to hypnotize the approaching guest.

The door-bell rang. Miss Katie, in her haste, turned the blaze of the lamp lower instead of higher, and hastened noiselessly downstairs into the hall. She turned the key, the door opened, and Mr. Tansey side-stepped in.

"Why, the i-de-a!" exclaimed Miss Katie, "is this you, Mr. Tansey? It's after midnight. Aren't you ashamed to wake me up at such an hour to let you in? You're just *awful*!"

"I was late," said Tansey, brilliantly.

"I should think you were! Ma was awfully worried about you. When you weren't in by ten, that hateful Tom McGill said you were out calling on another—said you were out calling on some young lady. I just despise Mr. McGill. Well, I'm not going to scold you anymore, Mr. Tansey, if it *is* a little late—Oh! I turned it the wrong way!"

Miss Katie gave a little scream. Absent-mindedly she had turned the blaze of the lamp entirely out instead of higher. It was very dark.

Tansey heard a musical, soft giggle, and breathed an entrancing odor of heliotrope. A groping light hand touched his arm.

"How awkward I was! Can you find your way—Sam?"

"I—I think I have a match, Miss K-Katie."

A scratching sound; a flame; a glow of light held at arm's length by the recreant follower of Destiny illuminating a tableau which shall end the ignominious chronicle—a maid with unkissed, curling, contemptuous lips slowly lifting the lamp chimney and allowing the wick to ignite; then waving a scornful and abjuring hand toward the staircase—the unhappy Tansey, erstwhile champion in the prophetic lists of fortune, ingloriously ascending to his just and certain doom, while (let us imagine) half within the wings stands the imminent figure of Fate jerking wildly at the wrong strings, and mixing things up in her usual able manner.

MEMOIRS OF A YELLOW DOG

I DON'T suppose it will knock any of you people off your perch to read a contribution from an animal. Mr. Kipling and a good many others have demonstrated the fact that animals can express themselves in remunerative English, and no magazine goes to press nowadays without an animal story in it, except the old-style monthlies that are still running pictures of Bryan and the Mont Pelée horror.

But you needn't look for any stuck-up literature in my piece, such as Bearoo, the bear, and Snakoo, the snake, and Tammanoo, the tiger, talk in the jungle books. A yellow dog that's spent most of his life in a cheap New York flat, sleeping in a corner on an old sateen underskirt (the one she spilled port wine on at the Lady Longshoremen's banquet), mustn't be expected to perform any tricks with the art of speech.

I was born a yellow pup; date, locality, pedigree, and weight unknown. The first thing I can recollect, an old woman had me in a basket at Broadway and Twenty-third trying to sell me to a fat lady. Old Mother Hubbard was boosting me to beat the band as a genuine Pomeranian-Hambletonian-Red-Irish-Cochin-China-Stoke-Pogis fox terrier. The fat lady chased a V around among the samples of gros grain flannelette in her shopping bag till she cornered it, and gave up. From that moment I was a pet—a mamma's own wootsey squidlums. Say, gentle reader, did you ever have a two-hundred-pound woman breathing a flavor of Camembert cheese and Peau d'Espagne pick you up and wallop her nose all over you, remarking all the time in an Emma Eames tone of voice: "Oh, oo's um oodlum, doodlum, woodlum, toodlum, bitsy-witsy skoodlums?"

From a pedigreed yellow pup I grew up to be an anonymous yellow cur looking like a cross between an Angora cat and a box of lemons.

But my mistress never tumbled. She thought that the two primeval pups that Noah chased into the ark were but a collateral branch of my ancestors. It took two policemen to keep her from entering me at the Madison Square Garden for the Siberian bloodhound prize.

I'll tell you about that flat. The house was the ordinary thing in New York, paved with Parian marble in the entrance hall and cobblestones above the first floor. Our flat was three fl—well, not flights—climbs up. My mistress rented it unfurnished, and put in the regular things—1903 antique upholstered parlor set, oil chromo of geishas in a Harlem tea house, rubber plant, and husband.

By Sirius! there was a biped I felt sorry for. He was a little man with sandy hair and whiskers a good deal like mine. Henpecked?—well, toucans and flamingoes and pelicans all had their bills in him. He wiped the dishes and listened to my mistress tell about the cheap, ragged things the lady with the squirrel-skin coat on the second floor hung out on her line to dry. And every evening while she was getting supper she made him take me out on the end of a string for a walk.

If men knew how women pass the time when they are alone they'd never marry. Laura Lean Jibbey, peanut brittle, a little almond cream on the neck muscles, dishes unwashed, half an hour's talk with the iceman, reading a package of old letters, a couple of pickles and two bottles of malt extract, one hour peeking through a hole in the window shade into the flat across the air-shaft—that's about all there is to it. Twenty minutes before time for him to come home from work she straightens up the house, fixes her rat so it won't show, and gets out a lot of sewing for a ten-minute bluff.

I led a dog's life in that flat. 'Most all day I lay there in my corner watching that fat woman kill time. I slept sometimes and had pipe dreams about being out chasing cats into basements and growling at old ladies with black mittens, as a dog was intended to do. Then she would pounce upon me with a lot of that drivelling poodle palaver and kiss me on the nose—but what could I do? A dog can't chew cloves.

I began to feel sorry for Hubby, dog my cats if I didn't. We looked so much alike that people noticed it when we went out; so we shook the streets that Morgan's cab drives down, and took to climbing the piles of last December's snow on the streets where cheap people live.

One evening when we were thus promenading, and I was trying to look like a prize St. Bernard, and the old man was trying to look like he wouldn't have murdered the first organ-grinder he heard play Mendelssohn's wedding-march, I looked up at him and said, in my way:

"What are you looking so sour about, you oakum trimmed lobster? She don't kiss you. You don't have to sit on her lap and listen to talk that would make the book of a musical comedy sound like the maxims of Epictetus. You ought to be thankful you're not a dog. Brace up, Benedick, and bid the blues begone."

The matrimonial mishap looked down at me with almost canine intelligence in his face.

"Why, doggie," says he, "good doggie. You almost look like you could speak. What is it, doggie—Cats?"

Cats! Could speak!

But, of course, he couldn't understand. Humans were denied the speech of animals. The only common ground of communication upon which dogs and men can get together is in fiction.

In the flat across the hall from us lived a lady with a black-and-tan terrier. Her husband strung it and took it out every evening, but he always came home cheerful and whistling. One day I touched noses with the black-and-tan in the hall, and I struck him for an elucidation.

"See, here, Wiggle-and-Skip," I says, "you know that it ain't the nature of a real man to play dry nurse to a dog in public. I never saw one leashed to a bow-wow yet that didn't look like he'd like to lick every other man that looked at him. But your boss comes in every day as perky and set up as an amateur prestidigitator doing the egg trick. How does he do it? Don't tell me he likes it."

"Him?" says the black-and-tan. "Why, he uses Nature's Own Remedy. He gets spifflicated. At first when we go out he's as shy as the man on the steamer who would rather play pedro when they make 'em all jackpots. By the time we've been in eight saloons he don't care whether the thing on the end of his line is a dog or a catfish. I've lost two inches of my tail trying to sidestep those swinging doors."

The pointer I got from that terrier—vaudeville please copy—set me to thinking.

One evening about six o'clock my mistress ordered him to get busy and do the ozone act for Lovey. I have concealed it until now, but that is what she called me. The black-and-tan was called "Tweetness." I consider that I have the bulge on him as far as you could chase a rabbit. Still "Lovey" is something of a nomenclatural tin can on the tail of one's self-respect.

At a quiet place on a safe street I tightened the line of my custodian in front of an attractive, refined saloon. I made a dead-ahead scramble for the doors, whining like a dog in the press despatches that lets the family know that little Alice is bogged while gathering lilies in the brook.

"Why, darn my eyes," says the old man, with a grin; "darn my eyes if the saffron-colored son of a seltzer lemonade ain't asking me in to take a drink. Lemme see—how long's it been since I saved shoe leather by keeping one foot on the foot-rest? I believe I'll—"

I knew I had him. Hot Scotches he took, sitting at a table. For an hour he kept the Campbells coming. I sat by his side rapping for the waiter with my tail, and eating free lunch such as mamma in her flat never equalled with her homemade truck bought at a delicatessen store eight minutes before papa comes home.

When the products of Scotland were all exhausted except the rye bread the old man unwound me from the table leg and played me outside like a fisherman plays a salmon. Out there he took off my collar and threw it into the street.

"Poor doggie," says he; "good doggie. She shan't kiss you any more. 'S a darned shame. Good doggie, go away and get run over by a street car and be happy."

I refused to leave. I leaped and frisked around the old man's legs happy as a pug on a rug.

"You old flea-headed woodchuck-chaser," I said to him—"you moon-baying, rabbit-pointing, egg-stealing old beagle, can't you see that I don't want to leave you? Can't you see that we're both Pups in the Wood and the missis is the cruel uncle after you with the dish towel and me with the flea liniment and a pink bow to tie on my tail. Why not cut that all out and be pards forever more?"

Maybe you'll say he didn't understand—maybe he didn't. But he kind of got a grip on the Hot Scotches, and stood still for a minute, thinking.

"Doggie," says he, finally, "we don't live more than a dozen lives on this earth, and very few of us live to be more than three hundred. If I ever see that flat any more I'm a flat, and if you do you're flatter; and that's no flattery. I'm offering sixty to one that Westward Ho wins out by the length of a dachshund."

There was no string, but I frolicked along with my master to the Twenty-third Street ferry. And the cats on the route saw reason to give thanks that prehensile claws had been given them.

On the Jersey side my master said to a stranger who stood eating a currant bun:

"Me and my doggie, we are bound for the Rocky Mountains."

But what pleased me most was when my old man pulled both of my ears until I howled, and said:

"You common, monkey-headed, rat-tailed, sulphur-colored son of a door mat, do you know what I'm going to call you?"

I thought of "Lovey," and I whined dolefully.

"I'm going to call you 'Pete,' " says my master; and if I'd had five tails I couldn't have done enough wagging to do justice to the occasion.

THE COMPLETE LIFE OF JOHN HOPKINS

THERE is a saying that no man has tasted the full flavor of life until he has known poverty, love, and war. The justness of this reflection commends it to the lover of condensed philosophy. The three conditions embrace about all there is in life worth knowing. A surface thinker might deem that wealth should be added to the list. Not so. When a poor man finds a long-hidden quarter-dollar that has slipped through a rip into his vest lining, he sounds the pleasure of life with a deeper plummet than any millionaire can hope to cast.

It seems that the wise executive power that rules life has thought best to drill man in these three conditions; and none may escape all three. In rural places the terms do not mean so much. Poverty is less pinching; love is temperate; war shrinks to contests about boundary lines and the neighbors' hens. It is in the cities that our epigram gains in truth and vigor; and it has remained for one John Hopkins to crowd the experience into a rather small space of time.

The Hopkins flat was like a thousand others. There was a rubber plant in one window; a flea-bitten terrier sat in the other, wondering when he was to have his day.

John Hopkins was like a thousand others. He worked at twenty dollars per week in a nine-story, red-brick building at either Insurance, Buckle's Hoisting Engines, Chiropody, Loans, Pulleys, Boas Renovated, Waltz Guaranteed in Five Lessons, or Artificial Limbs. It is not for us to wring Mr. Hopkins's avocation from these outward signs that be.

Mrs. Hopkins was like a thousand others. The auriferous tooth, the sedentary disposition, the Sunday afternoon wanderlust, the draft upon the delicatessen store for home-made comforts, the furor for department store marked-down sales, the feeling of superiority to the lady in the third-floor front who wore genuine ostrich tips and had two names over her bell, the mucilaginous hours during which she remained glued to the window-sill, the vigilant avoidance of the instalment man, the tireless patronage of the acoustics of the dumb-waiter shaft—all the attributes of the Gotham flat-dweller were hers.

One moment yet of sententiousness and the story moves.

In the Big City large and sudden things happen. You round a corner and thrust the rib of your umbrella into the eye of your old friend from Kootenai Falls. You stroll out to pluck a Sweet William in the park—and lo! bandits attack you—you are ambulanced to the hospital—you marry your nurse; are divorced—get squeezed while short on U.P.S. and D.O.W.N.S.—stand in the bread line—marry an heiress, take out your laundry and pay your club dues—seemingly all in the wink of an eye. You travel the streets, and a finger beckons to you, a handkerchief is dropped for you, a brick is dropped upon you, the elevator cable or your bank breaks, a *table d'hôte* or your wife disagrees with you, and Fate tosses you about like cork crumbs in wine opened by an un-feed waiter. The City is a sprightly youngster, and you are red paint upon its toy, and you get licked off.

John Hopkins sat, after a compressed dinner, in his glove-fitting straight-front flat. He sat upon a hornblende couch and gazed, with satiated eyes, at Art Brought Home to the People in the shape of "The Storm" tacked against the wall. Mrs. Hopkins discoursed droningly of the dinner smells from the flat across the hall. The flea-bitten terrier gave Hopkins a look of disgust, and showed a man-hating tooth.

Here was neither poverty, love, nor war; but upon such barren stems may be grafted those essentials of a complete life.

John Hopkins sought to inject a few raisins of conversation into the tasteless dough of existence. "Putting a new elevator in at the office," he said, discarding the nominative noun, "and the boss has turned out his whiskers."

"You don't mean it!" commented Mrs. Hopkins.

"Mr. Whipples," continued John, "wore his new spring suit down today. I liked it fine. It's a gray with—" He stopped, suddenly stricken by a need that made itself known to him. "I believe I'll walk down to the corner and get a five-cent cigar," he concluded.

John Hopkins took his hat and picked his way down the musty halls and stairs of the flat-house.

The evening air was mild, and the streets shrill with the careless cries of children playing games controlled by mysterious rhythms and phrases. Their elders held the doorways and steps with leisurely pipe and gossip. Paradoxically, the fire-escapes supported lovers in couples who made no attempt to fly the mounting conflagration they were there to fan.

The corner cigar store aimed at by John Hopkins was kept by a man named Freshmayer, who looked upon the earth as a sterile promontory.

Hopkins, unknown in the store, entered and called genially for his "bunch of spinach, carfare grade." This imputation deepened the pessimism of Freshmayer; but he set out a brand that came perilously near to filling the order. Hopkins bit off the roots of his purchase, and lighted up at the swinging gas jet. Feeling in his pockets to make payment, he found not a penny there.

"Say, my friend," he explained, frankly, "I've come out without any change. Hand you that nickel first time I pass."

Joy surged in Freshmayer's heart. Here was corroboration of his belief that the world was rotten and man a peripatetic evil. Without a word he rounded the end of his counter and made earnest onslaught upon his customer. Hopkins was no man to serve as a punching-bag for a pessimistic tobacconist. He quickly bestowed upon Freshmayer a colorado-maduro eye in return for the ardent kick that he received from that dealer in goods for cash only.

The impetus of the enemy's attack forced the Hopkins line back to the sidewalk. There the conflict raged; the pacific wooden Indian, with his carven smile, was overturned, and those of the street who delighted in carnage pressed round to view the zealous joust.

But then came the inevitable cop and imminent inconvenience for both the attacker and attacked. John Hopkins was a peaceful citizen, who worked at rebuses of nights in a flat, but he was not without the fundamental spirit of resistance that comes with the battle-rage. He knocked the policeman into a grocer's sidewalk display of goods and gave Freshmayer a punch that caused him temporarily to regret that he had not made it a rule to extend a five-cent line of credit to certain customers. Then Hopkins took spiritedly to his heels down the side-

CIGARS
3d

walk, closely followed by the cigar-dealer and the policeman, whose uniform testified to the reason in the grocer's sign that read: "Eggs cheaper than anywhere else in the city."

As Hopkins ran he became aware of a big, low, red, racing automobile that kept abreast of him in the street. This auto steered in to the side of the sidewalk, and the man guiding it motioned to Hopkins to jump into it. He did so without slackening his speed, and fell into the Turkey-red upholstered seat beside the chauffeur. The big machine, with a diminuendo cough, flew away like an albatross down the avenue into which the street emptied.

The driver of the auto sped his machine without a word. He was masked beyond guess in the goggles and diabolic garb of the chauffeur.

"Much obliged, old man," called Hopkins, gratefully. "I guess you've got sporting blood in you, all right, and don't admire the sight of two men trying to soak one. Little more and I'd have been pinched."

The chauffeur made no sign that he had heard. Hopkins shrugged a shoulder and chewed at his cigar, to which his teeth had clung grimly throughout the mêlée.

Ten minutes and the auto turned into the open carriage entrance of a noble mansion of brown stone, and stood still. The chauffeur leaped out, and said:

"Come quick. The lady, she will explain. It is the great honor you will have, monsieur. Ah, that milady could call upon Armand to do this thing! But, no, I am only one chauffeur."

With vehement gestures the chauffeur conducted Hopkins into the house. He was ushered into a small but luxurious reception chamber. A lady, young, and possessing the beauty of visions, rose from a chair. In her eyes smouldered a becoming anger. Her high-arched, thread-like brows were ruffled into a delicious frown.

"Milady," said the chauffeur, bowing low, "I have the honor to relate to you that I went to the house of Monsieur Long and found him to be not at home. As I came back I see this gentleman in combat against—how you say—greatest odds. He is fighting with five—ten—thirty men—gendarmes, *aussi*. Yes, milady, he what you call 'swat' one—three—eight policemans. If that Monsieur Long is out I say to myself this gentleman he will serve milady so well, and I bring him here."

"Very well, Armand," said the lady, "you may go." She turned to Hopkins.

"I sent my chauffeur," she said, "to bring my cousin, Walter Long. There is a man in this house who has treated me with insult and abuse. I have complained to my aunt, and she laughs at me. Armand says you are brave. In these prosaic days men who are both brave and chivalrous are few. May I count upon your assistance?"

John Hopkins thrust the remains of his cigar into his coat pocket. He looked upon this winning creature and felt his first thrill of romance. It was a knightly love, and contained no disloyalty to the flat with the flea-bitten terrier and the lady of his choice. He had married her after a picnic of the Lady Label Stickers' Union, Lodge No. 2, on a dare and a bet of new hats and chowder all around with his friend, Billy McManus. This angel who was begging him to come to her rescue was something too heavenly for chowder, and as for hats—golden, jewelled crowns for her!

"Say," said John Hopkins, "just show me the guy that you've got the grouch at. I've neglected my talents as a scrapper heretofore, but this is my busy night."

"He is in there," said the lady, pointing to a closed door. "Come. Are you sure that you do not falter or fear?"

"Me?" said John Hopkins. "Just give me one of those roses in the bunch you are wearing, will you?"

The lady gave him a red, red rose. John Hopkins kissed it, stuffed it into his vest pocket, opened the door and walked into the room. It was a handsome library, softly but brightly lighted. A young man was there, reading.

"Books on etiquette is what you want to study," said John Hopkins, abruptly. "Get up here, and I'll give you some lessons. Be rude to a lady, will you?"

The young man looked mildly surprised. Then he arose languidly, dextrously caught the arms of John Hopkins and conducted him irresistibly to the front door of the house.

"Beware, Ralph Branscombe," cried the lady, who had followed, "what you do to the gallant man who has tried to protect me."

The young man shoved John Hopkins gently out the door and then closed it.

"Bess," he said calmly, "I wish you would quit reading historical novels. How in the world did that fellow get in here?"

"Armand brought him," said the young lady. "I think you are awfully mean not to let me have that St. Bernard. I sent Armand for Walter. I was so angry with you."

"Be sensible, Bess," said the young man, taking her arm. "That dog isn't safe. He has bitten two or three people around the kennels. Come now, let's go tell auntie we are in good humor again."

Arm in arm, they moved away.

John Hopkins walked to his flat. The janitor's five-year-old daughter was playing on the steps. Hopkins gave her a nice red rose and walked upstairs.

Mrs. Hopkins was philandering with curl-papers.

"Get your cigar?" she asked, disinterestedly.

"Sure," said Hopkins, "and I knocked around awhile outside. It's a nice night."

He sat upon the hornblende sofa, took out the stump of his cigar, lighted it, and gazed at the graceful figures in "The Storm" on the opposite wall.

"I was telling you," said he, "about Mr. Whipple's suit. It's a gray, with an invisible check, and it looks fine."

THE LONESOME ROAD

BROWN as a coffee-berry, rugged, pistoled, spurred, wary, indefeasible, I saw my old friend, Deputy-Marshal Buck Caperton, stumble, with jingling rowels, into a chair in the marshal's outer office.

And because the court-house was almost deserted at that hour, and because Buck would sometimes relate to me things that were out of print, I followed him in and tricked him into talk through knowledge of a weakness he had. For, cigarettes rolled with sweet corn husk were as honey to Buck's palate; and though he could finger the trigger of a forty-five with skill and suddenness, he never could learn to roll a cigarette.

It was through no fault of mine (for I rolled the cigarettes tight and smooth), but the upshot of some whim of his own, that instead of to an Odyssey of the chaparral, I listened to—a dissertation upon matrimony! This from Buck Caperton! But I maintain that the cigarettes were impeccable, and crave absolution for myself.

"We just brought in Jim and Bud Granberry," said Buck. "Train robbing, you know. Held up the Aransas Pass last month. We caught 'em in the Twenty-Mile pear flat, south of the Nueces."

"Have much trouble corralling them?" I asked, for here was the meat that my hunger for epics craved.

"Some," said Buck; and then, during a little pause, his thoughts stampeded off the trail. "It's kind of queer about women," he went on, "and the place they're supposed to occupy in botany. If I was asked to classify them I'd say they was a human loco weed. Ever see a bronc that had been chewing loco? Ride him up to a puddle of water two feet wide, and he'll give a snort and fall back on you. It looks as big as the

Mississippi River to him. Next trip he'd walk into a cañon a thousand feet deep thinking it was a prairie-dog hole. Same way with a married man.

"I was thinking of Perry Rountree, that used to be my sidekicker before he committed matrimony. In them days me and Perry hated indisturbances of any kind. We roamed around considerable, stirring up the echoes and making 'em attend to business. Why, when me and Perry wanted to have some fun in a town it was a picnic for the census takers. They just counted the marshal's posse that it took to subdue us, and there was your population. But then there came along this Mariana Goodnight girl and looked at Perry sideways, and he was all bridle-wise and saddle-broke before you could skin a yearling.

"I wasn't even asked to the wedding. I reckon the bride had my pedigree and the front elevation of my habits all mapped out, and she decided that Perry would trot better in double harness without any unconverted mustang like Buck Caperton whickering around on the matrimonial range. So it was six months before I saw Perry again.

"One day I was passing on the edge of town, and I see something like a man in a little yard by a little house with a sprinkling-pot squirting water on a rose-bush. Seemed to me, I'd seen something like it before, and I stopped at the gate, trying to figure out its brands. 'Twas not Perry Rountree, but 'twas the kind of a curdled jellyfish matrimony had made out of him.

"Homicide was what that Mariana had perpetrated. He was looking well enough, but he had on a white collar and shoes, and you could tell in a minute that he'd speak polite and pay taxes and stick his little finger out while drinking, just like a sheep man or a citizen. Great skyrockets! but I hated to see Perry all corrupted and Willie-ized like that.

"He came out to the gate, and shook hands; and I says, with scorn, and speaking like a paroquet with the pip: 'Beg pardon—Mr. Rountree, I believe. Seems to me I sagatiated in your associations once, if I am not mistaken.'

" 'Oh, go to the devil, Buck,' says Perry, polite, as I was afraid he'd be.

" 'Well, then,' says I, 'you poor, contaminated adjunct of a sprinkling-pot and degraded household pet, what did you go and do it for? Look at you, all decent and unriotous, and only fit to sit on juries and mend the wood-house door. You was a man once. I have hostility for all such acts. Why don't you go in the house and count the tidies or set the clock, and not stand out here in the atmosphere? A jack-rabbit might come along and bite you.'

" 'Now, Buck,' says Perry, speaking mild, and some sorrowful, 'you don't understand. A married man has got to be different. He feels different from a tough old cloudburst like you. It's sinful to waste time pulling up towns just to look at their roots, and playing faro and looking upon red liquor, and such restless policies as them.'

" 'There was a time,' I says, and I expect I sighed when I mentioned it, 'when a certain domesticated little Mary's lamb I could name was some instructed himself in the line of pernicious sprightliness. I never expected, Perry, to see you reduced down from a full-grown pestilence to such a frivolous fraction of a man. Why,' says I, 'you've got a necktie on; and you speak a senseless kind of indoor drivel that reminds me of a storekeeper or a lady. You look to me like you might tote an umbrella and wear suspenders, and go home of nights.'

" 'The little woman,' says Perry, 'has made some improvements, I believe. You can't understand, Buck. I haven't been away from the house at night since we was married.'

"We talked on awhile, me and Perry, and, as sure as I live, that man interrupted me in the middle of my talk to tell me about six tomato plants he had growing in his garden. Shoved his agricultural degradation right up under my nose while I was telling him about the fun we had tarring and feathering that faro dealer at California Pete's layout! But by and by Perry shows a flicker of sense.

" 'Buck,' says he, 'I'll have to admit that it is a little dull at times. Not that I'm not perfectly happy with the little woman, but a man seems to require some excitement now and then. Now, I'll tell you: Mariana's gone visiting this afternoon, and she won't be home till seven o'clock. That's the limit for both of us—seven o'clock. Neither of us ever stays out a minute after that time unless we are together. Now, I'm glad you came along, Buck,' says Perry, 'for I'm feeling just like having one more rip-roaring razoo with you for the sake of old times. What you say to us putting in the afternoon having fun—I'd like it fine,' says Perry.

"I slapped that old captive range-rider half across his little garden.

" 'Get your hat, you old dried-up alligator,' I shouts, 'you ain't dead yet. You're part human, anyhow, if you did get all bogged up in matrimony. We'll take this town to pieces and see what makes it tick. We'll make all kinds of profligate demands upon the science of cork pulling. You'll grow horns yet, old muley cow,' says I, punching Perry in the ribs, 'if you trot around on the trail of vice with your Uncle Buck.'

" 'I'll have to be home by seven, you know,' says Perry again.

" 'Oh, yes,' says I, winking to myself, for I knew the kind of seven o'clocks Perry Rountree got back by after he once got to passing repartee with the bartenders.

"We goes down to the Gray Mule saloon—that old 'dobe building by the depot.

" 'Give it a name,' says I, as soon as we got one hoof on the foot-rest.

" 'Sarsaparilla,' says Perry.

"You could have knocked me down with a lemon peeling.

" 'Insult me as much as you want to,' I says to Perry, 'but don't startle the bartender. He may have heart-disease. Come on, now; your tongue got twisted. The tall glasses,' I orders, 'and the bottle in the left-hand corner of the ice chest.'

" 'Sarsaparilla,' repeats Perry, and then his eyes get animated, and I see he's got some great scheme in his mind he wants to emit.

" 'Buck,' he says, all interested, 'I'll tell you what! I want to make this a red-letter day. I've been keeping close at home, and I want to turn myself a-loose. We'll have the highest old time you ever saw. We'll go in the back room here and play checkers till half-past six.'

"I leaned against the bar, and I says to Gotch-eared Mike, who was on watch:

" 'For God's sake don't mention this. You know what Perry used to be. He's had the fever, and the doctor says we must humor him.'

" 'Give us the checker-board and the men, Mike,' says Perry. 'Come on, Buck, I'm just wild to have some excitement.'

"I went in the back room with Perry. Before we closed the door, I says to Mike:

" 'Don't ever let it straggle out from under your hat that you seen Buck Caperton fraternal with sarsaparilla or *persona grata* with a checker-board, or I'll make a swallow-fork in your other ear.'

"I locked the door and me and Perry played checkers. To see that poor old humiliated piece of household bric-a-brac sitting there and sniggering out loud whenever he jumped a man, and all obnoxious with animation when he got into my king row, would have made a sheep-dog sick with mortification. Him that was once satisfied only when he was pegging six boards at keno or giving the faro dealers nervous prostration—to see him pushing them checkers about like Sally Louisa at a school-children's party—why, I was all smothered up with mortification.

"And I sits there playing the black men, all sweating for fear some-body I knew would find it out. And I thinks to myself some about this marrying business, and how it seems to be the same kind of a game as that Mrs. Delilah played. She give her old man a haircut, and every-body knows what a man's head looks like after a woman cuts his hair. And then when the Pharisees came around to guy him he was so 'shamed he went to work and kicked the whole house down on top of the whole outfit. 'Them married men,' thinks I, 'lose all their spirit and instinct for riot and foolishness. They won't drink, they won't buck the tiger, they won't even fight. What do they want to go and stay married for?' I asks myself.

"But Perry seems to be having hilarity in considerable quantities.

" 'Buck old hoss,' says he, 'isn't this just the hell-roaringest time we ever had in our lives? I don't know when I've been stirred up so. You see, I've been sticking pretty close to home since I married, and I haven't been on a spree in a long time.'

" 'Spree!' Yes, that's what he called it. Playing checkers in the back room of the Gray Mule! I suppose it did seem to him a little more immoral and nearer to a prolonged debauch than standing over six tomato plants with a sprinkling-pot.

"Every little bit Perry looks at his watch and says:

" 'I got to be home, you know, Buck, at seven.'

" 'All right,' I'd say. 'Romp along and move. This here excitement's killing me. If I don't reform some, and loosen up the strain of this checkered dissipation I won't have a nerve left.'

"It might have been half-past six when commotions began to go on outside in the street. We heard a yelling and a six-shootering, and a lot of galloping and maneuvers.

" 'What's that?' I wonders.

" 'Oh, some nonsense outside,' says Perry. 'It's your move. We just got time to play this game.'

" 'I'll just take a peep through the window,' says I, 'and see. You can't expect a mere mortal to stand the excitement of having a king jumped and listen to an unidentified conflict going on at the same time.'

"The Gray Mule saloon was one of them old Spanish 'dobe buildings, and the back room only had two little windows a foot wide, with iron bars in 'em. I looked out one, and I see the cause of the ruckus.

"There was the Trimble gang—ten of 'em—the worst outfit of desperadoes and horse-thieves in Texas, coming up the street shooting right and left. They was coming right straight for the Gray Mule. Then they got past the range of my sight, but we heard 'em ride up to the front door, and then they socked the place full of lead. We heard the big looking-glass behind the bar knocked all to pieces and the bottles crashing. We could see Gotch-eared Mike in his apron running across the plaza like a coyote, with the bullets puffing up the dust all around him. Then the gang went to work in the saloon, drinking what they wanted and smashing what they didn't.

"Me and Perry both knew that gang, and they knew us. The year before Perry married, him and me was in the same ranger company—and we fought that outfit down on the San Miguel, and brought back Ben Trimble and two others for murder.

" 'We can't get out,' says I. 'We'll have to stay in here till they leave.'

"Perry looked at his watch.

" 'Twenty-five to seven,' says he. 'We can finish that game. I got two men on you. It's your move, Buck. I got to be home at seven, you know.'

"We sat down and went on playing. The Trimble gang had a roughhouse for sure. They were getting good and drunk. They'd drink awhile and holler awhile, and then they'd shoot up a few bottles and glasses. Two or three times they came and tried to open our door. Then there was some more shooting outside, and I looked out the window again. Ham Gossett, the town marshal, had a posse in the houses and stores across the street, and was trying to bag a Trimble or two through the windows.

"I lost that game of checkers. I'm free in saying that I lost three kings that I might have saved if I had been corralled in a more peaceful pasture. But that drivelling married man sat there and cackled when he won a man like an unintelligent hen picking up a grain of corn.

"When the game was over Perry gets up and looks at his watch.

" 'I've had a glorious time, Buck,' says he, 'but I'll have to be going now. It's a quarter to seven, and I got to be home by seven, you know.'

"I thought he was joking.

" 'They'll clear out or be dead drunk in half an hour or an hour,' says I. 'You ain't that tired of being married that you want to commit any more sudden suicide, are you?' says I, giving him the laugh.

" 'One time,' says Perry, 'I was half an hour late getting home. I met Mariana on the street looking for me. If you could have seen her, Buck—but you don't understand. She knows what a wild kind of a snoozer I've been, and she's afraid something will happen. I'll never be late getting home again. I'll say good-bye to you now, Buck.'

"I got between him and the door.

" 'Married man,' says I, 'I know you was christened a fool the minute the preacher tangled you up, but don't you never sometimes think one little think on a human basis? There's ten of that gang in there, and they're pizen with whiskey and desire for murder. They'll drink you up like a bottle of booze before you get halfway to the door. Be intelligent, now, and use at least wild-hog sense. Sit down and wait till we have some chance to get out without being carried in baskets.'

" 'I got to be home by seven, Buck,' repeats this henpecked thing of little wisdom, like an unthinking poll parrot. 'Mariana,' says he, ' 'll be looking out for me.' And he reaches down and pulls a leg out of the checker table. 'I'll go through this Trimble outfit,' says he, 'like a cottontail through a brush corral. I'm not pestered any more with a desire to engage in ruckuses, but I got to be home by seven. You lock the door after me, Buck. And don't you forget—I won three out of them five games. I'd play longer, but Mariana—'

" 'Hush up, you old locoed road runner,' I interrupts. 'Did you ever notice your Uncle Buck locking doors against trouble? I'm not married,' says I, 'but I'm as big a d——n fool as any Mormon. One from four leaves three,' says I, and I gathers out another leg of the table. 'We'll get home by seven,' says I, 'whether it's the heavenly one or the other. May I see you home?' says I, 'you sarsaparilla-drinking, checker-playing glutton for death and destruction.'

"We opened the door easy, and then stampeded for the front. Part of the gang was lined up at the bar; part of 'em was passing over the drinks, and two or three was peeping out the door and window taking shots at the marshal's crowd. The room was so full of smoke we got halfway to the front door before they noticed us. Then I heard Berry Trimble's voice somewhere yell out:

" 'How'd that Buck Caperton get in here?' and he skinned the side of my neck with a bullet. I reckon he felt bad over that miss, for Berry's the best shot south of the Southern Pacific Railroad. But the smoke in the saloon was some too thick for good shooting.

"Me and Perry smashed over two of the gang with our table legs, which didn't miss like the guns did, and as we run out the door I grabbed a Winchester from a fellow who was watching the outside, and I turned and regulated the account of Mr. Berry.

"Me and Perry got out and around the corner all right. I never much expected to get out, but I wasn't going to be intimidated by that married man. According to Perry's idea, checkers was the event of the day, but if I am any judge of gentle recreations that little table-leg parade through the Gray Mule saloon deserved the headlines in the bill of particulars.

" 'Walk fast,' says Perry, 'it's two minutes to seven, and I got to be home by—'

" 'Oh, shut up,' says I. 'I had an appointment as chief performer at an inquest at seven, and I'm not kicking about not keeping it.'

"I had to pass by Perry's little house. His Mariana was standing at the gate. We got there at five minutes past seven. She had on a blue wrapper, and her hair was pulled back smooth like little girls do when they want to look grown-folksy. She didn't see us till we got close, for she was gazing up the other way. Then she backed around, and saw

Perry, and a kind of a look scooted around over her face—danged if I can describe it. I heard her breathe long, just like a cow when you turn her calf in the lot, and she says: 'You're late, Perry.'

"Five minutes,' says Perry, cheerful. 'Me and old Buck was having a game of checkers.'

"Perry introduces me to Mariana, and they ask me to come in. No, sir-ee. I'd had enough truck with married folks for that day. I says I'll be going along, and that I've spent a very pleasant afternoon with my old partner—'especially,' says I, just to jostle Perry, 'during that game when the table legs came all loose.' But I'd promised him not to let her know anything.

"I've been worrying over that business ever since it happened," continued Buck. "There's one thing about it that's got me all twisted up, and I can't figure it out."

"What was that?" I asked, as I rolled and handed Buck the last cigarette.

"Why, I'll tell you: When I saw the look that little woman give Perry when she turned round and saw him coming back to the ranch safe—why was it I got the idea all in a minute that that look of hers was worth more than the whole caboodle of us—sarsaparilla, checkers, and all, and that the d——n fool in the game wasn't named Perry Rountree at all?"

LOST ON DRESS PARADE

MR. TOWERS CHANDLER was pressing his evening suit in his hall bedroom. One iron was heating on a small gas stove; the other was being pushed vigorously back and forth to make the desirable crease that would be seen later on extending in straight lines from Mr. Chandler's patent leather shoes to the edge of his low-cut vest. So much of the hero's toilet may be intrusted to our confidence. The remainder may be guessed by those whom genteel poverty has driven to ignoble expedient. Our next view of him shall be as he descends the steps of his lodging-house immaculately and correctly clothed; calm, assured, handsome—in appearance the typical New York young clubman setting out, slightly bored, to inaugurate the pleasures of the evening.

Chandler's honorarium was eighteen dollars per week. He was employed in the office of an architect. He was twenty-two years old; he considered architecture to be truly an art; and he honestly believed—though he would not have dared to admit it in New York—that the Flatiron Building was inferior in design to the great cathedral in Milan.

Out of each week's earning Chandler set aside one dollar. At the end of each ten weeks with the extra capital thus accumulated, he purchased one gentleman's evening from the bargain counter of stingy old Father Time. He arrayed himself in the regalia of millionaires and presidents; he took himself to the quarter where life is brightest and showiest, and there dined with taste and luxury. With ten dollars a man may, for a few hours, play the wealthy idler to perfection. The sum is ample for a well-considered meal, a bottle bearing a respectable label, commensurate tips, a smoke, cab fare, and the ordinary etceteras.

This one delectable evening culled from each dull seventy was to

Chandler a source of renascent bliss. To the society bud comes but one debut; it stands alone sweet in her memory when her hair has whitened; but to Chandler each ten weeks brought a joy as keen, as thrilling, as new, as the first had been. To sit among *bon vivants* under palms in the swirl of concealed music, to look upon the *habitués* of such a paradise and to be looked upon by them—what is a girl's first dance and short-sleeved tulle compared with this?

Up Broadway Chandler moved with the vespertine dress parade. For this evening he was an exhibit as well as a gazer. For the next sixty-nine evenings he would be dining in cheviot and worsted at dubious *table d'hôtes*, at whirlwind lunch counters, on sandwiches and beer in his hall bedroom. He was willing to do that, for he was a true son of the great city of razzle-dazzle, and to him one evening in the limelight made up for many dark ones.

Chandler protracted his walk until the Forties began to intersect the great and glittering primrose way, for the evening was yet young, and when one is of the *beau monde* only one day in seventy, one loves to protract the pleasure. Eyes bright, sinister, curious, admiring, provocative, alluring, were bent upon him, for his garb and air proclaimed him a devotee to the hour of solace and pleasure.

At a certain corner he came to a standstill, proposing to himself the question of turning back toward the showy and fashionable restaurant in which he usually dined on the evenings of his especial luxury. Just then a girl scudded lightly around the corner, slipped on a patch of icy snow, and fell plump upon the sidewalk.

Chandler assisted her to her feet with instant and solicitous courtesy. The girl hobbled to the wall of the building, leaned against it, and thanked him demurely.

"I think my ankle is strained," she said. "It twisted when I fell."

"Does it pain you much?" inquired Chandler.

"Only when I rest my weight upon it. I think I will be able to walk in a minute or two."

"If I can be of any further service," suggested the young man, "I will call a cab, or—"

"Thank you," said the girl, softly but heartily. "I am sure you need not trouble yourself any further. It was so awkward of me. And my shoe heels are horridly common-sense; I can't blame them at all."

Chandler looked at the girl and found her swiftly drawing his interest. She was pretty in a refined way; and her eye was both merry and kind. She was inexpensively clothed in a plain black dress that suggested a sort of uniform such as shop-girls wear. Her glossy dark-brown hair showed its coils beneath a cheap hat of black straw whose only ornament was a velvet ribbon and bow. She could have posed as a model for the self-respecting working girl of the best type.

A sudden idea came into the head of the young architect. He would ask this girl to dine with him. Here was the element that his splendid but solitary periodic feasts had lacked. His brief season of elegant luxury would be doubly enjoyable if he could add to it a lady's society. This girl was a lady, he was sure—her manner and speech settled that. And in spite of her extremely plain attire he felt that he would be pleased to sit at table with her.

These thoughts passed swiftly through his mind, and he decided to ask her. It was a breach of etiquette, of course, but oftentimes wage-earning girls waived formalities in matters of this kind. They were generally shrewd judges of men; and thought better of their own judgment than they did of useless conventions. His ten dollars, discreetly expended, would enable the two to dine very well indeed. The dinner would no doubt be a wonderful experience thrown into the dull routine of the girl's life; and her lively appreciation of it would add to his own triumph and pleasure.

"I think," he said to her, with frank gravity, "that your foot needs a longer rest than you suppose. Now, I am going to suggest a way in which you can give it that and at the same time do me a favor. I was on my way to dine all by my lonely self when you came tumbling around the corner. You come with me and we'll have a cozy dinner and a pleasant talk together, and by that time your game ankle will carry you home very nicely, I am sure."

The girl looked quickly up into Chandler's clear, pleasant countenance. Her eyes twinkled once very brightly, and then she smiled ingenuously.

"But we don't know each other—it wouldn't be right, would it?" she said, doubtfully.

"There is nothing wrong about it," said the young man, candidly. "I'll introduce myself—permit me—Mr. Towers Chandler. After our dinner, which I will try to make as pleasant as possible, I will bid you good-evening, or attend you safely to your door, whichever you prefer."

"But, dear me!" said the girl, with a glance at Chandler's faultless attire. "In this old dress and hat!"

"Never mind that," said Chandler, cheerfully. "I'm sure you look more charming in them than anyone we shall see in the most elaborate dinner toilette."

"My ankle does hurt yet," admitted the girl, attempting a limping step. "I think I will accept your invitation, Mr. Chandler. You may call me—Miss Marian."

"Come then, Miss Marian," said the young architect, gaily, but with perfect courtesy; "you will not have far to walk. There is a very respectable and good restaurant in the next block. You will have to lean on my arm—so—and walk slowly. It is lonely dining all by one's self. I'm just a little bit glad that you slipped on the ice."

When the two were established at a well-appointed table, with a promising waiter hovering in attendance, Chandler began to experience the real joy that his regular outing always brought to him.

The restaurant was not so showy or pretentious as the one farther down Broadway, which he always preferred, but it was nearly so. The tables were well filled with prosperous-looking diners, there was a good orchestra, playing softly enough to make conversation a possible pleasure, and the cuisine and service were beyond criticism. His companion, even in her cheap hat and dress, held herself with an air that added distinction to the natural beauty of her face and figure. And it is certain that she looked at Chandler, with his animated but self-possessed manner and his kindling and frank blue eyes, with something not far from admiration in her own charming face.

Then it was that the Madness of Manhattan, the Frenzy of Fuss and Feathers, the Bacillus of Brag, the Provincial Plague of Pose, seized upon Towers Chandler. He was on Broadway, surrounded by pomp and style, and there were eyes to look at him. On the stage of that comedy he had assumed to play the one-night part of a butterfly of fashion and an idler of means and taste. He was dressed for the part, and all his good angels had not the power to prevent him from acting it.

So he began to prate to Miss Marian of clubs, of teas, of golf and riding and kennels and cotillions and tours abroad and threw out hints of a yacht lying at Larchmont. He could see that she was vastly impressed by this vague talk, so he endorsed his pose by random insinuations concerning great wealth, and mentioned familiarly a few names that are handled reverently by the proletariat. It was Chandler's short little day, and he was wringing from it the best that could be had, as he saw it. And yet once or twice he saw the pure gold of this girl shine through the mist that his egotism had raised between him and all objects.

"This way of living that you speak of," she said, "sounds so futile and purposeless. Haven't you any work to do in the world that might interest you more?"

"My dear Miss Marian," he exclaimed—"work! Think of dressing every day for dinner, of making half a dozen calls in an afternoon—with a policeman at every corner ready to jump into your auto and take you to the station, if you get up any greater speed than a donkey cart's gait. We do-nothings are the hardest workers in the land."

The dinner was concluded, the waiter generously feed, and the two walked out to the corner where they had met. Miss Marian walked very well now; her limp was scarcely noticeable.

"Thank you for a nice time," she said, frankly. "I must run home now. I liked the dinner very much, Mr. Chandler."

He shook hands with her, smiling cordially, and said something about a game of bridge at his club. He watched her for a moment, walking rather rapidly eastward, and then he found a cab to drive him slowly homeward.

In his chilly bedroom Chandler laid away his evening clothes for a sixty-nine days' rest. He went about it thoughtfully.

"That was a stunning girl," he said to himself. "She's all right, too, I'd be sworn, even if she does have to work. Perhaps if I'd told her the truth instead of all that razzle-dazzle we might—but, confound it! I had to play up to my clothes."

Thus spoke the brave who was born and reared in the wigwams of the tribe of the Manhattans.

The girl, after leaving her entertainer, sped swiftly crosstown until she arrived at a handsome and sedate mansion two squares to the east, facing on that avenue which is the highway of Mammon and the auxiliary gods. Here she entered hurriedly and ascended to a room where a handsome young lady in an elaborate housedress was looking anxiously out the window.

"Oh, you madcap!" exclaimed the elder girl, when the other entered. "When will you quit frightening us this way? It is two hours since you ran out in that rag of an old dress and Marie's hat. Mamma has been so alarmed. She sent Louis in the auto to try to find you. You are a bad, thoughtless Puss."

The elder girl touched a button, and a maid came in a moment.

"Marie, tell Mamma that Miss Marian has returned."

"Don't scold, Sister. I only ran down to Mme. Theo's to tell her to use mauve insertion instead of pink. My costume and Marie's hat were just what I needed. Everyone thought I was a shop-girl, I am sure."

"Dinner is over, dear; you stayed so late."

"I know. I slipped on the sidewalk and turned my ankle. I could not walk, so I hobbled into a restaurant and sat there until I was better. That is why I was so long."

The two girls sat in the window seat, looking out at the lights and the stream of hurrying vehicles in the avenue. The younger one cuddled down with her head in her sister's lap.

"We will have to marry someday," she said dreamily—"both of us. We have so much money that we will not be allowed to disappoint the public. Do you want me to tell you the kind of a man I could love, Sis?"

"Go on, you scatterbrain," smiled the other.

"I could love a man with dark and kind blue eyes, who is gentle and respectful to poor girls, who is handsome and good and does not try to flirt. But I could love him only if he had an ambition, an object, some work to do in the world. I would not care how poor he was if I could help him build his way up. But, sister dear, the kind of man we always meet—the man who lives an idle life between society and his clubs—I could not love a man like that, even if his eyes were blue and he were ever so kind to poor girls whom he met in the street."

THE ROMANCE OF A BUSY BROKER

PITCHER, confidential clerk in the office of Harvey Maxwell, broker, allowed a look of mild interest and surprise to visit his usually expressionless countenance when his employer briskly entered at half-past nine in company with his young lady stenographer. With a snappy "Good-morning, Pitcher," Maxwell dashed at his desk as though he were intending to leap over it, and then plunged into the great heap of letters and telegrams waiting there for him.

The young lady had been Maxwell's stenographer for a year. She was beautiful in a way that was decidedly unstenographic. She forewent the pomp of the alluring pompadour. She wore no chains, bracelets, or lockets. She had not the air of being about to accept an invitation to luncheon. Her dress was gray and plain, but it fitted her figure with fidelity and discretion. In her neat black turban hat was the gold-green wing of a macaw. On this morning she was softly and shyly radiant. Her eyes were dreamily bright, her cheeks genuine peach-blow, her expression a happy one, tinged with reminiscence.

Pitcher, still mildly curious, noticed a difference in her ways this morning. Instead of going straight into the adjoining room, where her desk was, she lingered, slightly irresolute, in the outer office. Once she moved over by Maxwell's desk near enough for him to be aware of her presence.

The machine sitting at that desk was no longer a man; it was a busy New York broker, moved by buzzing wheels and uncoiling springs.

"Well—what is it? Anything?" asked Maxwell sharply. His opened mail lay like a bank of stage snow on his crowded desk. His keen gray eye, impersonal and brusque, flashed upon her half impatiently.

"Nothing," answered the stenographer, moving away with a little smile.

"Mr. Pitcher," she said to the confidential clerk, "did Mr. Maxwell say anything yesterday about engaging another stenographer?"

"He did," answered Pitcher. "He told me to get another one. I notified the agency yesterday afternoon to send over a few samples this morning. It's nine forty-five o'clock, and not a single picture hat or piece of pineapple chewing gum has showed up yet."

"I will do the work as usual, then," said the young lady, "until someone comes to fill the place." And she went to her desk at once and hung the black turban hat with the gold-green macaw wing in its accustomed place.

He who has been denied the spectacle of a busy Manhattan broker during a rush of business is handicapped for the profession of anthropology. The poet sings of the "crowded hour of glorious life." The broker's hour is not only crowded, but the minutes and seconds are hanging to all the straps and packing both front and rear platforms.

And this day was Harvey Maxwell's busy day. The ticker began to reel out jerkily its fitful coils of tape, the desk telephone had a chronic attack of buzzing. Men began to throng into the office and call at him over the railing, jovially, sharply, viciously, excitedly. Messenger boys ran in and out with messages and telegrams. The clerks in the office jumped about like sailors during a storm. Even Pitcher's face relaxed into something resembling animation.

On the Exchange there were hurricanes and landslides and snowstorms and glaciers and volcanoes, and those elemental disturbances were reproduced in miniature in the broker's offices. Maxwell shoved his chair against the wall and transacted business after the manner of a toe dancer. He jumped from ticker to phone, from desk to door with the trained agility of a harlequin.

In the midst of this growing and important stress the broker became suddenly aware of a high-rolled fringe of golden hair under a nodding canopy of velvet and ostrich tips, an imitation sealskin sacque, and a string of beads as large as hickory nuts, ending near the floor with a silver heart. There was a self-possessed young lady connected with these accessories; and Pitcher was there to construe her.

"Lady from the Stenographer's Agency to see about the position," said Pitcher.

Maxwell turned half around, with his hands full of papers and ticker tape.

"What position?" he asked, with a frown.

"Position of stenographer," said Pitcher. "You told me yesterday to call them up and have one sent over this morning."

"You are losing your mind, Pitcher," said Maxwell. "Why should I have given you any such instructions? Miss Leslie has given perfect satisfaction during the year she has been here. The place is hers as long as she chooses to retain it. There's no place open here, madam. Countermand that order with the agency, Pitcher, and don't bring any more of 'em in here."

The silver heart left the office, swinging and banging itself independently against the office furniture as it indignantly departed. Pitcher seized a moment to remark to the bookkeeper that the "old man" seemed to get more absent-minded and forgetful every day of the world.

The rush and pace of business grew fiercer and faster. On the floor they were pounding half a dozen stocks in which Maxwell's customers were heavy investors. Orders to buy and sell were coming and going as swift as the flight of swallows. Some of his own holdings were imperilled, and the man was working like some high-geared, delicate, strong machine—strung to full tension, going at full speed, accurate, never hesitating, with the proper word and decision and act ready and prompt as clockwork. Stocks and bonds, loans and mortgages, margins and securities—here was a world of finance, and there was no room in it for the human world or the world of nature.

When the luncheon hour drew near there came a slight lull in the uproar.

Maxwell stood by his desk with his hands full of telegrams and memoranda, with a fountain pen over his right ear and his hair hanging in disorderly strings over his forehead. His window was open, for the beloved janitress Spring had turned on a little warmth through the waking registers of the earth.

And through the window came a wandering—perhaps a lost—odor—a delicate, sweet odor of lilac that fixed the broker for a moment immovable. For this odor belonged to Miss Leslie; it was her own, and hers only.

The odor brought her vividly, almost tangibly, before him. The world of finance dwindled suddenly to a speck. And she was in the next room—twenty steps away.

"By George, I'll do it now," said Maxwell, half aloud. "I'll ask her now. I wonder I didn't do it long ago."

He dashed into the inner office with the haste of a short trying to cover. He charged upon the desk of the stenographer.

She looked up at him with a smile. A soft pink crept over her cheek, and her eyes were kind and frank. Maxwell leaned one elbow on her desk. He still clutched fluttering papers with both hands and the pen was above his ear.

"Miss Leslie," he began hurriedly, "I have but a moment to spare. I want to say something in that moment. Will you be my wife? I haven't had time to make love to you in the ordinary way, but I really do love you. Talk quick, please—those fellows are clubbing the stuffing out of Union Pacific."

"Oh, what are you talking about?" exclaimed the young lady. She rose to her feet and gazed upon him, round-eyed.

"Don't you understand?" said Maxwell, restively. "I want you to marry me. I love you, Miss Leslie. I wanted to tell you, and I snatched a minute when things had slackened up a bit. They're calling me for the phone now. Tell 'em to wait a minute, Pitcher. Won't you, Miss Leslie?"

The stenographer acted very queerly. At first she seemed overcome with amazement; then tears flowed from her wondering eyes; and then she smiled sunnily through them, and one of her arms slid tenderly about the broker's neck.

"I know now," she said, softly. "It's this old business that has driven everything else out of your head for the time. I was frightened at first. Don't you remember, Harvey? We were married last evening at eight o'clock in the Little Church Around the Corner."

THE THIRD INGREDIENT

THE (so-called) Vallambrosa Apartment-House is not an apartment-house. It is composed of two old-fashioned, brownstone-front residences welded into one. The parlor floor of one side is gay with the wraps and headgear of a modiste; the other is lugubrious with the sophistical promises and grisly display of a painless dentist. You may have a room there for two dollars a week or you may have one for twenty dollars. Among the Vallambrosa's roomers are stenographers, musicians, brokers, shop-girls, space-rate writers, art students, wire-tappers, and other people who lean far over the banister-rail when the door-bell rings.

This treatise shall have to do with but two of the Vallambrosians—though meaning no disrespect to the others.

At six o'clock one afternoon Hetty Pepper came back to her third-floor rear $3.50 room in the Vallambrosa with her nose and chin more sharply pointed than usual. To be discharged from the department store where you have been working four years, and with only fifteen cents in your purse, does have a tendency to make your features appear more finely chiseled.

And now for Hetty's thumb-nail biography while she climbs the two flights of stairs.

She walked into the Biggest Store one morning four years before with seventy-five other girls, applying for a job behind the waist department counter. The phalanx of wage-earners formed a bewildering scene of beauty, carrying a total mass of blond hair sufficient to have justified the horseback gallops of a hundred Lady Godivas.

The capable, cool-eyed, impersonal, young, bald-headed man whose task it was to engage six of the contestants, was aware of a feeling of suffocation as if he were drowning in a sea of frangipani, while white clouds, hand-embroidered, floated about him. And then a sail hove in sight. Hetty Pepper, homely of countenance, with small, contemptuous, green eyes and chocolate-colored hair, dressed in a suit of plain burlap and a common-sense hat, stood before him with every one of her twenty-nine years of life unmistakably in sight.

"You're on!" shouted the bald-headed young man, and was saved. And that is how Hetty came to be employed in the Biggest Store. The story of her rise to an eight-dollar-a-week salary is the combined stories of Hercules, Joan of Arc, Una, Job, and Little-Red-Riding-Hood. You shall not learn from me the salary that was paid her as a beginner. There is a sentiment growing about such things, and I want no millionaire store-proprietors climbing the fire-escape of my tenement-house to throw dynamite bombs into my skylight boudoir.

The story of Hetty's discharge from the Biggest Store is so nearly a repetition of her engagement as to be monotonous.

In each department of the store there is an omniscient, omnipresent, and omnivorous person carrying always a mileage book and a red necktie, and referred to as a "buyer." The destinies of the girls in his department who live on (see Bureau of Victual Statistics)—so much per week are in his hands.

This particular buyer was a capable, cool-eyed, impersonal, young, bald-headed man. As he walked along the aisles of his department he seemed to be sailing on a sea of frangipani, while white clouds, machine-embroidered, floated around him. Too many sweets bring surfeit. He looked upon Hetty Pepper's homely countenance, emerald eyes, and chocolate-colored hair as a welcome oasis of green in a desert of cloying beauty. In a quiet angle of a counter he pinched her arm kindly, three inches above the elbow. She slapped him three feet away with one good blow of her muscular and not especially lily-white right. So, now you know why Hetty Pepper came to leave the Biggest Store at thirty minutes' notice, with one dime and a nickel in her purse.

This morning's quotations list the price of rib beef at six cents per (butcher's) pound. But on the day that Hetty was "released" by the B. S. the price was seven and one-half cents. That fact is what makes this story possible. Otherwise, the extra four cents would have—

GORDON GRANT

But the plot of nearly all the good stories in the world is concerned with shorts who were unable to cover; so you can find no fault with this one.

Hetty mounted with her rib beef to her $3.50 third-floor back. One hot, savory beef-stew for supper, a night's good sleep, and she would be fit in the morning to apply again for the tasks of Hercules, Joan of Arc, Una, Job, and Little-Red-Riding-Hood.

In her room she got the granite-ware stewpan out of the 2 x 4-foot china—er—I mean earthenware closet, and began to dig down in a rats'-nest of paper bags for the potatoes and onions. She came out with her nose and chin just a little sharper pointed.

There was neither a potato nor an onion. Now, what kind of a beef-stew can you make out of simply beef? You can make oyster-soup without oysters, turtle-soup without turtles, coffee-cake without coffee, but you can't make beef-stew without potatoes and onions.

But rib beef alone, in an emergency, can make an ordinary pine door look like a wrought-iron gambling-house portal to the wolf. With salt and pepper and a tablespoonful of flour (first well stirred in a little cold water) 'twill serve—'tis not so deep as a lobster à la Newburg nor so wide as a church festival doughnut; but 'twill serve.

Hetty took her stewpan to the rear of the third-floor hall. According to the advertisements of the Vallambrosa there was running water to be found there. Between you and me and the water-meter, it only ambled or walked through the faucets; but technicalities have no place here. There was also a sink where housekeeping roomers often met to dump their coffee-grounds and glare at one another's kimonos.

At this sink Hetty found a girl with heavy, gold-brown, artistic hair and plaintive eyes, washing two large "Irish" potatoes. Hetty knew the Vallambrosa as well as anyone not owning "double hextra-magnifying eyes" could compass its mysteries. The kimonos were her encyclopedia, her "Who's What?" her clearing-house of news, of goers and comers. From a rose-pink kimono edged with Nile green she had learned that the girl with the potatoes was a miniature-painter living in a kind of attic—or "studio," as they prefer to call it—on the top floor. Hetty was not certain in her mind what a miniature was; but it certainly wasn't a house; because house-painters, although they wear splashy overalls and poke ladders in your face on the street, are known to indulge in a riotous profusion of food at home.

The potato girl was quite slim and small, and handled her potatoes as an old bachelor uncle handles a baby who is cutting teeth. She had a dull shoemaker's knife in her right hand, and she had begun to peel one of the potatoes with it.

Hetty addressed her in the punctiliously formal tone of one who intends to be cheerfully familiar with you in the second round.

"Beg pardon," she said, "for butting into what's not my business, but if you peel them potatoes you lose out. They're new Bermudas. You want to scrape 'em. Lemme show you."

She took a potato and the knife, and began to demonstrate.

"Oh, thank you," breathed the artist. "I didn't know. And I *did* hate to see the thick peeling go; it seemed such a waste. But I thought they always had to be peeled. When you've got only potatoes to eat, the peelings count, you know."

"Say, kid," said Hetty, staying her knife, "you ain't up against it, too, are you?"

The miniature artist smiled starvedly.

"I suppose I am. Art—or, at least, the way I interpret it—doesn't seem to be much in demand. I have only these potatoes for my dinner. But they aren't so bad boiled and hot, with a little butter and salt."

"Child," said Hetty, letting a brief smile soften her rigid features, "Fate has sent me and you together. I've had it handed to me in the neck, too; but I've got a chunk of meat in my room as big as a lap-dog. And I've done everything to get potatoes except pray for 'em. Let's me and you bunch our commissary departments and make a stew of 'em. We'll cook it in my room. If we only had an onion to go in it! Say, kid, you haven't got a couple of pennies that've slipped down into the lining of your last winter's sealskin, have you? I could step down to the corner and get one at old Giuseppe's stand. A stew without an onion is worse'n a matinée without candy."

"You may call me Cecilia," said the artist. "No; I spent my last penny three days ago."

"Then we'll have to cut the onion out instead of slicing it in," said Hetty. "I'd ask the janitress for one, but I don't want 'em hep just yet to the fact that I'm pounding the asphalt for another job. But I wish we did have an onion."

In the shop-girl's room the two began to prepare their supper. Cecilia's part was to sit on the couch helplessly and beg to be allowed to do something, in the voice of a cooing ring-dove. Hetty prepared the rib beef, putting it in cold salted water in the stewpan and setting it on the one-burner gas-stove.

"I wish we had an onion," said Hetty, as she scraped the two potatoes.

On the wall opposite the couch was pinned a flaming, gorgeous advertising picture of one of the new ferry-boats of the P.U.F.F. Railroad that had been built to cut down the time between Los Angeles and New York City one-eighth of a minute.

Hetty, turning her head during her continuous monologue, saw tears running from her guest's eyes as she gazed on the idealized presentment of the speeding, foam-girdled transport.

"Why, say, Cecilia, kid," said Hetty, poising her knife, "is it as bad art as that? I ain't a critic; but I thought it kind of brightened up the room. Of course, a manicure-painter could tell it was a bum picture in a minute. I'll take it down if you say so. I wish to the holy Saint Potluck we had an onion."

But the miniature miniature-painter had tumbled down, sobbing, with her nose indenting the hard-woven drapery of the couch. Something was here deeper than the artistic temperament offended at crude lithography.

Hetty knew. She had accepted her role long ago. How scant the words with which we try to describe a single quality of a human being! When we reach the abstract we are lost. The nearer to Nature that the babbling of our lips comes, the better do we understand. Figuratively (let us say), some people are Bosoms, some are Hands, some are Heads, some are Muscles, some are Feet, some are Backs for burdens.

Hetty was a Shoulder. Hers was a sharp, sinewy shoulder; but all her life people had laid their heads upon it, metaphorically or actually, and had left there all or half their troubles. Looking at Life anatomically, which is as good a way as any, she was preordained to be a Shoulder. There were few truer collar-bones anywhere than hers.

Hetty was only thirty-three, and she had not yet outlived the little pang that visited her whenever the head of youth and beauty leaned upon her for consolation. But one glance in her mirror always served as an instantaneous pain-killer. So she gave one pale look into the crinkly old looking-glass on the wall above the gas-stove, turned down the flame a little lower from the bubbling beef and potatoes, went over to the couch, and lifted Cecilia's head to its confessional.

"Go on and tell me, honey," she said. "I know now that it ain't art that's worrying you. You met him on a ferry-boat, didn't you? Go on, Cecilia, kid, and tell your—your Aunt Hetty about it."

But youth and melancholy must first spend the surplus of sighs and tears that waft and float the barque of romance to its harbor in the delectable isles. Presently, through the stringy tendons that formed the bars of the confessional, the penitent—or was it the glorified communicant of the sacred flame?—told her story without art or illumination.

"It was only three days ago. I was coming back on the ferry from Jersey City. Old Mr. Schrum, an art dealer, told me of a rich man in Newark who wanted a miniature of his daughter painted. I went to see him and showed him some of my work. When I told him the price would be fifty dollars he laughed at me like a hyena. He said an enlarged crayon twenty times the size would cost him only eight dollars.

"I had just enough money to buy my ferry ticket back to New York. I felt as if I didn't want to live another day. I must have looked as I felt, for I saw *him* on the row of seats opposite me, looking at me as if he understood. He was nice-looking, but oh, above everything else, he looked kind. When one is tired or unhappy or hopeless, kindness counts more than anything else.

"When I got so miserable that I couldn't fight against it any longer, I got up and walked slowly out the rear door of the ferry-boat cabin. No one was there, and I slipped quickly over the rail and dropped into the water. Oh, friend Hetty, it was cold, cold!

"For just one moment I wished I was back in the old Vallambrosa, starving and hoping. And then I got numb, and didn't care. And then I felt that somebody else was in the water close by me, holding me up. *He* had followed me, and jumped in to save me.

"Somebody threw a thing like a big, white doughnut at us, and he made me put my arms through the hole. Then the ferry-boat backed, and they pulled us on board. Oh, Hetty, I was so ashamed of my wickedness in trying to drown myself; and, besides, my hair had all tumbled down and was sopping wet, and I was such a sight.

"And then some men in blue clothes came around; and *he* gave them his card, and I heard him tell them he had seen me drop my purse on the edge of the boat outside the rail, and in leaning over to get it I had fallen overboard. And then I remembered having read in the papers that people who try to kill themselves are locked up in cells with people who try to kill other people, and I was afraid.

"But some ladies on the boat took me downstairs to the furnace-room and got me nearly dry and did up my hair. When the boat landed, *he* came and put me in a cab. He was all dripping himself, but laughed as if he thought it was all a joke. He begged me, but I wouldn't tell him my name nor where I lived, I was so ashamed."

"You were a fool, child," said Hetty, kindly. "Wait till I turn the light up a bit. I wish to Heaven we had an onion."

"Then he raised his hat," went on Cecilia, "and said: 'Very well. But I'll find you, anyhow. I'm going to claim my rights of salvage.' Then he gave money to the cab-driver and told him to take me where I wanted to go, and walked away. What is 'salvage,' Hetty?"

"The edge of a piece of goods that ain't hemmed," said the shop-girl. "You must have looked pretty well frazzled out to the little hero boy."

"It's been three days," moaned the miniature-painter, "and he hasn't found me yet."

"Extend the time," said Hetty. "This is a big town. Think of how many girls he might have to see soaked in water with their hair down before he would recognize you. The stew's getting on fine—but oh, for an onion! I'd even use a piece of garlic if I had it."

The beef and potatoes bubbled merrily, exhaling a mouth-watering savor that yet lacked something, leaving a hunger on the palate, a haunting, wistful desire for some lost and needful ingredient.

"I came near drowning in that awful river," said Cecilia, shuddering.

"It ought to have more water in it," said Hetty; "the stew, I mean. I'll go get some at the sink."

"It smells good," said the artist.

"That nasty old North River?" objected Hetty. "It smells to me like soap factories and wet setter-dogs—oh, you mean the stew. Well, I wish we had an onion for it. Did he look like he had money?"

"First, he looked kind," said Cecilia. "I'm sure he was rich; but that matters so little. When he drew out his bill-folder to pay the cabman you couldn't help seeing hundreds and thousands of dollars in it. And I looked over the cab doors and saw him leave the ferry station in a motor-car; and the chauffeur gave him his bearskin to put on, for he was sopping wet. And it was only three days ago."

"What a fool!" said Hetty, shortly.

"Oh, the chauffeur wasn't wet," breathed Cecilia. "And he drove the car away very nicely."

"I mean *you*," said Hetty. "For not giving him your address."

"I never give my address to chauffeurs," said Cecilia, haughtily.

"I wish we had one," said Hetty, disconsolately.

"What for?"

"For the stew, of course—oh, I mean an onion."

Hetty took a pitcher and started to the sink at the end of the hall.

A young man came down the stairs from above just as she was opposite the lower step. He was decently dressed, but pale and haggard. His eyes were dull with the stress of some burden of physical or mental woe. In his hand he bore an onion—a pink, smooth, solid, shining onion as large around as a ninety-eight-cent alarm-clock.

Hetty stopped. So did the young man. There was something Joan of Arc-ish, Herculean, and Una-ish in the look and pose of the shop-lady—she had cast off the roles of Job and Little-Red-Riding-Hood. The young man stopped at the foot of the stairs and coughed distractedly. He felt marooned, held up, attacked, assailed, levied upon, sacked, assessed, panhandled, browbeaten, though he knew not why. It was the look in Hetty's eyes that did it. In them he saw the Jolly Roger fly to the masthead and an able seaman with a dirk between his teeth scurry up the ratlines and nail it there. But as yet he did not know that the cargo he carried was the thing that had caused him to be so nearly blown out of the water without even a parley.

"*Beg* your pardon," said Hetty, as sweetly as her dilute acetic acid tones permitted, "but did you find that onion on the stairs? There was a hole in the paper bag; and I've just come out to look for it."

The young man coughed for half a minute. The interval may have given him the courage to defend his own property. Also, he clutched his pungent prize greedily, and, with a show of spirit, faced his grim waylayer.

"No," he said huskily, "I didn't find it on the stairs. It was given to me by Jack Bevens, on the top floor. If you don't believe it, ask him. I'll wait until you do."

"I know about Bevens," said Hetty, sourly. "He writes books and things up there for the paper-and-rags man. We can hear the postman guy him all over the house when he brings them thick envelopes back. Say—do you live in the Vallambrosa?"

"I do not," said the young man. "I come to see Bevens sometimes. He's my friend. I live two blocks west."

"What are you going to do with the onion?—*begging* your pardon," said Hetty.

"I'm going to eat it."

"Raw?"

"Yes: as soon as I get home."

"Haven't you got anything else to eat with it?"

The young man considered briefly.

"No," he confessed; "there's not another scrap of anything in my diggings to eat. I think old Jack is pretty hard up for grub in his shack, too. He hated to give up the onion, but I worried him into parting with it."

"Man," said Hetty, fixing him with her world-sapient eyes, and laying a bony but impressive finger on his sleeve, "you've known trouble, too, haven't you?"

"Lots," said the onion owner, promptly. "But this onion is my own property, honestly come by. If you will excuse me, I must be going."

"Listen," said Hetty, paling a little with anxiety. "Raw onion is a mighty poor diet. And so is a beef-stew without one. Now, if you're Jack Bevens's friend, I guess you're nearly right. There's a little lady—a friend of mine—in my room there at the end of the hall. Both of us are out of luck; and we had just potatoes and meat between us. They're stewing now. But it ain't got any soul. There's something lacking to it. There's certain things in life that are naturally intended to fit and belong together. One is pink cheese-cloth and green roses, and one is ham and eggs, and one is Irish and trouble. And the other one is beef and potatoes *with* onions. And still another one is people who are up against it and other people in the same fix."

The young man went into a protracted paroxysm of coughing. With one hand he hugged his onion to his bosom.

"No doubt; no doubt," said he, at length. "But, as I said, I must be going, because—"

Hetty clutched his sleeve firmly.

"Don't be a fool, Little Brother. Don't eat raw onions. Chip it in toward the dinner and line yourself inside with the best stew you ever licked a spoon over. Must two ladies knock a young gentleman down and drag him inside for the honor of dining with 'em? No harm shall befall you, Little Brother. Loosen up and fall into line."

The young man's pale face relaxed into a grin.

"Believe I'll go you," he said, brightening. "If my onion is good as a credential, I'll accept the invitation gladly."

"It's good as that, but better as seasoning," said Hetty. "You come and stand outside the door till I ask my lady friend if she has any objections. And don't run away with that letter of recommendation before I come out."

Hetty went into her room and closed the door. The young man waited outside.

"Cecilia, kid," said the shop-girl, oiling the sharp saw of her voice as well as she could, "there's an onion outside. With a young man attached. I've asked him in to dinner. You ain't going to kick, are you?"

"Oh, dear!" said Cecilia, sitting up and patting her artistic hair. She cast a mournful glance at the ferry-boat poster on the wall.

"Nit," said Hetty. "It ain't him. You're up against real life now. I believe you said your hero friend had money and automobiles. This is a poor skeezicks that's got nothing to eat but an onion. But he's easy-spoken and not a freshy. I imagine he's been a gentleman, he's so low down now. And we need the onion. Shall I bring him in? I'll guarantee his behavior."

"Hetty, dear," sighed Cecilia, "I'm so hungry. What difference does it make whether he's a prince or a burglar? I don't care. Bring him in if he's got anything to eat with him."

Hetty went back into the hall. The onion man was gone. Her heart missed a beat, and a gray look settled over her face except on her nose and cheek-bones. And then the tides of life flowed in again, for she saw him leaning out of the front window at the other end of the hall. She hurried there. He was shouting to someone below. The noise of the street overpowered the sound of her footsteps. She looked down over his shoulder, saw whom he was speaking to, and heard his words. He pulled himself in from the window-sill and saw her standing over him.

Hetty's eyes bored into him like two steel gimlets.

"Don't lie to me," she said, calmly. "What were you going to do with that onion?"

The young man suppressed a cough and faced her resolutely. His manner was that of one who had been bearded sufficiently.

"I was going to eat it," said he, with emphatic slowness; "just as I told you before."

"And you have nothing else to eat at home?"

"Not a thing."

"What kind of work do you do?"

"I am not working at anything just now."

"Then why," said Hetty, with her voice set on its sharpest edge, "do you lean out of windows and give orders to chauffeurs in green automobiles in the street below?"

The young man flushed, and his dull eyes began to sparkle.

"Because, madam," said he, in *accelerando* tones, "I pay the chauffeur's wages and I own the automobile—and also this onion—this onion, madam."

He flourished the onion within an inch of Hetty's nose. The shop-lady did not retreat a hair's-breadth.

"Then why do you eat onions," she said, with biting contempt, "and nothing else?"

"I never said I did," retorted the young man, heatedly. "I said I had nothing else to eat where I live. I am not a delicatessen storekeeper."

"Then why," pursued Hetty, inflexibly, "were you going to eat a raw onion?"

"My mother," said the young man, "always made me eat one for a cold. Pardon my referring to a physical infirmity; but you may have noticed that I have a very, very severe cold. I was going to eat the onion and go to bed. I wonder why I am standing here and apologizing to you for it."

"How did you catch this cold?" went on Hetty, suspiciously.

The young man seemed to have arrived at some extreme height of feeling. There were two modes of descent open to him—a burst of rage or a surrender to the ridiculous. He chose wisely; and the empty hall echoed his hoarse laughter.

"You're a dandy," said he. "And I don't blame you for being careful. I don't mind telling you. I got wet. I was on a North River ferry a few days ago when a girl jumped overboard. Of course, I—"

Hetty extended her hand, interrupting his story.

"Give me the onion," she said.

The young man set his jaw a trifle harder.

"Give me the onion," she repeated.

He grinned, and laid it in her hand.

Then Hetty's infrequent, grim, melancholy smile showed itself. She took the young man's arm and pointed with her other hand to the door of her room.

"Little Brother," she said, "go in there. The little fool you fished out of the river is there waiting for you. Go on in. I'll give you three minutes before I come. Potatoes is in there, waiting. Go on in, Onions."

After he had tapped at the door and entered, Hetty began to peel and wash the onion at the sink. She gave a gray look at the gray roofs outside, and the smile on her face vanished by little jerks and twitches.

"But it's us," she said, grimly, to herself, "it's *us* that furnishes the beef."

THE CLARION CALL

HALF of this story can be found in the records of the Police Department; the other half belongs behind the business counter of a newspaper office.

One afternoon two weeks after Millionaire Norcross was found in his apartment murdered by a burglar, the murderer, while strolling serenely down Broadway, ran plump against Detective Barney Woods.

"Is that you, Johnny Kernan?" asked Woods, who had been near-sighted in public for five years.

"No less," cried Kernan, heartily. "If it isn't Barney Woods, late and early of old Saint Jo! You'll have to show me! What are you doing East? Do the green-goods circulars get out that far?"

"I've been in New York some years," said Woods. "I'm on the city detective force."

"Well, well!" said Kernan, breathing smiling joy and patting the detective's arm.

"Come into Muller's," said Woods, "and let's hunt a quiet table. I'd like to talk to you awhile."

It lacked a few minutes to the hour of four. The tides of trade were not yet loosed, and they found a quiet corner of the café. Kernan, well dressed, slightly swaggering, self-confident, seated himself opposite the little detective, with his pale, sandy mustache, squinting eyes, and ready-made cheviot suit.

"What business are you in now?" asked Woods. "You know you left Saint Jo a year before I did."

"I'm selling shares in a copper mine," said Kernan. "I may establish an office here. Well, well! and so old Barney is a New York detective. You always had a turn that way. You were on the police in Saint Jo after I left there, weren't you?"

"Six months," said Woods. "And now there's one more question, Johnny. I've followed your record pretty close ever since you did that hotel job in Saratoga, and I never knew you to use your gun before. Why did you kill Norcross?"

Kernan stared for a few moments with concentrated attention at the slice of lemon in his high-ball; and then he looked at the detective with a sudden, crooked, brilliant smile.

"How did you guess it, Barney?" he asked, admiringly. "I swear I thought the job was as clean and as smooth as a peeled onion. Did I leave a string hanging out anywhere?"

Woods laid upon the table a small gold pencil intended for a watch-charm.

"It's the one I gave you the last Christmas we were in Saint Jo. I've got your shaving mug yet. I found this under a corner of the rug in Norcross's room. I warn you to be careful what you say. I've got it put on to you, Johnny. We were old friends once, but I must do my duty. You'll have to go to the chair for Norcross."

Kernan laughed.

"My luck stays with me," said he. "Who'd have thought old Barney was on my trail!" He slipped one hand inside his coat. In an instant Woods had a revolver against his side.

"Put it away," said Kernan, wrinkling his nose. "I'm only investigating. Aha! It takes nine tailors to make a man, but one can do a man up. There's a hole in that vest pocket. I took that pencil off my chain and slipped it in there in case of a scrap. Put up your gun, Barney, and I'll tell you why I had to shoot Norcross. The old fool started down the hall after me, popping at the buttons on the back of my coat with a peevish little twenty-two and I had to stop him. The old lady was a darling. She just lay in bed and saw her twelve-thousand-dollar diamond necklace go without a chirp, while she begged like a panhandler to have back a little thin gold ring with a garnet worth about three dollars. I guess she married old Norcross for his money, all right. Don't they hang on to the little trinkets from the Man Who Lost Out, though? There were six rings, two brooches, and a chatelaine watch. Fifteen thousand would cover the lot."

"I warned you not to talk," said Woods.

"Oh, that's all right," said Kernan. "The stuff is in my suit-case at the hotel. And now I'll tell you why I'm talking. Because it's safe. I'm talking to a man I know. You owe me a thousand dollars, Barney Woods, and even if you wanted to arrest me your hand wouldn't make the move."

"I haven't forgotten," said Woods. "You counted out twenty fifties without a word. I'll pay it back someday. That thousand saved me and—well, they were piling my furniture out on the sidewalk when I got back to the house."

"And so," continued Kernan, "you being Barney Woods, born as true as steel, and bound to play a white man's game, can't lift a finger to arrest the man you're indebted to. Oh, I have to study men as well as Yale locks and window fastenings in my business. Now, keep quiet while I ring for the waiter. I've had a thirst for a year or two that worries me a little. If I'm ever caught the lucky sleuth will have to divide honors with old boy Booze. But I never drink during business hours. After a job I can crook elbows with my old friend Barney with a clear conscience. What are you taking?"

The waiter came with the little decanters and the siphon and left them alone again.

"You've called the turn," said Woods, as he rolled the little gold pencil about with a thoughtful forefinger. "I've got to pass you up. I can't lay a hand on you. If I'd a-paid that money back—but I didn't, and that settles it. It's a bad break I'm making, Johnny, but I can't dodge it. You helped me once, and it calls for the same."

"I knew it," said Kernan, raising his glass, with a flushed smile of self-appreciation. "I can judge men. Here's to Barney, for—'he's a jolly good fellow.' "

"I don't believe," went on Woods quietly, as if he were thinking aloud, "that if accounts had been square between you and me, all the money in all the banks in New York could have bought you out of my hands tonight."

"I know it couldn't," said Kernan. "That's why I knew I was safe with you."

"Most people," continued the detective, "look sideways at my business. They don't class it among the fine arts and the professions. But I've always taken a kind of fool pride in it. And here is where I go 'busted.' I guess I'm a man first and a detective afterward. I've got to let you go, and then I've got to resign from the force. I guess I can drive an express wagon. Your thousand dollars is further off than ever, Johnny."

"Oh, you're welcome to it," said Kernan, with a lordly air. "I'd be willing to call the debt off, but I know you wouldn't have it. It was a lucky day for me when you borrowed it. And now, let's drop the subject. I'm off to the West on a morning train. I know a place out there where I can negotiate the Norcross sparks. Drink up, Barney, and forget your troubles. We'll have a jolly time while the police are knocking their heads together over the case. I've got one of my Sahara thirsts on tonight. But I'm in the hands—the unofficial hands—of my old friend Barney, and I won't even dream of a cop."

And then, as Kernan's ready finger kept the button and the waiter working, his weak point—a tremendous vanity and arrogant egotism, began to show itself. He recounted story after story of his successful plunderings, ingenious plots, and infamous transgressions until Woods, with all his familiarity with evil-doers, felt growing within him a cold abhorrence toward the utterly vicious man who had once been his benefactor.

"I'm disposed of, of course," said Woods, at length. "But I advise you to keep under cover for a spell. The newspapers may take up this Norcross affair. There has been an epidemic of burglaries and manslaughter in town this summer."

The word sent Kernan into a high glow of sullen and vindictive rage.

"To h——l with the newspapers," he growled. "What do they spell but brag and blow and boodle in box-car letters? Suppose they do take up a case—what does it amount to? The police are easy enough to fool; but what do the newspapers do? They send a lot of pin-head reporters around to the scene; and they make for the nearest saloon and have beer while they take photos of the bartender's oldest daughter in evening dress, to print as the fiancée of the young man in the tenth story, who thought he heard a noise below on the night of the murder. That's about as near as the newspapers ever come to running down Mr. Burglar."

"Well, I don't know," said Woods, reflecting. "Some of the papers have done good work in that line. There's the *Morning Mars,* for instance. It warmed up two or three trails, and got the man after the police had let 'em get cold."

"I'll show you," said Kernan, rising, and expanding his chest. "I'll show you what I think of newspapers in general, and your *Morning Mars* in particular."

Three feet from their table was the telephone-booth. Kernan went inside and sat at the instrument, leaving the door open. He found a number in the book, took down the receiver and made his demand upon Central. Woods sat still, looking at the sneering, cold, vigilant face waiting close to the transmitter, and listened to the words that came from the thin, truculent lips curved into a contemptuous smile.

"That the *Morning Mars*? . . . I want to speak to the managing editor . . . Why, tell him it's someone who wants to talk to him about the Norcross murder.

"You the editor? . . . All right. . . . I am the man who killed old Norcross . . . Wait! Hold the wire; I'm not the usual crank . . . Oh, there isn't the slightest danger. I've just been discussing it with a detective friend of mine. I killed the old man at two-thirty A.M. two weeks ago tomorrow. . . . Have a drink with you? Now, hadn't you better leave that kind of talk to your funny man? Can't you tell whether a man's guying you or whether you're being offered the biggest scoop your dull dishrag of a paper ever had? . . . Well, that's so; it's a bobtail scoop—but you can hardly expect me to phone in my name and address. . . . Why? Oh, because I heard you make a specialty of solving mysterious crimes that stump the police. . . . No, that's not all. I want to tell you that your rotten, lying, penny sheet is of no more use in tracking an intelligent murderer or highwayman than a blind poodle would be. . . . What? . . . Oh, no, this isn't a rival newspaper office; you're getting it straight. I did the Norcross job, and I've got the jewels in my suit-case at—'the name of the hotel could not be learned'—you recognize that phrase, don't you? I thought so. You've used it often enough. Kind of rattles you, doesn't it, to have the mysterious villain call up your great, big, all-powerful organ of right and justice and good government and tell you what a helpless old gas-bag you are? . . . Cut that out; you're not that big a fool—no, you don't think I'm a fraud. I can tell it by your voice. . . . Now, listen, and I'll give you a pointer that will prove it to you. Of course you've had this murder case worked over by your staff of bright young blockheads. Half of the second button on old Mrs. Norcross's nightgown is broken off. I saw it when I took the garnet ring off her finger. I thought it was a ruby. . . . Stop that! it won't work."

Kernan turned to Woods with a diabolic smile.

"I've got him going. He believes me now. He didn't quite cover the transmitter with his hand when he told somebody to call up Central on another phone and get our number. I'll give him just one more dig, and then we'll make a 'get-away.'

"Hello! . . . Yes. I'm here yet. You didn't think I'd run from such a little subsidized, turn-coat rag of a newspaper, did you? . . . Have me inside of forty-eight hours? Say, will you quit being funny? Now, you let grown men alone and attend to your business of hunting up divorce cases and street-car accidents and printing the filth and scandal that you make your living by. Good-bye, old boy—sorry I haven't time to call on you. I'd feel perfectly safe in your sanctum asinorum. Tra-la!"

"He's as mad as a cat that's lost a mouse," said Kernan, hanging up the receiver and coming out. "And now, Barney, my boy, we'll go to a show and enjoy ourselves until a reasonable bedtime. Four hours' sleep for me, and then the west-bound."

The two dined in a Broadway restaurant. Kernan was pleased with himself. He spent money like a prince of fiction. And then a weird and gorgeous musical comedy engaged their attention. Afterward there was a late supper in a grillroom, with champagne, and Kernan at the height of his complacency.

Half-past three in the morning found them in a corner of an all-night café, Kernan still boasting in a vapid and rambling way, Woods thinking moodily over the end that had come to his usefulness as an upholder of the law.

But, as he pondered, his eye brightened with a speculative light.

"I wonder if it's possible," he said to himself, "I wonder if it's pos-si-ble!"

And then outside the café the comparative stillness of the early morning was punctured by faint, uncertain cries that seemed mere fireflies of sound, some growing louder, some fainter, waxing and waning amid the rumble of milk wagons and infrequent cars. Shrill cries they were when near—well-known cries that conveyed many meanings to the ears of those of the slumbering millions of the great city who waked to hear them. Cries that bore upon their significant, small volume the weight of a world's woe and laughter and delight and stress. To some, cowering beneath the protection of a night's ephemeral cover, they brought news of the hideous, bright day; to others, wrapped in happy sleep, they announced a morning that would dawn blacker than sable night. To many of the rich they brought a besom to sweep away what had been theirs while the stars shone; to the poor they brought—another day.

All over the city the cries were starting up, keen and sonorous, heralding the chances that the slipping of one cogwheel in the machinery of time had made; apportioning to the sleepers while they lay at the mercy of fate, the vengeance, profit, grief, reward, and doom that the new figure in the calendar had brought them. Shrill and yet plaintive were the cries, as if the young voices grieved that so much evil and so little good was in their irresponsible hands. Thus echoed in the streets of the helpless city the transmission of the latest decrees of the gods, the cries of the newsboys—the Clarion Call of the Press.

Woods flipped a dime to the waiter, and said:

"Get me a *Morning Mars*."

When the paper came he glanced at its first page, and then tore a leaf out of his memorandum book and began to write on it with the little gold pencil.

"What's the news?" yawned Kernan.

Woods flipped over to him the piece of writing:

The New York *Morning Mars:*

Please pay to the order of John Kernan the one thousand dollars reward coming to me for his arrest and conviction.

BARNARD WOODS.

"I kind of thought they would do that," said Woods, "when you were jollying 'em so hard. Now, Johnny, you'll come to the police station with me."

THE MEMENTO

MISS LYNNETTE D'ARMANDE turned her back on Broadway. This was but tit for tat, because Broadway had often done the same thing to Miss D'Armande. Still, the "tats" seemed to have it, for the ex-leading lady of the "Reaping the Whirlwind" company had everything to ask of Broadway, while there was no vice-versa.

So Miss Lynnette D'Armande turned the back of her chair to her window that overlooked Broadway, and sat down to stitch in time the lisle-thread heel of a black silk stocking. The tumult and glitter of the roaring Broadway beneath her window had no charm for her; what she greatly desired was the stifling air of a dressing-room on that fairyland street and the roar of an audience gathered in that capricious quarter. In the meantime, those stockings must not be neglected. Silk does wear out so, but—after all, isn't it just the only goods there is?

The Hotel Thalia looks on Broadway as Marathon looks on the sea. It stands like a gloomy cliff above the whirlpool where the tides of two great thoroughfares clash. Here the player-bands gather at the end of their wanderings, to loosen the buskin and dust the sock. Thick in the streets around it are booking-offices, theatres, agents, schools, and the lobster-palaces to which those thorny paths lead.

Wandering through the eccentric halls of the dim and fusty Thalia, you seem to have found yourself in some great ark or caravan about to sail, or fly, or roll away on wheels. About the house lingers a sense of unrest, of expectation, of transientness, even of anxiety and apprehension. The halls are a labyrinth. Without a guide, you wander like a lost soul in a Sam Loyd puzzle.

Turning any corner, a dressing-sack or a *cul-de-sac* may bring you up short. You meet alarming tragedians stalking in bath-robes in search of rumored bathrooms. From hundreds of rooms come the buzz of talk, scraps of new and old songs, and the ready laughter of the convened players.

Summer has come; their companies have disbanded, and they take their rest in their favorite caravansary, while they besiege the managers for engagements for the coming season.

At this hour of the afternoon the day's work of tramping the rounds of the agents' offices is over. Past you, as you ramble distractedly through the mossy halls, flit audible visions of houris, with veiled, starry eyes, flying tag-ends of things and a swish of silk, bequeathing to the dull hallways an odor of gaiety and a memory of frangipanni. Serious young comedians, with versatile Adam's apples, gather in doorways and talk of Booth. Far-reaching from somewhere comes the smell of ham and red cabbage, and the crash of dishes on the American plan.

The indeterminate hum of life in the Thalia is enlivened by the discreet popping—at reasonable and salubrious intervals—of beer-bottle corks. Thus punctuated, life in the genial hostel scans easily—the comma being the favorite mark, semicolons frowned upon, and periods barred.

Miss D'Armande's room was a small one. There was room for her rocker between the dresser and the washstand if it were placed longitudinally. On the dresser were its usual accoutrements, plus the ex-leading lady's collected souvenirs of road engagements and photographs of her dearest and best professional friends.

At one of these photographs she looked twice or thrice as she darned, and smiled friendlily.

"I'd like to know where Lee is just this minute," she said, half-aloud.

If you had been privileged to view the photograph thus flattered, you would have thought at the first glance that you saw the picture of a many-petalled white flower, blown through the air by a storm. But the floral kingdom was not responsible for that swirl of petalous whiteness.

You saw the filmy, brief skirt of Miss Rosalie Ray as she made a complete heels-over-head turn in her wistaria-entwined swing, far out from the stage, high above the heads of the audience. You saw the camera's inadequate representation of the graceful, strong kick, with which she, at this exciting moment, sent flying, high and far, the yellow silk garter that each evening spun from her agile limb and descended upon the delighted audience below.

You saw, too, amid the black-clothed, mainly masculine patrons of select vaudeville a hundred hands raised with the hope of staying the flight of the brilliant aerial token.

Forty weeks of the best circuits this act had brought Miss Rosalie Ray, for each of two years. She did other things during her twelve minutes—a song and dance, imitations of two or three actors who are but imitations of themselves, and a balancing feat with a step-ladder and feather-duster; but when the blossom-decked swing was let down from the flies, and Miss Rosalie sprang smiling into the seat, with the golden circlet conspicuous in the place whence it was soon to slide and become a soaring and coveted guerdon—then it was that the audience rose in its seat as a single man—or presumably so—and indorsed the specialty that made Miss Ray's name a favorite in the booking-offices.

At the end of the two years Miss Ray suddenly announced to her dear friend, Miss D'Armande, that she was going to spend the summer at an antediluvian village on the north shore of Long Island, and that the stage would see her no more.

Seventeen minutes after Miss Lynnette D'Armande had expressed her wish to know the whereabouts of her old chum, there were sharp raps at her door.

Doubt not that it was Rosalie Ray. At the shrill command to enter she did so, with something of a tired flutter, and dropped a heavy hand-bag on the floor. Upon my word, it was Rosalie, in a loose, travel-stained automobileless coat, closely tied brown veil with yard-long, flying ends, gray walking-suit, and tan oxfords with lavender overgaiters.

When she threw off her veil and hat, you saw a pretty enough face, now flushed and disturbed by some unusual emotion, and restless, large eyes with discontent marring their brightness. A heavy pile of dull auburn hair, hastily put up, was escaping in crinkly, waving strands and curling, small locks from the confining combs and pins.

The meeting of the two was not marked by the effusion vocal, gymnastical, osculatory, and catechetical that distinguishes the greetings of their unprofessional sisters in society. There was a brief clinch, two simultaneous labial dabs, and they stood on the same footing of the old days. Very much like the short salutations of soldiers or of travellers in foreign wilds are the welcomes between the strollers at the corners of their criss-cross roads.

"I've got the hall-room two flights up above yours," said Rosalie, "but I came straight to see you before going up. I didn't know you were here till they told me."

"I've been in since the last of April," said Lynnette. "And I'm going on the road with a 'Fatal Inheritance' company. We open next week in Elizabeth. I thought you'd quit the stage, Lee. Tell me about yourself."

Rosalie settled herself with a skilful wriggle on the top of Miss D'Armande's wardrobe trunk, and leaned her head against the papered wall. From long habit, thus can peripatetic leading ladies and their sisters make themselves as comfortable as though the deepest armchairs embraced them.

"I'm going to tell you, Lynn," she said, with a strangely sardonic and yet carelessly resigned look on her youthful face. "And then tomorrow I'll strike the old Broadway trail again, and wear some more paint off the chairs in the agents' offices. If anybody had told me any time in the last three months up to four o'clock this afternoon that I'd ever listen to that 'Leave-your-name-and-address' rot of the booking bunch again, I'd have given 'em the real Mrs. Fiske laugh. Loan me a handkerchief, Lynn. Gee! but those Long Island trains are fierce. I've got enough soft-coal cinders on my face to go on and play *Topsy* without using the cork. And, speaking of corks—got anything to drink, Lynn?"

Miss D'Armande opened a door of the washstand and took out a bottle.

"There's nearly a pint of Manhattan. There's a cluster of carnations in the drinking glass, but—"

"Oh, pass the bottle. Save the glass for company. Thanks! That hits the spot. The same to you. My first drink in three months!

"Yes, Lynn, I quit the stage at the end of last season. I quit it because I was sick of the life. And especially because my heart and soul were sick of men—of the kind of men we stage people have to be up against. You know what the game is to us—it's a fight against 'em all the way down the line from the manager who wants us to try his new motor-car to the bill-posters who want to call us by our front names.

"And the men we have to meet after the show are the worst of all. The stage-door kind, and the manager's friends who take us to supper and show their diamonds and talk about seeing 'Dan' and 'Dave' and 'Charlie' for us. They're beasts, and I hate 'em.

"I tell you, Lynn, it's the girls like us on the stage that ought to be pitied. It's girls from good homes that are honestly ambitious and work hard to rise in the profession, but never do get there. You hear a lot of sympathy sloshed around on chorus girls and their fifteen dollars a week. Piffle! There ain't a sorrow in the chorus that a lobster cannot heal.

"If there's any tears to shed, let 'em fall for the actress that gets a salary of from thirty to forty-five dollars a week for taking a leading part in a bum show. She knows she'll never do any better; but she hangs on for years, hoping for the 'chance' that never comes.

"And the fool plays we have to work in! Having another girl roll you around the stage by the hind legs in a 'Wheelbarrow Chorus' in a musical comedy is dignified drama compared with the idiotic things I've had to do in the thirty-centers.

"But what I hated most was the men—the men leering and blathering at you across tables, trying to buy you with Würzburger or Extra Dry, according to their estimate of your price. And the men in the audiences, clapping, yelling, snarling, crowding, writhing, gloating—like a lot of wild beasts, with their eyes fixed on you, ready to eat you up if you come in reach of their claws. Oh, how I hate 'em!

"Well, I'm not telling you much about myself, am I, Lynn?

"I had two hundred dollars saved up, and I cut the stage the first of the summer. I went over on Long Island and found the sweetest little village that ever was, called Soundport, right on the water. I was going to spend the summer there, and study up on elocution, and try to get a class in the fall. There was an old widow lady with a cottage near the beach who sometimes rented a room or two just for company, and she took me in. She had another boarder, too—the Reverend Arthur Lyle.

"Yes, he was the headliner. You're on, Lynn. I'll tell you all of it in a minute. It's only a one-act play.

"The first time he walked on, Lynn, I felt myself going; the first lines he spoke, he had me. He was different from the men in audiences. He was tall and slim, and you never heard him come in the room, but you *felt* him. He had a face like a picture of a knight—like one of that Round Table bunch—and a voice like a cello solo. And his manners!

"Lynn, if you'd take John Drew in his best drawing-room scene and compare the two, you'd have John arrested for disturbing the peace.

"I'll spare you the particulars; but in less than a month Arthur and I were engaged. He preached at a little one-night stand of a Methodist church. There was to be a parsonage the size of a lunch-wagon, and hens and honeysuckles when we were married. Arthur used to preach to me a good deal about Heaven, but he never could get my mind quite off those honeysuckles and hens.

"No; I didn't tell him I'd been on the stage. I hated the business and all that went with it; I'd cut it out forever, and I didn't see any use of stirring things up. I was a good girl, and I didn't have anything to confess, except being an elocutionist, and that was about all the strain my conscience would stand.

"Oh, I tell you, Lynn, I was happy. I sang in the choir and attended the sewing society, and recited that 'Annie Laurie' thing with the whistling stunt in it, 'in a manner bordering upon the professional,' as the weekly village paper reported it. And Arthur and I went rowing, and walking in the woods, and clamming, and that poky little village seemed to me the best place in the world. I'd have been happy to live there always, too, if—

"But one morning old Mrs. Gurley, the widow lady, got gossipy while I was helping her string beans on the back porch, and began to gush information, as folks who rent out their rooms usually do. Mr. Lyle was her idea of a saint on earth—as he was mine, too. She went over all his virtues and graces, and wound up by telling me that Arthur had had an extremely romantic love-affair, not long before, that had ended unhappily. She didn't seem to be on to the details, but she knew that he had been hit pretty hard. He was paler and thinner, she said, and he had some kind of a remembrance or keepsake of the lady in a little rosewood box that he kept locked in his desk drawer in his study.

" 'Several times,' says she, 'I've seen him gloomerin' over that box of evenings, and he always locks it up right away if anybody comes into the room.'

"Well, you can imagine how long it was before I got Arthur by the wrist and led him down stage and hissed in his ear.

"That same afternoon we were lazying around in a boat among the water-lilies at the edge of the bay.

" 'Arthur,' says I, 'you never told me you'd had another love-affair. But Mrs. Gurley did,' I went on, to let him know I knew. I hate to hear a man lie.

" 'Before you came,' says he, looking me frankly in the eye, 'there was a previous affection—a strong one. Since you know of it, I will be perfectly candid with you.'

" 'I am waiting,' says I.

" 'My dear Ida,' says Arthur—of course I went by my real name, while I was in Soundport—'this former affection was a spiritual one, in fact. Although the lady aroused my deepest sentiments, and was, as I thought, my ideal woman, I never met her, and never spoke to her. It was an ideal love. My love for you, while no less ideal, is different. You wouldn't let that come between us.'

" 'Was she pretty?' I asked.

" 'She was very beautiful,' said Arthur.

" 'Did you see her often?' I asked.

" 'Something like a dozen times,' says he.

" 'Always from a distance?' says I.

" 'Always from quite a distance,' says he.

" 'And you loved her?' I asked.

" 'She seemed my ideal of beauty and grace—and soul,' says Arthur.

" 'And this keepsake that you keep under lock and key, and moon over at times, is that a remembrance from her?'

" 'A memento,' says Arthur, 'that I have treasured.'

" 'Did she send it to you?'

" 'It came to me from her,' says he.

" 'In a roundabout way?' I asked.

" 'Somewhat roundabout,' says he, 'and yet rather direct.'

" 'Why didn't you ever meet her?' I asked. 'Were your positions in life so different?'

" 'She was far above me,' says Arthur. 'Now, Ida,' he goes on, 'this is all of the past. You're not going to be jealous, are you?'

" 'Jealous!' says I. 'Why, man, what are you talking about? It makes me think ten times as much of you as I did before I knew about it.'

"And it did, Lynn—if you can understand it. That ideal love was a new one on me, but it struck me as being the most beautiful and glorious thing I'd ever heard of. Think of a man loving a woman he'd never even spoken to, and being faithful just to what his mind and heart pictured her! Oh, it sounded great to me. The men I'd always known come at you with either diamonds, knock-out-drops or a raise of salary—and their ideals!—well, we'll say no more.

"Yes, it made me think more of Arthur than I did before. I couldn't be jealous of that far-away divinity that he used to worship, for I was going to have him myself. And I began to look upon him as a saint on earth, just as old lady Gurley did.

"About four o'clock this afternoon a man came to the house for Arthur to go and see somebody that was sick among his church bunch. Old lady Gurley was taking her afternoon snore on a couch, so that left me pretty much alone.

"In passing by Arthur's study I looked in, and saw his bunch of keys hanging in the drawer of his desk, where he'd forgotten 'em. Well, I guess we're all to the Mrs. Bluebeard now and then, ain't we, Lynn? I made up my mind I'd have a look at that memento he kept so secret. Not that I cared what it was—it was just curiosity.

"While I was opening the drawer I imagined one or two things it might be. I thought it might be a dried rosebud she'd dropped down to him from a balcony, or maybe a picture of her he'd cut out of a magazine, she being so high up in the world.

"I opened the drawer, and there was the rosewood casket about the size of a gent's collar box. I found the little key in the bunch that fitted it, and unlocked it and raised the lid.

"I took one look at that memento, and then I went to my room and packed my trunk. I threw a few things into my grip, gave my hair a flirt or two with a side-comb, put on my hat, and went in and gave the old lady's foot a kick. I'd tried awfully hard to use proper and correct language while I was there for Arthur's sake, and I had the habit down pat, but it left me then.

" 'Stop sawing gourds,' says I, 'and sit up and take notice. The ghost's about to walk. I'm going away from here, and I owe you eight dollars. The expressman will call for my trunk.'

"I handed her the money.

" 'Dear me, Miss Crosby!' says she. 'Is anything wrong? I thought you were pleased here. Dear me, young women are so hard to understand, and so different from what you expect 'em to be.'

" 'You're damn right,' says I. 'Some of 'em are. But you can't say that about men. *When you know one man you know 'em all!* That settles the human-race question.'

"And then I caught the four-thirty-eight, soft-coal unlimited; and here I am."

"You didn't tell me what was in the box, Lee," said Miss D'Armande, anxiously.

"One of those yellow silk garters that I used to kick off my leg into the audience during that old vaudeville swing act of mine. Is there any of the cocktail left, Lynn?"

NEMESIS AND THE CANDY MAN

WE SAIL at eight in the morning on the *Celtic*," said Honoria, plucking a loose thread from her lace sleeve.

"I heard so," said young Ives, dropping his hat, and muffing it as he tried to catch it, "and I came around to wish you a pleasant voyage."

"Of course you heard it," said Honoria, coldly sweet, "since we have had no opportunity of informing you ourselves."

Ives looked at her pleadingly, but with little hope. Outside in the street a high-pitched voice chanted, not unmusically, a commercial gamut of "Cand-ee-ee-ee-s! Nice, fresh cand-ee-ee-ee-ees!"

"It's our old candy man," said Honoria, leaning out the window and beckoning. "I want some of his motto kisses. There's nothing in the Broadway shops half so good."

The candy man stopped his pushcart in front of the old Madison Avenue home. He had a holiday and festival air unusual to street peddlers. His tie was new and bright red, and a horseshoe pin, almost life-size, glittered speciously from its folds. His brown, thin face was crinkled into a semi-foolish smile. Striped cuffs with dog-head buttons covered the tan on his wrists.

"I do believe he's going to get married," said Honoria, pityingly. "I never saw him taken that way before. And today is the first time in months that he has cried his wares, I am sure."

Ives threw a coin to the sidewalk. The candy man knows his customers. He filled a paper bag, climbed the old-fashioned stoop and handed it in.

"I remember—" said Ives.

"Wait," said Honoria.

She took a small portfolio from the drawer of a writing desk and from the portfolio a slip of flimsy paper one-quarter of an inch by two inches in size.

"This," said Honoria, inflexibly, "was wrapped about the first one we opened."

"It was a year ago," apologized Ives, as he held out his hand for it,

"As long as skies above are blue
To you, my love, I will be true."

This he read from the slip of flimsy paper.

"We were to have sailed a fortnight ago," said Honoria, gossipingly. "It has been such a warm summer. The town is quite deserted. There is nowhere to go. Yet I am told that one or two of the roof gardens are amusing. The singing—and the dancing—on one or two seem to have met with approval."

Ives did not wince. When you are in the ring you are not surprised when your adversary taps you on the ribs.

"I followed the candy man that time," said Ives, irrelevantly, "and gave him five dollars at the corner of Broadway."

He reached for the paper bag in Honoria's lap, took out one of the square, wrapped confections and slowly unrolled it.

"Sara Chillingworth's father," said Honoria, "has given her an automobile."

"Read that," said Ives, handing over the slip that had been wrapped around the square of candy.

"Life teaches us—how to live,
Love teaches us—to forgive."

Honoria's cheeks turned pink.

"Honoria!" cried Ives, starting up from his chair.

"Miss Clinton," corrected Honoria, rising like Venus from the bead on the surf. "I warned you not to speak that name again."

"Honoria," repeated Ives, "you must hear me. I know I do not deserve your forgiveness, but I must have it. There is a madness that possesses one sometimes for which his better nature is not responsible. I throw everything else but you to the winds. I strike off the chains that have bound me. I renounce the siren that lured me from you. Let the bought verse of that street peddler plead for me. It is you only whom I can love. Let your love forgive, and I swear to you that mine will be true 'as long as skies above are blue.' "

On the West Side, between Sixth and Seventh Avenues, an alley cuts the block in the middle. It perishes in a little court in the center of the block. The district is theatrical; the inhabitants, the bubbling froth of half a dozen nations. The atmosphere is bohemian, the language polyglot, the locality precarious.

In the court at the rear of the alley lived the candy man. At seven o'clock he pushed his cart into the narrow entrance, rested it upon the irregular stone slats, and sat upon one of the handles to cool himself. There was a great draft of cool wind through the alley.

There was a window above the spot where he always stopped his pushcart. In the cool of the afternoon, Mlle. Adèle, drawing card of the Aërial Roof Garden, sat at the window and took the air. Generally her ponderous mass of dark auburn hair was down, that the breeze might have the felicity of aiding Sidonie, the maid, in drying and airing it. About her shoulders—the point of her that the photographers always made the most of—was loosely draped a heliotrope scarf. Her arms to the elbow were bare—there were no sculptors there to rave over them—but even the stolid bricks in the walls of the alley should not have been so insensate as to disapprove. While she sat thus Félice, another maid, anointed and bathed the small feet that twinkled and so charmed the nightly Aërial audiences.

Gradually Mademoiselle began to notice the candy man stopping to mop his brow and cool himself beneath her window. In the hands of her maids she was deprived for the time of her vocation—the charming and binding to her chariot of man. To lose time was displeasing to Mademoiselle. Here was the candy man—no fit game for her darts, truly—but of the sex upon which she had been born to make war.

After casting upon him looks of unseeing coldness for a dozen times, one afternoon she suddenly thawed and poured down upon him a smile that put to shame the sweets upon his cart.

"Candy man," she said, cooingly, while Sidonie followed her impul-

sive dive, brushing the heavy auburn hair, "don't you think I am beautiful?"

The candy man laughed harshly, and looked up, with his thin jaw set, while he wiped his forehead with a red-and-blue handkerchief.

"Yer'd make a dandy magazine cover," he said, grudgingly. "Beautiful or not is for them that cares. It's not my line. If yer lookin' for bouquets apply elsewhere between nine and twelve. I think we'll have rain."

Truly, fascinating a candy man is like killing rabbits in a deep snow; but the hunter's blood is widely diffused. Mademoiselle tugged a great coil of hair from Sidonie's hands and let it fall out the window.

"Candy man, have you a sweetheart anywhere with hair as long and soft as that? And with an arm so round?" She flexed an arm like Galatea's after the miracle across the window-sill.

The candy man cackled shrilly as he arranged a stack of butterscotch that had tumbled down.

"Smoke up!" said he, vulgarly. "Nothin' doin' in the complimentary line. I'm too wise to be bamboozled by a switch of hair and a newly massaged arm. Oh, I guess you'll make good in the calcium, all right, with plenty of powder and paint on and the orchestra playing 'Under the Old Apple Tree.' But don't put on your hat and chase downstairs to fly to the Little Church Around the Corner with me. I've been up against peroxide and make-up boxes before. Say, all joking aside—don't you think we'll have rain?"

"Candy man," said Mademoiselle, softly, with her lips curving and her chin dimpling, "don't you think I'm pretty?"

The candy man grinned.

"Savin' money, ain't yer?" said he, "by bein' yer own press agent. I smoke, but I haven't seen yer mug on any of the five-cent cigar boxes. It'd take a new brand of woman to get me goin', anyway. I know 'em from side-combs to shoelaces. Gimme a good day's sales and steak-and-onions at seven and a pipe and an evenin' paper back there in the court, and I'll not trouble Lillian Russell herself to wink at me, if you please."

Mademoiselle pouted.

"Candy man," she said, softly and deeply, "yet you shall say that I am beautiful. All men say so and so shall you."

The candy man laughed and pulled out his pipe.

"Well," said he, "I must be goin' in. There is a story in the evenin' paper that I am readin'. Men are divin' in the seas for a treasure, and pirates are watchin' them from behind a reef. And there ain't a woman on land or water or in the air. Good-evenin'." And he trundled his pushcart down the alley and back to the musty court where he lived.

Incredibly to him who has not learned woman, Mademoiselle sat at the window each day and spread her nets for the ignominious game. Once she kept a grand cavalier waiting in her reception chamber for half an hour while she battered in vain the candy man's tough philosophy. His rough laugh chafed her vanity to its core. Daily he sat on his cart in the breeze of the alley while her hair was being ministered to, and daily the shafts of her beauty rebounded from his dull bosom pointless and ineffectual. Unworthy pique brightened her eyes. Pride-hurt she glowed upon him in a way that would have sent her higher adorers into an egoistic paradise. The candy man's hard eyes looked upon her with a half-concealed derision that urged her to the use of the sharpest arrow in her beauty's quiver.

One afternoon she leaned far over the sill, and she did not challenge and torment him as usual.

"Candy man," said she, "stand up and look into my eyes."

He stood up and looked into her eyes, with his harsh laugh like the sawing of wood. He took out his pipe, fumbled with it, and put it back into his pocket with a trembling hand.

"That will do," said Mademoiselle, with a slow smile. "I must go now to my *masseuse*. Good-evening."

The next evening at seven the candy man came and rested his cart under the window. But was it the candy man? His clothes were a bright new check. His necktie was a flaming red, adorned by a glittering horseshoe pin, almost life-size. His shoes were polished; the tan of his cheeks had paled—his hands had been washed. The window was empty, and he waited under it with his nose upward, like a hound hoping for a bone.

Mademoiselle came, with Sidonie carrying her load of hair. She looked at the candy man and smiled a slow smile that faded away into ennui. Instantly she knew that the game was bagged; and so quickly she wearied of the chase. She began to talk to Sidonie.

"Been a fine day," said the candy man, hollowly. "First time in a month I've felt first-class. Hit it up down old Madison, hollering out like I useter. Think it'll rain tomorrow?"

Mademoiselle laid two round arms on the cushion on the window-sill, and a dimpled chin upon them.

"Candy man," said she, softly, "do you not love me?"

The candy man stood up and leaned against the brick wall.

"Lady," said he, chokingly, "I've got eight hundred dollars saved up. Did I say you wasn't beautiful? Take it every bit of it and buy a collar for your dog with it."

A sound as of a hundred silvery bells tinkled in the room of Mademoiselle. The laughter filled the alley and trickled back into the court, as strange a thing to enter there as sunlight itself. Mademoiselle was amused. Sidonie, a wise echo, added a sepulchral but faithful contralto. The laughter of the two seemed at last to penetrate the candy man. He fumbled with his horseshoe pin. At length Mademoiselle, exhausted, turned her flushed, beautiful face to the window.

"Candy man," said she, "go away. When I laugh Sidonie pulls my hair. I can but laugh while you remain there."

"Here is a note for Mademoiselle," said Félice, coming to the window in the room.

"There is no justice," said the candy man, lifting the handle of his cart and moving away.

Three yards he moved, and stopped. Loud shriek after shriek came from the window of Mademoiselle. Quickly he ran back. He heard a body thumping upon the floor and a sound as though heels beat alternately upon it.

"What is it?" he called.

Sidonie's severe head came into the window.

"Mademoiselle is overcome by bad news," she said. "One whom she loved with all her soul has gone—you may have heard of him—he is Monsieur Ives. He sails across the ocean tomorrow. Oh, you men!"

DOUGHERTY'S EYE-OPENER

BIG JIM DOUGHERTY was a sport. He belonged to that race of men. In Manhattan it is a distinct race. They are the Caribs of the North—strong, artful, self-sufficient, clannish, honorable within the laws of their race, holding in lenient contempt neighboring tribes who bow to the measure of Society's tape-line. I refer, of course, to the titled nobility of sportdom. There is a class which bears as a qualifying adjective the substantive belonging to a wind instrument made of a cheap and base metal. But the tin mines of Cornwall never produced the material for manufacturing descriptive nomenclature for "Big Jim" Dougherty.

The habitat of the sport is the lobby or the outside corner of certain hotels and combination restaurants and cafés. They are mostly men of different sizes, running from small to large; but they are unanimous in the possession of a recently shaven, blue-black cheek and chin and dark overcoats (in season) with black velvet collars.

Of the domestic life of the sport little is known. It has been said that Cupid and Hymen sometimes take a hand in the game and copper the queen of hearts to lose. Daring theorists have averred—not content with simply saying—that a sport often contracts a spouse, and even incurs descendants. Sometimes he sits in the game of politics; and then at chowder picnics there is a revelation of a Mrs. Sport and little Sports in glazed hats with tin pails.

But mostly the sport is Oriental. He believes his women-folk should not be too patent. Somewhere behind grilles or flower-ornamented fire escapes they await him. There, no doubt, they tread on rugs from Teheran and are diverted by the bulbul and play upon the dulcimer and feed upon sweetmeats. But away from his home the sport is an integer.

He does not, as men of other races in Manhattan do, become the convoy in his unoccupied hours of fluttering laces and high heels that tick off delectably the happy seconds of the evening parade. He herds with his own race at corners, and delivers a commentary in his Carib lingo upon the passing show.

"Big Jim" Dougherty had a wife, but he did not wear a button portrait of her upon his lapel. He had a home in one of those brownstone, iron-railed streets on the West Side that look like a recently excavated bowling alley of Pompeii.

To this home of his Mr. Dougherty repaired each night when the hour was so late as to promise no further diversion in the arch domains of sport. By that time the occupant of the monogamistic harem would be in dreamland, the bulbul silenced and the hour propitious for slumber.

"Big Jim" always arose at twelve, meridian, for breakfast, and soon afterward he would return to the rendezvous of his "crowd."

He was always vaguely conscious that there was a Mrs. Dougherty. He would have received without denial the charge that the quiet, neat, comfortable little woman across the table at home was his wife. In fact, he remembered pretty well that they had been married for nearly four years. She would often tell him about the cute tricks of Spot, the canary, and the light-haired lady that lived in the window of the flat across the street.

"Big Jim" Dougherty even listened to this conversation of hers sometimes. He knew that she would have a nice dinner ready for him every evening at seven when he came for it. She sometimes went to matinées, and she had a talking machine with six dozen records. Once when her Uncle Amos blew in on a wind from up-state, she went with him to the Eden Musée. Surely these things were diversions enough for any woman.

One afternoon Mr. Dougherty finished his breakfast, put on his hat and got away fairly for the door. When his hand was on the knob he heard his wife's voice.

"Jim," she said, firmly, "I wish you would take me out to dinner this evening. It has been three years since you have been outside the door with me."

"Big Jim" was astounded. She had never asked anything like this before. It had the flavor of a totally new proposition. But he was a game sport.

"All right," he said. "You be ready when I come at seven. None of this 'wait two minutes till I primp an hour or two' kind of business, now, Dele."

"I'll be ready," said his wife, calmly.

At seven she descended the stone steps in the Pompeian bowling alley at the side of "Big Jim" Dougherty. She wore a dinner gown made of a stuff that the spiders must have woven, and of a color that a twilight sky must have contributed. A light coat with many admirably unnecessary capes and adorably inutile ribbons floated downward from her shoulders. Fine feathers do make fine birds; and the only reproach in the saying is for the man who refuses to give up his earnings to the ostrich-tip industry.

"Big Jim" Dougherty was troubled. There was a being at his side whom he did not know. He thought of the sober-hued plumage that this bird of paradise was accustomed to wear in her cage, and this winged revelation puzzled him. In some way she reminded him of the Delia Cullen that he had married four years before. Shyly and rather awkwardly he stalked at her right hand.

"After dinner I'll take you back home, Dele," said Mr. Dougherty, "and then I'll drop back up to Seltzer's with the boys. You can have swell chuck tonight if you want it. I made a winning on Anaconda yesterday; so you can go as far as you like."

Mr. Dougherty had intended to make the outing with his unwonted wife an inconspicuous one. Uxoriousness was a weakness that the precepts of the Caribs did not countenance. If any of his friends of the track, the billiard cloth, or the square circle had wives they had never complained of the fact in public. There were a number of *table d'hôte* places on the cross streets near the broad and shining way; and to one of these he had purposed to escort her, so that the bushel might not be removed from the light of his domesticity.

But while on the way Mr. Dougherty altered those intentions. He had been casting stealthy glances at his attractive companion and he was seized with the conviction that she was no selling plater. He resolved to parade with his wife past Seltzer's café, where at this time a number of his tribe would be gathered to view the daily evening procession. Yes; and he would take her to dine at Hoogley's, the swellest slow-lunch warehouse on the line, he said to himself.

The congregation of smooth-faced tribal gentlemen were on watch at Seltzer's. As Mr. Dougherty and his reorganized Delia passed they stared, momentarily petrified, and then removed their hats—a performance as unusual to them as was the astonishing innovation presented to their gaze by "Big Jim." On the latter gentleman's impassive face there appeared a slight flicker of triumph—a faint flicker, no more to be observed than the expression called there by the draft of little casino to a four-card spade flush.

Hoogley's was animated. Electric lights shone—as, indeed, they were expected to do. And the napery, the glassware, and the flowers also meritoriously performed the spectacular duties required of them. The guests were numerous, well-dressed, and gay.

A waiter—not necessarily obsequious—conducted "Big Jim" Dougherty and his wife to a table.

"Play that menu straight across for what you like, Dele," said "Big Jim." "It's you for a trough of the gilded oats tonight. It strikes me that maybe we've been sticking too fast to home fodder."

"Big Jim's" wife gave her order. He looked at her with respect. She had mentioned truffles; and he had not known that she knew what truffles were. From the wine list she designated an appropriate and desirable brand. He looked at her with some admiration.

She was beaming with the innocent excitement that woman derives from the exercise of her gregariousness. She was talking to him about a hundred things with animation and delight. And as the meal progressed her cheeks, colorless from a life indoors, took on a delicate flush. "Big Jim" looked around the room and saw that none of the women there had her charm. And then he thought of the three years she had suffered immurement, uncomplaining, and a flush of shame warmed him, for he carried fair play as an item in his creed.

But when the Honorable Patrick Corrigan, leader in Dougherty's district and a friend of his, saw them and came over to the table, matters got to the three-quarter stretch. The Honorable Patrick was a gallant man, both in deeds and words. As for the Blarney stone, his previous actions toward it must have been pronounced. Heavy damages for breach of promise could surely have been obtained had the Blarney stone seen fit to sue the Honorable Patrick.

"Jimmy, old man!" he called; he clapped Dougherty on the back; he shone like a midday sun upon Delia.

"Honorable Mr. Corrigan—Mrs. Dougherty," said "Big Jim."

The Honorable Patrick became a fountain of entertainment and admiration. The waiter had to fetch a third chair for him; he made another at the table, and the wineglasses were refilled.

"You selfish old rascal!" he exclaimed, shaking an arch finger at "Big Jim," "to have kept Mrs. Dougherty a secret from us."

And then "Big Jim" Dougherty, who was no talker, sat dumb, and saw the wife who had dined every evening for three years at home, blossom like a fairy flower. Quick, witty, charming, full of light and ready talk, she received the experienced attack of the Honorable Patrick on the field of repartee and surprised, vanquished, delighted him. She unfolded her long-closed petals and around her the room became a garden. They tried to include "Big Jim" in the conversation, but he was without a vocabulary.

And then a stray bunch of politicians and good fellows who lived for sport came into the room. They saw "Big Jim" and the leader, and over they came and were made acquainted with Mrs. Dougherty. And in a few minutes she was holding a salon. Half a dozen men surrounded her, courtiers all, and six found her capable of charming. "Big Jim" sat, grim, and kept saying to himself: "Three years, three years!"

The dinner came to an end. The Honorable Patrick reached for Mrs. Dougherty's cloak; but that was a matter of action instead of words, and Dougherty's big hand got it first by two seconds.

While the farewells were being said at the door the Honorable Patrick smote Dougherty mightily between the shoulders.

"Jimmy, me boy," he declared, in a giant whisper, "the madam is a jewel of the first water. Ye're a lucky dog."

"Big Jim" walked homeward with his wife. She seemed quite as pleased with the lights and show windows in the streets as with the admiration of the men in Hoogley's. As they passed Seltzer's they heard the sound of many voices in the café. The boys would be starting the drinks around now and discussing past performances.

At the door of their home Delia paused. The pleasure of the outing radiated softly from her countenance. She could not hope for Jim of evenings, but the glory of this one would lighten her lonely hours for a long time.

"Thank you for taking me out, Jim," she said, gratefully. "You'll be going back up to Seltzer's now, of course."

"To —— with Seltzer's," said "Big Jim," emphatically. "And d——n Pat Corrigan! Does he think I haven't got any eyes?"

And the door closed behind both of them.

THE FURNISHED ROOM

RESTLESS, shifting, fugacious as time itself is a certain vast bulk of the population of the red-brick district of the lower West Side. Homeless, they have a hundred homes. They flit from furnished room to furnished room, transients forever—transients in abode, transients in heart and mind. They sing "Home, Sweet Home" in ragtime; they carry their *lares et penates* in a bandbox; their vine is entwined about a picture hat; a rubber plant is their fig tree.

Hence the houses of this district, having had a thousand dwellers, should have a thousand tales to tell, mostly dull ones, no doubt; but it would be strange if there could not be found a ghost or two in the wake of all these vagrant guests.

One evening after dark a young man prowled among these crumbling red mansions, ringing their bells. At the twelfth he rested his lean hand-baggage upon the step and wiped the dust from his hatband and forehead. The bell sounded faint and far away in some remote, hollow depths.

To the door of this, the twelfth house whose bell he had rung, came a housekeeper who made him think of an unwholesome, surfeited worm that had eaten its nut to a hollow shell and now sought to fill the vacancy with edible lodgers.

He asked if there was a room to let.

"Come in," said the housekeeper. Her voice came from her throat; her throat seemed lined with fur. "I have the third floor back, vacant since a week back. Should you wish to look at it?"

The young man followed her up the stairs. A faint light from no particular source mitigated the shadows of the halls. They trod noiselessly upon a stair carpet that its own loom would have forsworn. It seemed to have become vegetable; to have degenerated in that rank, sunless air to lush lichen or spreading moss that grew in patches to the staircase and was viscid under the foot like organic matter. At each turn of the stairs were vacant niches in the wall. Perhaps plants had once been set within them. If so they had died in that foul and tainted air. It may be that statues of the saints had stood there, but it was not difficult to conceive that imps and devils had dragged them forth in the darkness and down to the unholy depths of some furnished pit below.

"This is the room," said the housekeeper, from her furry throat. "It's a nice room. It ain't often vacant. I had some most elegant people in it last summer—no trouble at all, and paid in advance to the minute. The water's at the end of the hall. Sprowls and Mooney kept it three months. They done a vaudeville sketch. Miss B'retta Sprowls—you may have heard of her—Oh, that was just the stage names—right there over the dresser is where the marriage certificate hung, framed. The gas is here, and you see there is plenty of closet room. It's a room everybody likes. It never stays idle long."

"Do you have many theatrical people rooming here?" asked the young man.

"They comes and goes. A good proportion of my lodgers is connected with the theatres. Yes, sir, this is the theatrical district. Actor people never stays long anywhere. I get my share. Yes, they comes and they goes."

He engaged the room, paying for a week in advance. He was tired, he said, and would take possession at once. He counted out the money. The room had been made ready, she said, even to towels and water. As the housekeeper moved away he put, for the thousandth time, the question that he carried at the end of his tongue.

"A young girl—Miss Vashner—Miss Eloise Vashner—do you remember such a one among your lodgers? She would be singing on the stage, most likely. A fair girl, of medium height and slender, with reddish, gold hair and a dark mole near her left eyebrow."

"No, I don't remember the name. Them stage people has names they change as often as their rooms. They comes and they goes. No, I don't call that one to mind."

No. Always no. Five months of ceaseless interrogation and the inevitable negative. So much time spent by day in questioning managers, agents, schools, and choruses; by night among the audiences of theatres from all-star casts down to music halls so low that he dreaded to find what he most hoped for. He who had loved her best had tried to find her. He was sure that since her disappearance from home this great, water-girt city held her somewhere, but it was like a monstrous quicksand, shifting its particles constantly, with no foundation, its upper granules of today buried tomorrow in ooze and slime.

The furnished room received its latest guest with a first glow of pseudo-hospitality, a hectic, haggard, perfunctory welcome like the specious smile of a demirep. The sophistical comfort came in reflected gleams from the decayed furniture, the ragged brocade upholstery of a couch and two chairs, a foot-wide cheap pier-glass between the two windows, from one or two gilt picture frames and a brass bedstead in a corner.

The guest reclined, inert, upon a chair, while the room, confused in speech as though it were an apartment in Babel, tried to discourse to him of its divers tenantry.

A polychromatic rug like some brilliant-flowered rectangular, tropical islet lay surrounded by a billowy sea of soiled matting. Upon the gay-papered wall were those pictures that pursue the homeless one from house to house—The Huguenot Lovers, The First Quarrel, The Wedding Breakfast, Psyche at the Fountain. The mantel's chastely severe outline was ingloriously veiled behind some pert drapery drawn rakishly askew like the sashes of the Amazonian ballet. Upon it was some desolate flotsam cast aside by the room's marooned when a lucky sail had borne them to a fresh port—a trifling vase or two, pictures of actresses, a medicine bottle, some stray cards out of a deck.

One by one, as the characters of a cryptograph become explicit, the little signs left by the furnished room's procession of guests developed a significance. The threadbare space in the rug in front of the dresser told that lovely women had marched in the throng. Tiny finger-prints on the wall spoke of little prisoners trying to feel their way to sun and air. A splattered stain, raying like the shadow of a bursting bomb, witnessed where a hurled glass or bottle had splintered with its contents against the wall. Across the pier-glass had been scrawled with a diamond in staggering letters the name "Marie." It seemed that the succession of dwellers in the furnished room had turned in fury—perhaps tempted beyond forbearance by its garish coldness—and wreaked upon it their passions. The furniture was chipped and bruised; the couch, distorted by bursting springs, seemed a horrible monster that had been slain during the stress of some grotesque convulsion. Some more potent upheaval had cloven a great slice from the marble mantel. Each plank in the floor owned its particular cant and shriek as from a separate and individual agony. It seemed incredible that all this malice and injury had been wrought upon the room by those who had called it for a time their home; and yet it may have been the cheated home instinct surviving blindly, the resentful rage at false household gods that had kindled their wrath. A hut that is our own we can sweep and adorn and cherish.

The young tenant in the chair allowed these thoughts to file, softshod, through his mind, while there drifted into the room furnished sounds and furnished scents. He heard in one room a tittering and incontinent, slack laughter; in others the monologue of a scold, the rattling of dice, a lullaby, and one crying dully; above him a banjo tinkled with spirit. Doors banged somewhere; the elevated trains roared intermittently; a cat yowled miserably upon a back fence. And he breathed the breath of the house—a dank savor rather than a smell—a cold, musty effluvium as from underground vaults mingled with the reeking exhalations of linoleum and mildewed and rotten woodwork.

Then, suddenly, as he rested there, the room was filled with the strong, sweet odor of mignonette. It came as upon a single buffet of wind with such sureness and fragrance and emphasis that it almost seemed a living visitant. And the man cried aloud: "What, dear?" as if he had been called, and sprang up and faced about. The rich odor clung to him and wrapped him around. He reached out his arms for it, all his senses for the time confused and commingled. How could one be peremptorily called by an odor? Surely it must have been a sound. But, was it not the sound that had touched, that had caressed him?

"She has been in this room," he cried, and he sprang to wrest from it a token, for he knew he would recognize the smallest thing that had belonged to her or that she had touched. This enveloping scent of mignonette, the odor that she had loved and made her own—whence came it?

The room had been but carelessly set in order. Scattered upon the flimsy dresser scarf were half a dozen hairpins—those discreet, indistinguishable friends of womankind, feminine of gender, infinite of mood, and uncommunicative of tense. These he ignored, conscious of their triumphant lack of identity. Ransacking the drawers of the dresser he came upon a discarded, tiny, ragged handkerchief. He pressed it to his face. It was racy and insolent with heliotrope; he hurled it to the floor. In another drawer he found odd buttons, a theatre programme, a pawnbroker's card, two lost marshmallows, a book on the divination of dreams. In the last was a woman's black satin hair-bow, which halted him, poised between ice and fire. But the black satin hair-bow also is femininity's demure, impersonal, common ornament, and tells no tales.

And then he traversed the room like a hound on the scent, skimming the walls, considering the corners of the bulging matting on his hands and knees, rummaging mantel and tables, the curtains and hangings, the drunken cabinet in the corner, for a visible sign, unable to perceive that she was there beside, around, against, within, above him, clinging to him, wooing him, calling him so poignantly through the finer senses that even his grosser ones became cognizant of the call. Once again he answered loudly: "Yes, dear!" and turned, wild-eyed, to gaze on vacancy, for he could not yet discern form and color and love, and outstretched arms in the odor of mignonette. Oh, God! whence that odor, and since when have odors had a voice to call? Thus he groped.

He burrowed in crevices and corners, and found corks and cigarettes. These he passed in passive contempt. But once he found in a fold of the matting a half-smoked cigar, and this he ground beneath his heel with a green and trenchant oath. He sifted the room from end to end. He found dreary and ignoble small records of many a peripatetic tenant; but of her whom he sought, and who may have lodged there, and whose spirit seemed to hover there, he found no trace.

And then he thought of the housekeeper.

He ran from the haunted room downstairs and to a door that showed a crack of light. She came out to his knock. He smothered his excitement as best he could.

"Will you tell me, madam," he besought her, "who occupied the room I have before I came?"

"Yes, sir. I can tell you again. 'Twas Sprowls and Mooney, as I said. Miss B'retta Sprowls it was in the theatres, but Missis Mooney she was. My house is well known for respectability. The marriage certificate hung, framed, on a nail over—"

"What kind of a lady was Miss Sprowls—in looks, I mean?"

"Why, black-haired, sir, short, and stout, with a comical face. They left a week ago Tuesday."

"And before they occupied it?"

"Why, there was a single gentleman connected with the draying business. He left owing me a week. Before him was Missis Crowder and her two children, that stayed four months; and back of them was old Mr. Doyle, whose sons paid for him. He kept the room six months. That goes back a year, sir, and further I do not remember."

He thanked her and crept back to his room. The room was dead. The essence that had vivified it was gone. The perfume of mignonette had departed. In its place was the old, stale odor of mouldy house furniture, of atmosphere in storage.

The ebbing of his hope drained his faith. He sat staring at the yellow, singing gaslight. Soon he walked to the bed and began to tear the sheets into strips. With the blade of his knife he drove them tightly into every crevice around windows and door. When all was snug and taut he turned out the light, turned the gas full on again, and laid himself gratefully upon the bed.

It was Mrs. McCool's night to go with the can for beer. So she fetched it and sat with Mrs. Purdy in one of those subterranean retreats where housekeepers foregather and the worm dieth seldom.

"I rented out my third floor, back, this evening," said Mrs. Purdy, across a fine circle of foam. "A young man took it. He went up to bed two hours ago."

"Now, did ye, Mrs. Purdy, ma'am?" said Mrs. McCool, with intense admiration. "You do be a wonder for rentin' rooms of that kind. And did ye tell him, then?" she concluded in a husky whisper, laden with mystery.

"Rooms," said Mrs. Purdy, in her furriest tones, "are furnished for to rent. I did not tell him, Mrs. McCool."

" 'Tis right ye are, ma'am; 'tis by renting rooms we kape alive. Ye have the rale sense for business, ma'am. There be many people will rayjict the rentin' of a room if they be tould a suicide has been after dyin' in the bed of it."

"As you say, we has our living to be making," remarked Mrs. Purdy.

"Yis, ma'am; 'tis true. 'Tis just one wake ago this day I helped ye lay out the third floor, back. A pretty slip of a colleen she was to be killin' herself wid the gas—a swate little face she had, Mrs. Purdy, ma'am."

"She'd a-been called handsome, as you say," said Mrs. Purdy, assenting but critical, "but for that mole she had a-growin' by her left eyebrow. Do fill up your glass again, Mrs. McCool."

THE HIGHER PRAGMATISM

I

WHERE to go for wisdom has become a question of serious import. The ancients are discredited; Plato is boiler-plate; Aristotle is tottering; Marcus Aurelius is reeling; Aesop has been copyrighted by Indiana; Solomon is too solemn; you couldn't get anything out of Epictetus with a pick.

The ant, which for many years served as a model of intelligence and industry in the school-readers, has been proven to be a doddering idiot and a waster of time and effort. The owl today is hooted at. Chautauqua conventions have abandoned culture and adopted diabolo. Graybeards give glowing testimonials to the vendors of patent hair-restorers. There are typographical errors in the almanacs published by the daily newspapers. College professors have become—

But there shall be no personalities.

To sit in classes, to delve into the encyclopedia or the past-performances page, will not make us wise. As the poet says, "Knowledge comes, but wisdom lingers." Wisdom is dew, which, while we know it not, soaks into us, refreshes us, and makes us grow. Knowledge is a strong stream of water turned on us through a hose. It disturbs our roots.

Then, let us rather gather wisdom. But how to do so requires knowledge. If we know a thing, we know it; but very often we are not wise to it that we are wise, and—

But let's go on with the story.

II

Once upon a time I found a ten-cent magazine lying on a bench in a little city park. Anyhow, that was the amount he asked me for when I sat on the bench next to him. He was a musty, dingy, and tattered magazine, with some queer stories bound in him, I was sure. He turned out to be a scrap-book.

"I am a newspaper reporter," I said to him, to try him. "I have been detailed to write up some of the experiences of the unfortunate ones who spend their evenings in this park. May I ask you to what you attribute your downfall in—"

I was interrupted by a laugh from my purchase—a laugh so rusty and unpractised that I was sure it had been his first for many a day.

"Oh, no, no," said he. "You ain't a reporter. Reporters don't talk that way. They pretend to be one of us, and say they've just got in on the blind baggage from St. Louis. I can tell a reporter on sight. Us park bums get to be fine judges of human nature. We sit here all day and watch the people go by. I can size up anybody who walks past my bench in a way that would surprise you."

"Well," I said, "go on and tell me. How do you size me up?"

"I should say," said the student of human nature with unpardonable hesitation, "that you was, say, in the contracting business—or maybe worked in a store—or was a sign-painter. You stopped in the park to finish your cigar, and thought you'd get a little free monologue out of me. Still, you might be a plasterer or a lawyer—it's getting kind of dark, you see. And your wife won't let you smoke at home."

I frowned gloomily.

"But, judging again," went on the reader of men, "I'd say you ain't got a wife."

"No," said I, rising restlessly. "No, no, no, I ain't. But I *will* have, by the arrows of Cupid! That is, if—"

My voice must have trailed away and muffled itself in uncertainty and despair.

"I see you have a story yourself," said the dusty vagrant—impudently, it seemed to me. "Suppose you take your dime back and spin your yarn for me. I'm interested myself in the ups and downs of unfortunate ones who spend their evenings in the park."

Somehow, that amused me. I looked at the frowsy derelict with more interest. I did have a story. Why not tell it to him? I had told none of my friends. I had always been a reserved and bottled-up man. It was psychical timidity or sensitiveness—perhaps both. And I smiled to myself in wonder when I felt an impulse to confide in this stranger and vagabond. "Jack," said I.

"Mack," said he.

"Mack," said I, "I'll tell you."

"Do you want the dime back in advance?" said he.

I handed him a dollar.

"The dime," said I, "was the price of listening to *your* story."

"Right on the point of the jaw," said he. "Go on."

And then, incredible as it may seem to the lovers in the world who confide their sorrows only to the night wind and the gibbous moon, I laid bare my secret to that wreck of all things that you would have supposed to be in sympathy with love.

I told him of the days and weeks and months that I had spent in adoring Mildred Telfair. I spoke of my despair, my grievous days and wakeful nights, my dwindling hopes and distress of mind. I even pictured to this night-prowler her beauty and dignity, the great sway she had in society, and the magnificence of her life as the elder daughter of an ancient race whose pride overbalanced the dollars of the city's millionaires.

"Why don't you cop the lady out?" asked Mack, bringing me down to earth and dialect again.

I explained to him that my worth was so small, my income so minute, and my fears so large that I hadn't the courage to speak to her of my worship. I told him that in her presence I could only blush and stammer, and that she looked upon me with a wonderful, maddening smile of amusement.

"She kind of moves in the professional class, don't she?" asked Mack.

"The Telfair family—" I began, haughtily.

"I mean professional beauty," said my hearer.

"She is greatly and widely admired," I answered, cautiously.

"Any sisters?"

"One."

"You know any more girls?"

"Why, several," I answered. "And a few others."

"Say," said Mack, "tell me one thing—can you hand out the dope to other girls? Can you chin 'em and make matinée eyes at 'em and squeeze 'em? You know what I mean. You're just shy when it comes to this particular dame—the professional beauty—ain't that right?"

"In a way you have outlined the situation with approximate truth," I admitted.

"I thought so," said Mack, grimly. "Now, that reminds me of my own case. I'll tell you about it."

I was indignant, but concealed it. What was this loafer's case or anybody's case compared with mine? Besides, I had given him a dollar and ten cents.

"Feel my muscle," said my companion, suddenly, flexing his biceps. I did so mechanically. The fellows in gyms are always asking you to do that. His arm was as hard as cast-iron.

"Four years ago," said Mack, "I could lick any man in New York outside of the professional ring. Your case and mine is just the same. I come from the West Side—between Thirtieth and Fourteenth—I won't give the number on the door. I was a scrapper when I was ten, and when I was twenty no amateur in the city could stand up four rounds with me. 'S a fact. You know Bill McCarty? No? He managed the smokers for some of them swell clubs. Well, I knocked out everything Bill brought up before me. I was a middle-weight, but could train down to a welter when necessary. I boxed all over the West Side at bouts and benefits and private entertainments, and was never put out once.

"But, say, the first time I put my foot in the ring with a professional I was no more than a canned lobster. I dunno how it was—I seemed to lose heart. I guess I got too much imagination. There was a formality and publicness about it that kind of weakened my nerve. I never won a fight in the ring. Light-weights and all kinds of scrubs used to sign up with my manager and then walk up and tap me on the wrist and see me fall. The minute I seen the crowd and a lot of gents in evening clothes down in front, and seen a professional come inside the ropes, I got as weak as ginger-ale.

"Of course, it wasn't long till I couldn't get no backers, and I didn't have any more chances to fight a professional—or many amateurs, either. But lemme tell you—I was as good as most men inside the ring or out. It was just that dumb, dead feeling I had when I was up against a regular that always done me up.

"Well, sir, after I had got out of the business, I got a mighty grouch on. I used to go round town licking private citizens and all kinds of unprofessionals just to please myself. I'd lick cops in dark streets and car-conductors and cab-drivers and draymen whenever I could start a row with 'em. It didn't make any difference how big they were, or how much science they had, I got away with 'em. If I'd only just have had the confidence in the ring that I had beating up the best men outside of it, I'd be wearing black pearls and heliotrope silk socks today.

"One evening I was walking along near the Bowery, thinking about things, when along comes a slumming-party. About six or seven they was, all in swallowtails, and these silk hats that don't shine. One of the gang kind of shoves me off the sidewalk. I hadn't had a scrap in three days, and I just says, 'De-light-ed!' and hits him back of the ear.

"Well, we had it. That Johnnie put up as decent a little fight as you'd want to see in the moving pictures. It was on a side street, and no cops around. The other guy had a lot of science, but it only took me about six minutes to lay him out.

"Some of the swallowtails dragged him up against some steps and began to fan him. Another one of 'em comes over to me and says:

" 'Young man, do you know what you've done?'

" 'Oh, beat it,' says I. 'I've done nothing but a little punching-bag work. Take Freddy back to Yale and tell him to quit studying sociology on the wrong side of the sidewalk.'

" 'My good fellow,' says he, 'I don't know who you are, but I'd like to. You've knocked out Reddy Burns, the champion middle-weight of the world! He came to New York yesterday, to try to get a match on with Jim Jeffries. If you—'

"But when I come out of my faint I was laying on the floor in a drug store saturated with aromatic spirits of ammonia. If I'd known that was Reddy Burns, I'd have got down in the gutter and crawled past him instead of handing him one like I did. Why, if I'd ever been in a ring and seen him climbing over the ropes, I'd have been all to the sal volatile.

CHOP
SUEY
UPSTAIRS

"So that's what imagination does," concluded Mack. "And, as I said, your case and mine is simultaneous. You'll never win out. You can't go up against the professionals. I tell you, it's a park bench for yours in this romance business."

Mack, the pessimist, laughed harshly.

"I'm afraid I don't see the parallel," I said, coldly. "I have only a very slight acquaintance with the prize-ring."

The derelict touched my sleeve with his forefinger, for emphasis, as he explained his parable.

"Every man," said he, with some dignity, "has got his lamps on something that looks good to him. With you, it's this dame that you're afraid to say your say to. With me, it was to win out in the ring. Well, you'll lose just like I did."

"Why do you think I shall lose?" I asked warmly.

" 'Cause," said he, "you're afraid to go in the ring. You dassen't stand up before a professional. Your case and mine is just the same. You're a amateur; and that means that you'd better keep outside of the ropes."

"Well, I must be going," I said, rising and looking with elaborate care at my watch.

When I was twenty feet away the park-bencher called to me.

"Much obliged for the dollar," he said. "And for the dime. But you'll never get 'er. You're in the amateur class."

"Serves you right," I said to myself, "for hobnobbing with a tramp. His impudence!"

But, as I walked, his words seemed to repeat themselves over and over again in my brain. I think I even grew angry at the man.

"I'll show him!" I finally said, aloud. "I'll show him that I can fight Reddy Burns, too—even knowing who he is."

I hurried to a telephone-booth and rang up the Telfair residence.

A soft, sweet voice answered. Didn't I know that voice? My hand holding the receiver shook.

"Is that *you?*" said I, employing the foolish words that form the vocabulary of every talker through the telephone.

"Yes, this is I," came back the answer in the low, clear-cut tones that are an inheritance of the Telfairs. "Who is it, please?"

"It's me," said I, less ungrammatically than egotistically. "It's me, and I've got a few things that I want to say to you right now and immediately and straight to the point."

"*Dear* me," said the voice. "Oh, it's you, Mr. Arden!"

I wondered if any accent on the first word was intended; Mildred was fine at saying things that you had to study out afterward.

"Yes," said I. "I hope so. And now to come down to brass tacks." I thought that rather a vernacularism, if there is such a word, as soon as I had said it; but I didn't stop to apologize. "You know, of course, that I love you, and that I have been in that idiotic state for a long time. I don't want any more foolishness about it—that is, I mean I want an answer from you right now. Will you marry me or not? Hold the wire, please. Keep out, Central. Hello, hello! Will you, or will you *not*?"

That was just the uppercut for Reddy Burns's chin. The answer came back:

"Why, Phil, dear, of course I will! I didn't know that you—that is, you never said—oh, come up to the house, please—I can't say what I want to over the phone. You are so importunate. But please come up to the house, won't you?"

Would I?

I rang the bell of the Telfair house violently. Some sort of a human came to the door and shooed me into the drawing-room.

"Oh, well," said I to myself, looking at the ceiling, "anyone can learn from anyone. That was a pretty good philosophy of Mack's, anyhow. He didn't take advantage of his experience, but I get the benefit of it. If you want to get into the professional class, you've got to—"

I stopped thinking then. Someone was coming down the stairs. My knees began to shake. I knew then how Mack had felt when a professional began to climb over the ropes. I looked around foolishly for a door or a window by which I might escape. If it had been any other girl approaching, I mightn't have—

But just then the door opened, and Bess, Mildred's younger sister, came in. I'd never seen her look so much like a glorified angel. She walked straight up to me, and—and—

I'd never noticed before what perfectly wonderful eyes and hair Elizabeth Telfair had.

"Phil," she said, in the Telfair, sweet, thrilling tones, "why didn't you tell me about it before? I thought it was Sister you wanted all the time, until you telephoned to me a few minutes ago!"

I suppose Mack and I always will be hopeless amateurs. But, as the thing has turned out in my case, I'm mighty glad of it.

RUS IN URBE

CONSIDERING men in relation to money, there are three kinds whom I dislike: men who have more money than they can spend; men who have more money than they do spend; and men who spend more money than they have. Of the three varieties, I believe I have the least liking for the first. But, as a man, I liked Spencer Grenville North pretty well, although he had something like two or ten or thirty millions—I've forgotten exactly how many.

I did not leave town that summer. I usually went down to a village on the south shore of Long Island. The place was surrounded by duck-farms, and the ducks and dogs and whippoorwills and rusty windmills made so much noise that I could sleep as peacefully as if I were in my own flat six doors from the elevated railroad in New York. But that summer I did not go. Remember that. One of my friends asked me why I did not. I replied: "Because, old man, New York is the finest summer resort in the world." You have heard that phrase before. But that is what I told him.

I was press agent that year for Binkley & Bing, the theatrical managers and producers. Of course you know what a press agent is. Well, he is not. That is the secret of being one.

Binkley was touring France in his new C. & N. Williamson car, and Bing had gone to Scotland to learn curling, which he seemed to associate in his mind with hot tongs rather than with ice. Before they left they gave me June and July, on salary, for my vacation, which act was in accord with their large spirit of liberality. But I remained in New York, which I had decided was the finest summer resort in—

But I said that before.

On July the tenth, North came to town from his camp in the Adirondacks. Try to imagine a camp with sixteen rooms, plumbing, eider-down quilts, a butler, a garage, solid silver plate, and a long-distance telephone. Of course it was in the woods—if Mr. Pinchot wants to preserve the forests let him give every citizen two or ten or thirty million dollars, and the trees will all gather around the summer camps, as the Birnam woods came to Dunsinane, and be preserved.

North came to see me in my three rooms and bath, extra charge for light when used extravagantly or all night. He slapped me on the back (I would rather have my shins kicked any day), and greeted me with outdoor obstreperousness and revolting good spirits. He was insolently brown and healthy-looking, and offensively well dressed.

"Just ran down for a few days," said he, "to sign some papers and stuff like that. My lawyer wired me to come. Well, you indolent cockney, what are you doing in town? I took a chance and telephoned, and they said you were here. What's the matter with that Utopia on Long Island where you used to take your typewriter and your villainous temper every summer? Anything wrong with the—er—swans, weren't they, that used to sing on the farms at night?"

"Ducks," said I. "The songs of swans are for luckier ears. They swim and curve their necks in artificial lakes on the estates of the wealthy to delight the eyes of the favorites of Fortune."

"Also in Central Park," said North, "to delight the eyes of immigrants and bummers. I've seen 'em there lots of times. But why are you in the city so late in the summer?"

"New York City," I began to recite, "is the finest sum—"

"No, you don't," said North, emphatically. "You don't spring that old one on me. I know you know better. Man, you ought to have gone up with us this summer. The Prestons are there, and Tom Volney and the Monroes and Lulu Stanford and the Miss Kennedy and her aunt that you liked so well."

"I never liked Miss Kennedy's aunt," I said.

"I didn't say you did," said North. "We are having the greatest time we've ever had. The pickerel and trout are so ravenous that I believe they would swallow your hook with a Montana copper-mine prospectus fastened on it. And we've a couple of electric launches; and I'll tell you what we do every night or two—we tow a rowboat behind each one with a big phonograph and a boy to change the discs in 'em. On the water, and twenty yards behind you, they are not so bad. And there are passably good roads through the woods where we go motoring. I shipped two cars up there. And the Pinecliff Inn is only three miles away. You know the Pinecliff. Some good people are there this season, and we run over to the dances twice a week. Can't you go back with me for a week, old man?"

I laughed. "Northy," said I—"if I may be so familiar with a millionaire, because I hate both the names Spencer and Grenville—your invitation is meant kindly, but—the city in the summer-time for me. Here, while the *bourgeoisie* is away, I can live as Nero lived—barring, thank heaven, the fiddling—while the city burns at ninety in the shade. The tropics and the zones wait upon me like handmaidens. I sit under Florida palms and eat pomegranates while Boreas himself, electrically conjured up, blows upon me his Arctic breath. As for trout, you know, yourself, that Jean, at Maurice's, cooks them better than anyone else in the world."

"Be advised," said North. "My chef has pinched the blue ribbon from the lot. He lays some slices of bacon inside the trout, wraps it all in corn-husks—the husks of green corn, you know—buries them in hot ashes and covers them with live coals. We build fires on the bank of the lake and have fish suppers."

"I know," said I. "And the servants bring down tables and chairs and damask cloths, and you eat with silver forks. I know the kind of camps that you millionaires have. And there are champagne pails set about, disgracing the wild flowers, and, no doubt, Madame Tetrazzini to sing in the boat pavilion after the trout."

"Oh no," said North, concernedly, "we were never as bad as that. We did have a variety troupe up from the city three or four nights, but they weren't stars by as far as light can travel in the same length of time. I always like a few home comforts even when I'm roughing it. But don't tell me you prefer to stay in the city during summer. I don't believe it. If you do, why did you spend your summers there for the last four years, even sneaking away from town on a night train, and refusing to tell your friends where this Arcadian village was?"

"Because," said I, "they might have followed me and discovered it.

But since then I have learned that Amaryllis has come to town. The coolest things, the freshest, the brightest, the choicest, are to be found in the city. If you've nothing on hand this evening I will show you."

"I'm free," said North, "and I have my light car outside. I suppose, since you've been converted to the town, that your idea of rural sport is to have a little whirl between bicycle cops in Central Park and then a mug of sticky ale in some stuffy rathskeller under a fan that can't stir up as many revolutions in a week as Nicaragua can in a day."

"We'll begin with the spin through the Park, anyhow," I said. I was choking with the hot, stale air of my little apartment, and I wanted that breath of the cool to brace me for the task of proving to my friend that New York was the greatest—and so forth.

"Where can you find air any fresher or purer than this?" I asked, as we sped into Central's boskiest dell.

"Air!" said North, contemptuously. "Do you call this air?—this muggy vapor, smelling of garbage and gasoline smoke. Man, I wish you could get one sniff of the real Adirondack article in the pine woods at daylight."

"I have heard of it," said I. "But for fragrance and tang and a joy in the nostrils I would not give one puff of sea breeze across the bay, down on my little boat dock on Long Island, for ten of your turpentine-scented tornadoes."

"Then why," asked North, a little curiously, "don't you go there instead of staying cooped up in this Greater Bakery?"

"Because," said I, doggedly, "I have discovered that New York is the greatest summer—"

"Don't say that again," interrupted North, "unless you've actually got a job as General Passenger Agent of the Subway. You can't really believe it."

I went to some trouble to try to prove my theory to my friend. The Weather Bureau and the season had conspired to make the argument worthy of an able advocate.

The city seemed stretched on a broiler directly above the furnaces of Avernus. There was a kind of tepid gaiety afoot and awheel in the boulevards, mainly evinced by languid men strolling about in straw hats and evening clothes, and rows of idle taxicabs with their flags up, looking like a blockaded Fourth of July procession. The hotels kept up a specious brilliancy and hospitable outlook, but inside one saw vast empty caverns, and the footrails at the bars gleamed brightly from long disacquaintance with the sole-leather of customers. In the crosstown streets the steps of the old brownstone houses were swarming with "stoopers," that motley race hailing from skylight room and basement, bringing out their straw doorstep mats to sit and fill the air with strange noises and opinions.

North and I dined on the top of a hotel; and here, for a few minutes, I thought I had made a score. An east wind, almost cool, blew across the roofless roof. A capable orchestra concealed in a bower of wistaria played with sufficient judgment to make the art of music probable and the art of conversation possible.

Some ladies in reproachless summer gowns at other tables gave animation and color to the scene. And an excellent dinner, mainly from the refrigerator, seemed to successfully back my judgment as to summer resorts. But North grumbled all during the meal, and cursed his lawyers and prated so of his confounded camp in the woods that I began to wish he would go back there and leave me in my peaceful city retreat.

After dining we went to a roof-garden vaudeville that was being much praised. There we found a good bill, an artificially cooled atmosphere, cold drinks, prompt service, and a gay, well-dressed audience. North was bored.

"If this isn't comfortable enough for you on the hottest August night for five years," I said, a little sarcastically, "you might think about the kids down in Delancey and Hester Streets lying out on the fire-escapes with their tongues hanging out, trying to get a breath of air that hasn't been fried on both sides. The contrast might increase your enjoyment."

"Don't talk Socialism," said North. "I gave five hundred dollars to the free ice fund on the first of May. I'm contrasting these stale, artificial, hollow, wearisome 'amusements' with the enjoyment a man can get in the woods. You should see the firs and pines do skirt-dances during a storm; and lie down flat and drink out of a mountain branch at the end of a day's tramp after the deer. That's the only way to spend a summer. Get out and live with nature."

"I agree with you absolutely," said I, with emphasis.

For one moment I had relaxed my vigilance, and had spoken my true sentiments. North looked at me long and curiously.

"Then why, in the name of Pan and Apollo," he asked, "have you been singing this deceitful paean to summer in town?"

I suppose I looked my guilt.

"Ha," said North, "I see. May I ask her name?"

"Annie Ashton," said I, simply. "She played Nannette in Binkley & Bing's production of *The Silver Cord*. She is to have a better part next season."

"Take me to see her," said North.

Miss Ashton lived with her mother in a small hotel. They were out of the West, and had a little money that bridged the seasons. As press agent of Binkley & Bing I had tried to keep her before the public. As Robert James Vandiver I had hoped to withdraw her; for if ever one was made to keep company with said Vandiver and smell the salt breeze on the south shore of Long Island and listen to the ducks quack in the watches of the night, it was the Ashton set forth above.

But she had a soul above ducks—above nightingales; aye, even above birds of paradise. She was very beautiful, with quiet ways, and seemed genuine. She had both taste and talent for the stage, and she liked to stay at home and read and make caps for her mother. She was unvaryingly kind and friendly with Binkley & Bing's press agent. Since the theatre had closed she had allowed Mr. Vandiver to call in an unofficial role. I had often spoken to her of my friend, Spencer Grenville North; and so, as it was early, the first turn of the vaudeville being not yet over, we left to find a telephone.

Miss Ashton would be very glad to see Mr. Vandiver and Mr. North.

We found her fitting a new cap on her mother. I never saw her look more charming.

North made himself disagreeably entertaining. He was a good talker, and had a way with him. Besides, he had two, ten, or thirty millions, I've forgotten which. I incautiously admired the mother's cap, whereupon she brought out her store of a dozen or two, and I took a course in edgings and frills. Even though Annie's fingers had pinked, or ruched, or hemmed, or whatever you do to 'em, they palled upon me. And I could hear North drivelling to Annie about his odious Adirondack camp.

Two days after that I saw North in his motor-car with Miss Ashton and her mother. On the next afternoon he dropped in on me.

"Bobby," said he, "this old burg isn't such a bad proposition in the summer-time, after all. Since I've been knocking around it looks better to me. There are some first-rate musical comedies and light operas on the roofs and in the outdoor gardens. And if you hunt up the right places and stick to soft drinks, you can keep about as cool here as you can in the country. Hang it! when you come to think of it, there's nothing much to the country, anyhow. You get tired and sunburned and lonesome, and you have to eat any old thing that the cook dishes up to you."

"It makes a difference, doesn't it?" said I.

"It certainly does. Now, I found some whitebait yesterday, at Maurice's, with a new sauce that beats anything in the trout line I ever tasted."

"It makes a difference, doesn't it?" I said.

"Immense. The sauce is the main thing with whitebait."

"It makes a difference, doesn't it?" I asked, looking him straight in the eye. He understood.

"Look here, Bob," he said, "I was going to tell you. I couldn't help it. I'll play fair with you, but I'm going in to win. She is the 'one particular' for me."

"All right," said I. "It's a fair field. There are no rights for you to encroach upon."

On Thursday afternoon Miss Ashton invited North and myself to have tea in her apartment. He was devoted, and she was more charming than usual. By avoiding the subject of caps I managed to get a word or two into and out of the talk. Miss Ashton asked me in a make-conversational tone something about the next season's tour.

"Oh," said I, "I don't know about that. I'm not going to be with Binkley and Bing next season."

"Why, I thought," said she, "that they were going to put the Number One road company under your charge. I thought you told me so."

"They were," said I, "but they won't. I'll tell you what I'm going to do. I'm going to the south shore of Long Island and buy a small cottage I know there on the edge of the bay. And I'll buy a catboat and a rowboat and a shotgun and a yellow dog. I've got money enough to do it. And I'll smell the salt wind all day when it blows from the sea and the pine odor when it blows from the land. And, of course, I'll write plays until I have a trunk full of 'em on hand.

"And the next thing and the biggest thing I'll do will be to buy that duck-farm next door. Few people understand ducks. I can watch 'em for hours. They can march better than any company in the National Guard, and they can play 'follow my leader' better than the entire Democratic party. Their voices don't amount to much, but I like to hear 'em. They wake you up a dozen times a night, but there's a homely sound about their quacking that is more musical to me than the cry of 'Fresh strawber-rees!' under your window in the morning when you want to sleep.

"And," I went on, enthusiastically, "do you know the value of ducks besides their beauty and intelligence and order and sweetness of voice? Picking their feathers gives you an unfailing and never ceasing income. On a farm that I know the feathers were sold for four hundred dollars in one year. Think of that! And the ones shipped to the market will bring in more money than that. Yes, I am for the ducks and the salt breeze coming over the bay. I think I shall get a Chinese cook, and with him and the dog and the sunsets for company I shall do well. No more of this dull, baking, senseless, roaring city for me."

Miss Ashton looked surprised. North laughed.

"I am going to begin one of my plays tonight," I said, "so I must be going." And with that I took my departure.

A few days later Miss Ashton telephoned to me, asking me to call at four in the afternoon. I did.

"You have been very good to me," she said, hesitatingly, "and I thought I would tell you. I am going to leave the stage."

"Yes," said I, "I suppose you will. They usually do when there's so much money."

"There is no money," she said, "or very little. Our money is almost gone."

"But I am told," said I, "that he has something like two or ten or thirty millions—I have forgotten which."

"I know what you mean," she said. "I will not pretend that I do not. I am not going to marry Mr. North."

"Then why are you leaving the stage?" I asked, severely. "What else can you do to earn a living?"

She came closer to me, and I can see the look in her eyes yet as she spoke.

"I can pick ducks," she said.

We sold the first year's feathers for three hundred fifty dollars.

THE RATHSKELLER AND THE ROSE

MISS POSIE CARRINGTON had earned her success. She began life handicapped by the family name of "Boggs," in the small town known as Cranberry Corners. At the age of eighteen she had acquired the name of "Carrington" and a position in the chorus of a metropolitan burlesque company. Thence upward she had ascended by the legitimate and delectable steps of "broiler," member of the famous "Dickey-bird" octette, in the successful musical comedy, "Fudge and Fellows," leader of the potato-bug dance in "Fol-de-Rol," and at length to the part of the maid " 'Toinette" in "The King's Bath-Robe," which captured the critics and gave her her chance. And when we come to consider Miss Carrington she is in the heyday of flattery, fame, and fizz; and that astute manager, Herr Timothy Goldstein, has her signature to iron-clad papers that she will star the coming season in Dyde Rich's new play, "Paresis by Gaslight."

Promptly there came to Herr Timothy a capable twentieth-century young character actor by the name of Highsmith, who besought engagement as "Sol Haytosser," the comic and chief male character part in "Paresis by Gaslight."

"My boy," said Goldstein, "take the part if you can get it. Miss Carrington won't listen to any of my suggestions. She has turned down half a dozen of the best imitators of the rural dub in the city. She declares she won't set a foot on the stage unless 'Haytosser' is the best that can be raked up. She was raised in a village, you know, and when a Broadway orchid sticks a straw in his hair and tries to call himself a clover blossom she's on, all right. I asked her, in a sarcastic vein, if she thought Denman Thompson would make any kind of a show in the part. 'Oh, no,' says she. 'I don't want him or John Drew or Jim Corbett or any of these swell actors that don't know a turnip from a turnstile. I want the real article.' So, my boy, if you want to play 'Sol Haytosser' you will have to convince Miss Carrington. Luck be with you."

Highsmith took the train the next day for Cranberry Corners. He remained in that forsaken and inanimate village three days. He found the Boggs family and corkscrewed their history unto the third and fourth generation. He amassed the facts and the local color of Cranberry Corners. The village had not grown as rapidly as had Miss Carrington. The actor estimated that it had suffered as few actual changes since the departure of its solitary follower of Thespis as had a stage upon which "four years is supposed to have elapsed." He absorbed Cranberry Corners and returned to the city of chameleon changes.

It was in the rathskeller that Highsmith made the hit of his histrionic career. There is no need to name the place; there is but one rathskeller where you could hope to find Miss Posie Carrington after a performance of "The King's Bath-Robe."

There was a jolly small party at one of the tables that drew many eyes. Miss Carrington, petite, marvellous, bubbling, electric, fame-drunken, shall be named first. Herr Goldstein follows, sonorous, curly-haired, heavy, a trifle anxious, as some bear that had caught, somehow, a butterfly in his claws. Next, a man condemned to a newspaper, sad, courted, armed, analyzing for press agent's dross every sentence that was poured over him, eating his à la Newburg in the silence of greatness. To conclude, a youth with parted hair, a name that is ochre to red journals and gold on the back of a supper check. These sat at a table while the musicians played, while waiters moved in the mazy performance of their duties with their backs toward all who desired their service, and all was bizarre and merry because it was nine feet below the level of the sidewalk.

At 11:45 a being entered the rathskeller. The first violin perceptibly flatted a C that should have been natural; the clarinet blew a bubble instead of a grace note; Miss Carrington giggled and the youth with parted hair swallowed an olive seed.

Exquisitely and irreproachably rural was the new entry. A lank, disconcerted, hesitating young man it was, flaxen-haired, gaping of mouth, awkward, stricken to misery by the lights and company. His clothing was butternut, with bright blue tie, showing four inches of bony wrist and white-socked ankle. He upset a chair, sat in another one, curled a foot around a table leg, and cringed at the approach of a waiter.

"You may fetch me a glass of lager beer," he said, in response to the discreet questioning of the servitor.

The eyes of the rathskeller were upon him. He was as fresh as a collard and as ingenuous as a hay rake. He let his eye rove about the place as one who regards, big-eyed, hogs in the potato patch. His gaze rested at length upon Miss Carrington. He rose and went to her table with a lateral, shining smile and a blush of pleased trepidation.

"How're ye, Miss Posie?" he said in accents not to be doubted. "Don't ye remember me—Bill Summers—the Summerses that lived back of the blacksmith shop? I reckon I've growed up some since ye left Cranberry Corners.

" 'Liza Perry 'lowed I might see ye in the city while I was here. You know 'Liza married Benny Stanfield, and she says—"

"Ah, say!" interrupted Miss Carrington, brightly, "Lize Perry is never married—what! Oh, the freckles of her!"

"Married in June," grinned the gossip, "and livin' in the old Tatum Place. Ham Riley perfessed religion; old Mrs. Blithers sold her place to Cap'n Spooner; the youngest Waters girl run away with a music teacher; the court-house burned up last March; your uncle Wiley was elected constable; Matilda Hoskins died from runnin' a needle in her hand, and Tom Beedle is courtin' Sallie Lathrop—they say he don't miss a night but what he's settin' on their porch."

"The wall-eyed thing!" exclaimed Miss Carrington, with asperity. "Why, Tom Beedle once—say, you folks, excuse me awhile—this is an old friend of mine—Mr.—what was it? Yes, Mr. Summers—Mr. Goldstein, Mr. Ricketts, Mr.—Oh, what's yours? 'Johnny' 'll do—come on over here and tell me some more."

She swept him to an isolated table in a corner. Herr Goldstein shrugged his fat shoulders and beckoned to the waiter. The newspaper man brightened a little and mentioned absinthe. The youth with parted hair was plunged into melancholy. The guests of the rathskeller laughed, clinked glasses, and enjoyed the comedy that Posie Carrington was treating them to after her regular performance. A few cynical ones whispered "press agent" and smiled wisely.

Posie Carrington laid her dimpled and desirable chin upon her hands, and forgot her audience—a faculty that had won her laurels for her.

"I don't seem to recollect any Bill Summers," she said, thoughtfully gazing straight into the innocent blue eyes of the rustic young man. "But I know the Summerses, all right. I guess there ain't many changes in the old town. You see any of my folks lately?"

And then Highsmith played his trump. The part of "Sol Haytosser" called for pathos as well as comedy. Miss Carrington should see that he could do that as well.

"Miss Posie," said "Bill Summers," "I was up to your folkeses house jist two or three days ago. No, there ain't many changes to speak of. The lilac bush by the kitchen window is over a foot higher, and the elm in the front yard died and had to be cut down. And yet it don't seem the same place that it used to be."

"How's ma?" asked Miss Carrington.

"She was settin' by the front door, crocheting a lamp-mat when I saw her last," said "Bill." "She's older'n she was, Miss Posie. But everything in the house looked jest the same. Your ma asked me to set down. 'Don't touch that willow rocker, William,' says she. 'It ain't been moved since Posie left; and that's the apron she was hemmin', layin' over the arm of it, jist as she flung it. I'm in hopes,' she goes on, 'that Posie'll finish runnin' out that hem someday.' "

Miss Carrington beckoned peremptorily to a waiter.

"A pint of extra dry," she ordered, briefly; "and give the check to Goldstein."

"The sun was shinin' in the door," went on the chronicler from Cranberry, "and your ma was settin' right in it. I asked her if she hadn't better move back a little. 'William,' says she, 'when I get sot down and lookin' down the road, I can't bear to move. Never a day,' says she, 'but what I set here every minute that I can spare and watch over them palin's for Posie. She went away down that road in the night, for we seen her little shoe tracks in the dust, and somethin' tells me she'll come back that way ag'in when she's weary of the world and begins to think about her old mother.'

"When I was comin' away," concluded Bill, "I pulled this off'n the bush by the front steps. I thought maybe I might see you in the city, and I knowed you'd like somethin' from the old home."

He took from his coat pocket a rose—a drooping, yellow, velvet, odorous rose that hung its head in the foul atmosphere of that tainted rathskeller like a virgin bowing before the hot breath of the lions in a Roman arena.

Miss Carrington's penetrating but musical laugh rose above the orchestra's rendering of "Bluebells."

"Oh, say!" she cried, with glee, "ain't those poky places the limit? I just know that two hours at Cranberry Corners would give me the horrors now. Well, I'm awful glad to have seen you, Mr. Summers. I guess I'll hustle around to the hotel now and get my beauty sleep."

She thrust the yellow rose into the bosom of her wonderful, dainty, silken garments, stood up and nodded imperiously at Herr Goldstein.

Her three companions and "Bill Summers" attended her to her cab. When her flounces and streamers were all safely tucked inside she dazzled them with au revoirs from her shining eyes and teeth.

"Come around to the hotel and see me, Bill, before you leave the city," she called as the glittering cab rolled away.

Highsmith, still in his make-up, went with Herr Goldstein to a café booth.

"Bright idea, eh?" asked the smiling actor. "Ought to land 'Sol Haytosser' for me, don't you think? The little lady never once tumbled."

"I didn't hear your conversation," said Goldstein, "but your make-up and acting was O.K. Here's to your success. You'd better call on Miss Carrington early tomorrow and strike her for the part. I don't see how she can keep from being satisfied with your exhibition of ability."

At 11:45 A.M. on the next day Highsmith, handsome, dressed in the latest mode, confident, with a fuchsia in his button-hole, sent up his card to Miss Carrington in her select apartment hotel.

He was shown up and received by the actress's French maid.

"I am sorree," said Mlle. Hortense, "but I am to say this to all. It is with great regret. Mees Carrington have cancelled all engagements on the stage and have returned to live in that—how you call that town? Cranberry Cornaire!"

THE RENAISSANCE AT CHARLEROI

GRANDEMONT CHARLES was a little Creole gentleman, aged thirty-four, with a bald spot on the top of his head and the manners of a prince. By day he was a clerk in a cotton broker's office in one of those cold, rancid mountains of oozy brick, down near the levee in New Orleans. By night, in his three-story-high *chambre garnier* in the old French Quarter he was again the last male descendant of the Charles family, that noble house that had lorded it in France, and had pushed its way smiling, rapiered, and courtly into Louisiana's early and brilliant days. Of late years the Charleses had subsided into the more republican but scarcely less royally carried magnificence and ease of plantation life along the Mississippi. Perhaps Grandemont was even Marquis de Brassé. There was that title in the family. But a Marquis on seventy-five dollars per month! *Vraiment!* Still, it has been done on less.

Grandemont had saved out of his salary the sum of six hundred dollars. Enough, you would say, for any man to marry on. So, after a silence of two years on that subject, he reopened that most hazardous question to Mlle. Adèle Fauquier, riding down to Meade d'Or, her father's plantation. Her answer was the same that it had been any time during the last ten years: "First find my brother, Monsieur Charles."

This time he had stood before her, perhaps discouraged by a love so long and hopeless, being dependent upon a contingency so unreasonable, and demanded to be told in simple words whether she loved him or no.

Adèle looked at him steadily out of her gray eyes that betrayed no secrets and answered, a little more softly:

"Grandemont, you have no right to ask that question unless you can do what I ask of you. Either bring back brother Victor to us or the proof that he died."

Somehow, though five times thus rejected, his heart was not so heavy when he left. She had not denied that she loved. Upon what shallow waters can the bark of passion remain afloat! Or, shall we play the doctrinaire, and hint that at thirty-four the tides of life are calmer and cognizant of many sources instead of but one—as at four-and-twenty?

Victor Fauquier would never be found. In those early days of his disappearance there was money to the Charles name, and Grandemont had spent the dollars as if they were picayunes in trying to find the lost youth. Even then he had had small hope of success, for the Mississippi gives up a victim from its oily tangles only at the whim of its malign will.

A thousand times had Grandemont conned in his mind the scene of Victor's disappearance. And, at each time that Adèle had set her stubborn but pitiful alternative against his suit, still clearer it repeated itself in his brain.

The boy had been the family favorite; daring, winning, reckless. His unwise fancy had been captured by a girl on the plantation—the daughter of an overseer. Victor's family was in ignorance of the intrigue, as far as it had gone. To save them the inevitable pain that his course promised, Grandemont strove to prevent it. Omnipotent money smoothed the way. The overseer and his daughter left, between a sunset and dawn, for an undesignated bourne. Grandemont was confident that this stroke would bring the boy to reason. He rode over to Meade d'Or to talk with him. The two strolled out of the house and grounds, crossed the road, and, mounting the levee, walked its broad path while they conversed. A thundercloud was hanging, imminent, above, but, as yet, no rain fell. At Grandemont's disclosure of his interference in the clandestine romance, Victor attacked him, in a wild and sudden fury. Grandemont, though of slight frame, possessed muscles of iron. He caught the wrists amid a shower of blows descending upon him, bent the lad backward and stretched him upon the levee path. In a little while the gust of passion was spent, and he was allowed to rise. Calm now, but a powder mine where he had been but a whiff of the tantrums, Victor extended his hand toward the dwelling house of Meade d'Or.

"You and they," he cried, "have conspired to destroy my happiness. None of you shall ever look upon my face again."

Turning, he ran swiftly down the levee, disappearing in the darkness. Grandemont followed as well as he could, calling to him, but in vain. For longer than an hour he pursued the search. Descending the side of the levee, he penetrated the rank density of weeds and willows that undergrew the trees until the river's edge, shouting Victor's name. There was never an answer, though once he thought he heard a bubbling scream from the dun waters sliding past. Then the storm broke, and he returned to the house drenched and dejected.

There he explained the boy's absence sufficiently, he thought, not speaking of the tangle that had led to it, for he hoped that Victor would return as soon as his anger had cooled. Afterward, when the threat was made good and they saw his face no more, he found it difficult to alter his explanations of that night, and there clung a certain mystery to the boy's reasons for vanishing as well as to the manner of it.

It was on that night that Grandemont first perceived a new and singular expression in Adèle's eyes whenever she looked at him. And through the years following that expression was always there. He could not read it, for it was born of a thought she would never otherwise reveal.

Perhaps, if he had known that Adèle had stood at the gate on that unlucky night, where she had followed, lingering, to await the return of her brother and lover, wondering why they had chosen so tempestuous an hour and so black a spot to hold converse—if he had known that a sudden flash of lightning had revealed to her sight that short, sharp struggle as Victor was sinking under his hands, he might have explained everything, and she—

I know not what she would have done. But one thing is clear—there was something besides her brother's disappearance between Grandemont's pleadings for her hand and Adèle's "yes." Ten years had passed, and what she had seen during the space of that lightning flash remained an indelible picture. She had loved her brother, but was she holding out for the solution of that mystery or for the "Truth"? Women have been known to reverence it, even as an abstract principle. It is said there have been a few who, in the matter of their affections, have considered a life to be a small thing as compared with a lie. That I do not know. But, I wonder, had Grandemont cast himself at her feet crying that his hand had sent Victor to the bottom of that inscrutable river, and that he could no longer sully his love with a lie, I wonder if—I wonder what she would have done!

But, Grandemont Charles, Arcadian little gentleman, never guessed the meaning of that look in Adèle's eyes; and from this last bootless payment of his devoirs he rode away as rich as ever in honor and love, but poor in hope.

That was in September. It was during the first winter month that Grandemont conceived his idea of the *renaissance*. Since Adèle would never be his, and wealth without her were useless trumpery, why need he add to that hoard of slowly harvested dollars? Why should he even retain that hoard?

Hundreds were the cigarettes he consumed over his claret, sitting at the little polished tables in the Royal Street cafés while thinking over his plan. By and by he had it perfect. It would cost, beyond doubt, all the money he had, but—*le jeu vaut la chandelle*—for some hours he would be once more a Charles of Charleroi. Once again should the nineteenth of January, that most significant day in the fortunes of the house of Charles, be fittingly observed. On that date the French king had seated a Charles by his side at table; on that date Armand Charles, Marquis de Brassé, landed, like a brilliant meteor, in New Orleans; it was the date of his mother's wedding; of Grandemont's birth. Since Grandemont could remember until the breaking up of the family that anniversary had been the synonym for feasting, hospitality, and proud commemoration.

Charleroi was the old family plantation, lying some twenty miles down the river. Years ago the estate had been sold to discharge the debts of its too-bountiful owners. Once again it had changed hands, and now the must and mildew of litigation had settled upon it. A question of heirship was in the courts, and the dwelling house of

GORDON GRANT
'17

Charleroi, unless the tales told of ghostly powdered and laced Charleses haunting its unechoing chambers were true, stood uninhabited.

Grandemont found the solicitor in chancery who held the keys pending the decision. He proved to be an old friend of the family. Grandemont explained briefly that he desired to rent the house for two or three days. He wanted to give a dinner at his old home to a few friends. That was all.

"Take it for a week—a month, if you will," said the solicitor; "but do not speak to me of rental." With a sigh he concluded: "The dinners I have eaten under that roof, *mon fils*!"

There came to many of the old, established dealers in furniture, china, silverware, decorations, and household fittings at their stores on Canal, Chartres, St. Charles, and Royal Streets, a quiet young man with a little bald spot on the top of his head, distinguished manners, and the eye of a connoisseur, who explained what he wanted. To hire the complete and elegant equipment of a dining-room, hall, reception-room, and cloak-rooms. The goods were to be packed and sent, by boat, to the Charleroi landing, and would be returned within three or four days. All damage or loss to be promptly paid for.

Many of those old merchants knew Grandemont by sight, and the Charleses of old by association. Some of them were of Creole stock and felt a thrill of responsive sympathy with the magnificently indiscreet design of this impoverished clerk who would revive but for a moment the ancient flame of glory with the fuel of his savings.

"Choose what you want," they said to him. "Handle everything carefully. See that the damage bill is kept low, and the charges for the loan will not oppress you."

To the wine merchants next; and here a doleful slice was lopped from the six hundred. It was an exquisite pleasure to Grandemont once more to pick among the precious vintages. The champagne bins lured him like the abodes of sirens, but these he was forced to pass. With his six hundred he stood before them as a child with a penny stands before a French doll. But he bought with taste and discretion of other wines—Chablis, Moselle, Château d'Or, Hochheimer, and port of right age and pedigree.

The matter of the cuisine gave him some studious hours until he suddenly recollected André—André, their old chef—the most sublime master of French Creole cookery in the Mississippi Valley. Perhaps he was yet somewhere about the plantation. The solicitor had told him that the place was still being cultivated, in accordance with a compromise agreement between the litigants.

On the next Sunday after the thought Grandemont rode, horseback, down to Charleroi. The big square house with its two long ells looked blank and cheerless with its closed shutters and doors.

The shrubbery in the yard was ragged and riotous. Fallen leaves from the grove littered the walks and porches. Turning down the lane at the side of the house, Grandemont rode on to the quarters of the plantation hands. He found the workers just streaming back from church, careless, happy, and bedecked in gay yellows, reds, and blues.

Yes, André was still there; his wool a little grayer; his mouth as wide; his laughter as ready as ever. Grandemont told him of his plan, and the old chef swayed with pride and delight. With a sigh of relief, knowing that he need have no further concern until the serving of that dinner was announced, he placed in André's hands a liberal sum for the cost of it, giving *carte blanche* for its creation.

Among the blacks were also a number of the old house servants. Absalom, the former major domo, and a half-dozen of the younger men, once waiters and attachés of the kitchen, pantry, and other domestic departments, crowded around to greet "*M'shi Grande*." Absalom guaranteed to marshal, of these, a corps of assistants that would perform with credit the serving of the dinner.

After distributing a liberal largesse among the faithful, Grandemont rode back to town well pleased. There were many other smaller details to think of and provide for, but eventually the scheme was complete, and now there remained only the issuance of the invitations to his guests.

Along the river within the scope of a score of miles dwelt some half-dozen families with whose princely hospitality that of the Charleses had been contemporaneous. They were the proudest and most august of the old régime. Their small circle had been a brilliant one; their social relations close and warm; their houses full of rare welcome and discriminating bounty. Those friends, said Grandemont, should once more, if never again, sit at Charleroi on a nineteenth of January to celebrate the festal day of his house.

Grandemont had his cards of invitation engraved. They were expensive, but beautiful. In one particular their good taste might have been disputed; but the Creole allowed himself that one feather in the cap of his fugacious splendor. Might he not be allowed, for the one day of the *renaissance,* to be "Grandemont du Puy Charles, of Charleroi"? He sent the invitations out early in January so that the guests might not fail to receive due notice.

At eight o'clock on the morning of the nineteenth, the lower coast steamboat *River Belle* gingerly approached the long unused landing at Charleroi. The bridge was lowered, and a swarm of the plantation hands streamed along the rotting pier, bearing ashore a strange assortment of freight. Great shapeless bundles and bales and packets swathed in cloths and bound with ropes; tubs and urns of palms, evergreens, and tropical flowers; tables, mirrors, chairs, couches, carpets, and pictures—all carefully bound and padded against the dangers of transit.

Grandemont was among them, the busiest there. To the safe conveyance of certain large hampers eloquent with printed cautions to delicate handling he gave his superintendence, for they contained the fragile china and glassware. The dropping of one of those hampers would have cost him more than he could have saved in a year.

The last article unloaded, the *River Belle* backed off and continued her course down stream. In less than an hour everything had been conveyed to the house. And then came Absalom's task, directing the placing of the furniture and wares. There was plenty of help, for that day was always a holiday at Charleroi, and the Negroes did not suffer the old traditions to lapse. Almost the entire population of the quarters volunteered their aid. A score of picaninnies were sweeping at the leaves in the yard. In the big kitchen at the rear André was lording it with his old-time magnificence over his numerous sub-cooks and scullions. Shutters were flung wide; dust spun in clouds; the house echoed to voices and the tread of busy feet. The prince had come again, and Charleroi woke from its long sleep.

The full moon, as she rose across the river that night and peeped above the levee, saw a sight that had been long missing from her orbit.

The old plantation house shed a soft and alluring radiance from every window. Of its two-score rooms only four had been refurnished—the large reception chamber, the dining hall, and two smaller rooms for the convenience of the expected guests. But lighted wax candles were set in the windows of every room.

The dining hall was the *chef d'oeuvre*. The long table, set with twenty-five covers, sparkled like a winter landscape with its snowy napery and china and the icy gleam of crystal. The chaste beauty of the room had required small adornment. The polished floor burned to a glowing ruby with the reflection of candle light. The rich wainscoting reached halfway to the ceiling. Along and above this had been set the relieving lightness of a few water-color sketches of fruit and flower.

The reception chamber was fitted in a simple but elegant style. Its arrangement suggested nothing of the fact that on the morrow the room would again be cleared and abandoned to the dust and the spider. The entrance hall was imposing with palms and ferns and the light of an immense candelabrum.

At seven o'clock Grandemont, in evening dress, with pearls—a family passion—in his spotless linen, emerged from somewhere. The invitations had specified eight as the dining hour. He drew an armchair upon the porch, and sat there, smoking cigarettes and half dreaming.

The moon was an hour high. Fifty yards back from the gate stood the house, under its noble grove. The road ran in front, and then came the grass-grown levee and the insatiate river beyond. Just above the levee top a tiny red light was creeping down and a tiny green one was creeping up. Then the passing steamers saluted, and the hoarse din startled the drowsy silence of the melancholy lowlands. The stillness returned, save for the little voices of the night—the owl's recitative, the capriccio of the crickets, the concerto of the frogs in the grass. The picaninnies and the dawdlers from the quarters had been dismissed to their confines, and the mêlée of the day was reduced to an orderly and intelligent silence. The six colored waiters, in their white jackets, paced, cat-footed, about the table, pretending to arrange where all was beyond betterment. Absalom, in black and shining pumps, posed, superior, here and there where the lights set off his grandeur. And Grandemont rested in his chair, waiting for his guests.

He must have drifted into a dream—and an extravagant one—for he was master of Charleroi and Adèle was his wife. She was coming out to him now; he could hear her steps; he could feel her hand upon his shoulder—

"*Pardon moi, M'shi Grande*"—it was Absalom's hand touching him, it was Absalom's voice, speaking the *patois* of the blacks—"but it is eight o'clock."

Eight o'clock. Grandemont sprang up. In the moonlight he could see the row of hitching-posts outside the gate. Long ago the horses of the guests should have stood there. They were vacant.

A chanted roar of indignation, a just, waxing bellow of affront and dishonored genius came from André's kitchen, filling the house with rhythmic protest. The beautiful dinner, the pearl of a dinner, the little excellent superb jewel of a dinner! But one moment more of waiting and not even the thousand thunders of black pigs of the quarters would touch it!

"They are a little late," said Grandemont, calmly. "They will come soon. Tell André to hold back dinner. And ask him if, by some chance, a bull from the pastures has broken, roaring, into the house."

He seated himself again to his cigarettes. Though he had said it, he scarcely believed Charleroi would entertain company that night. For the first time in history the invitation of a Charles had been ignored. So simple in courtesy and honor was Grandemont and, perhaps, so serenely confident in the prestige of his name, that the most likely reasons for his vacant board did not occur to him.

Charleroi stood by a road travelled daily by people from those plantations whither his invitations had gone. No doubt even on the day before the sudden reanimation of the old house they had driven past and observed the evidences of long desertion and decay. They had looked at the corpse of Charleroi and then at Grandemont's invitations, and, though the puzzle or tasteless hoax or whatever the thing meant left them perplexed, they would not seek its solution by the folly of a visit to that deserted house.

The moon was now above the grove, and the yard was pied with deep shadows save where they lightened in the tender glow of outpouring candle light. A crisp breeze from the river hinted at the possibility of frost when the night should have become older. The grass at one side of the steps was specked with the white stubs of Grandemont's cigarettes. The cotton-broker's clerk sat in his chair with the smoke spiralling above him. I doubt that he once thought of the little fortune he had so impotently squandered. Perhaps it was compensation enough for him to sit thus at Charleroi for a few retrieved hours. Idly his mind wandered in and out many fanciful paths of memory. He smiled to himself as a paraphrased line of Scripture strayed into his mind: "A certain *poor* man made a feast."

He heard the sound of Absalom coughing a note of summons. Grandemont stirred. This time he had not been asleep—only drowsing.

"Nine o'clock, *M'shi Grande,*" said Absalom in the uninflected voice of a good servant who states a fact unqualified by personal opinion.

Grandemont rose to his feet. In their time all the Charleses had been proven, and they were gallant losers.

"Serve dinner," he said calmly. And then he checked Absalom's movement to obey, for something clicked the gate latch and was coming down the walk toward the house. Something that shuffled its feet and muttered to itself as it came. It stopped in the current of light at the foot of the steps and spake, in the universal whine of the gadding mendicant.

"Kind sir, could you spare a poor, hungry man, out of luck, a little to eat? And to sleep in the corner of a shed? For"—the thing concluded, irrelevantly—"I can sleep now. There are no mountains to dance reels in the night; and the copper kettles are all scoured bright. The iron band is still around my ankle, and a link, if it is your desire I should be chained."

It set a foot upon the step and drew up the rags that hung upon the limb. Above the distorted shoe, caked with the dust of a hundred leagues, they saw the link and the iron band. The clothes of the tramp were wreaked to piebald tatters by sun and rain and wear. A mat of brown, tangled hair and beard covered his head and face, out of which his eyes stared distractedly. Grandemont noticed that he carried in one hand a white, square card.

"What is that?" he asked.

"I picked it up, sir, at the side of the road." The vagabond handed the card to Grandemont. "Just a little to eat, sir. A little parched corn, a *tortilla,* or a handful of beans. Goat's meat I cannot eat. When I cut their throats they cry like children."

Grandemont held up the card. It was one of his own invitations to dinner. No doubt someone had cast it away from a passing carriage after comparing it with the tenantless house of Charleroi.

"From the hedges and highways bid them come," he said to himself, softly smiling. And then to Absalom: "Send Louis to me."

Louis, once his own body-servant, came promptly, in his white jacket.

"This gentleman," said Grandemont, "will dine with me. Furnish him with bath and clothes. In twenty minutes have him ready and dinner served."

Louis approached the disreputable guest with the suavity due to a visitor to Charleroi, and spirited him away to inner regions.

Promptly, in twenty minutes, Absalom announced dinner, and, a moment later, the guest was ushered into the dining hall where Grandemont waited, standing, at the head of the table. The attentions of Louis had transformed the stranger into something resembling the polite animal. Clean linen and an old evening suit that had been sent down from town to clothe a waiter had worked a miracle with his exterior. Brush and comb had partially subdued the wild disorder of his hair. Now he might have passed for no more extravagant a thing than one of those *poseurs* in art and music who affect such oddity of guise. The man's countenance and demeanor, as he approached the table, exhibited nothing of the awkwardness or confusion to be expected from his Arabian Nights change. He allowed Absalom to seat him at Grandemont's right hand with the manner of one thus accustomed to be waited upon.

"It grieves me," said Grandemont, "to be obliged to exchange names with a guest. My own name is Charles."

"In the mountains," said the wayfarer, "they call me Gringo. Along the roads they call me Jack."

"I prefer the latter," said Grandemont. "A glass of wine with you, Mr. Jack."

Course after course was served by the supernumerous waiters. Grandemont, inspired by the results of André's exquisite skill in cookery and his own in the selection of wines, became the model host, talkative, witty, and genial. The guest was fitful in conversation. His mind seemed to be sustaining a succession of waves of dementia followed by intervals of comparative lucidity. There was the glassy brightness of recent fever in his eyes. A long course of it must have been the cause of his emaciation and weakness, his distracted mind, and the dull pallor that showed even through the tan of wind and sun.

"Charles," he said to Grandemont—for thus he seemed to interpret his name—"you never saw the mountains dance, did you?"

"No, Mr. Jack," answered Grandemont, gravely, "the spectacle has been denied me. But, I assure you, I can understand it must be a diverting sight. The big ones, you know, white with snow on the tops, waltzing—*décolleté,* we may say."

"You first scour the kettles," said Mr. Jack, leaning toward him excitedly, "to cook the beans in the morning, and you lie down on the blanket and keep quite still. Then they come out and dance for you. You would go out and dance with them but you are chained every night to the center pole of the hut. You believe the mountains dance, don't you, Charlie?"

"I contradict no traveller's tales," said Grandemont, with a smile.

Mr. Jack laughed loudly. He dropped his voice to a confidential whisper.

"You are a fool to believe it," he went on. "They don't really dance. It's the fever in your head. It's the hard work and the bad water that does it. You are sick for weeks and there is no medicine. The fever comes on every evening, and then you are as strong as two men. One night the *compañia* are lying drunk with *mescal.* They have brought back sacks of silver dollars from a ride, and they drink to celebrate. In the night you file the chain in two and go down the mountain. You walk for miles—hundreds of them. By and by the mountains are all gone, and you come to the prairies. They do not dance at night; they are merciful, and you sleep. Then you come to the river, and it says things to you. You follow it down, down, but you can't find what you are looking for."

Mr. Jack leaned back in his chair, and his eyes slowly closed. The food and wine had steeped him in a deep calm. The tense strain had been smoothed from his face. The languor of repletion was claiming him. Drowsily he spoke again.

"It's bad manners—I know—to go to sleep—at table—but—that was—such a good dinner—Grande, old fellow."

Grande! The owner of the name started and set down his glass. How should this wretched tatterdemalion whom he had invited, Caliph-like, to sit at his feast know his name?

Not at first, but soon, little by little, the suspicion, wild and unreasonable as it was, stole into his brain. He drew out his watch with hands that almost balked him by their trembling, and opened the back case. There was a picture there—a photograph fixed to the inner side.

Rising, Grandemont shook Mr. Jack by the shoulder. The weary guest opened his eyes. Grandemont held the watch.

"Look at this picture, Mr. Jack. Have you ever—"

"*My sister Adèle!*"

The vagrant's voice rang loud and sudden through the room. He started to his feet, but Grandemont's arms were about him, and Grandemont was calling him "Victor!—Victor Fauquier! *Merci, merci, mon Dieu!*"

Too far overcome by sleep and fatigue was the lost one to talk that night. Days afterward, when the tropic *calentura* had cooled in his veins, the disordered fragments he had spoken were completed in shape and sequence. He told the story of his angry flight, of toils and calamities on sea and shore, of his ebbing and flowing fortune in southern lands, and of his latest peril when, held a captive, he served menially in a stronghold of bandits in the Sonora Mountains of Mexico. And of the fever that seized him there and his escape and delirium, during which he strayed, perhaps led by some marvellous instinct, back to the river on whose bank he had been born. And of the proud and stubborn thing in his blood that had kept him silent through all those years, clouding the honor of one, though he knew it not, and keeping apart two loving hearts. "What a thing is love!" you may say. And if I grant it, you shall say, with me: "What a thing is pride!"

On a couch in the reception chamber Victor lay, with a dawning understanding in his heavy eyes and peace in his softened countenance. Absalom was preparing a lounge for the transient master of Charleroi, who, tomorrow, would be again the clerk of a cotton broker, but also—

"Tomorrow," Grandemont was saying, as he stood by the couch of his guest, speaking the words with his face shining as must have shone the face of Elijah's charioteer when he announced the glories of that heavenly journey—"Tomorrow I will take you to Her."

THE CALIPH, CUPID, AND THE CLOCK

PRINCE MICHAEL, of the Electorate of Valleluna, sat on his favorite bench in the park. The coolness of the September night quickened the life in him like a rare, tonic wine. The benches were not filled; for park loungers, with their stagnant blood, are prompt to detect and fly home from the crispness of early autumn. The moon was just clearing the roofs of the range of dwellings that bounded the quadrangle on the east. Children laughed and played about the fine-sprayed fountain. In the shadowed spots fauns and hamadryads wooed, unconscious of the gaze of mortal eyes. A hand organ—Philomel by the grace of our stage carpenter, Fancy—fluted and droned in a side street. Around the enchanted boundaries of the little park street cars spat and mewed and the stilted trains roared like tigers and lions prowling for a place to enter. And above the trees shone the great, round, shining face of an illuminated clock in the tower of an antique public building.

Prince Michael's shoes were wrecked far beyond the skill of the carefullest cobbler. The ragman would have declined any negotiations concerning his clothes. The two weeks' stubble on his face was gray and brown and red and greenish yellow—as if it had been made up from individual contributions from the chorus of a musical comedy. No man existed who had money enough to wear so bad a hat as his.

Prince Michael sat on his favorite bench and smiled. It was a diverting thought to him that he was wealthy enough to buy every one of those close-ranged, bulky, window-lit mansions that faced him, if he chose. He could have matched gold, equipages, jewels, art treasures, estates, and acres with any Croesus in this proud city of Manhattan, and scarcely have entered upon the bulk of his holdings. He could have sat at table with reigning sovereigns. The social world, the world of art, the fellowship of the elect, adulation, imitation, the homage of the fairest, honors from the highest, praise from the wisest, flattery, esteem, credit, pleasure, fame—all the honey of life was waiting in the comb in the hive of the world for Prince Michael, of the Electorate of Valleluna, whenever he might choose to take it. But his choice was to sit in rags and dinginess on a bench in a park. For he had tasted of the fruit of the tree of life, and, finding it bitter in his mouth, had stepped out of Eden for a time to seek distraction close to the unarmored, beating heart of the world.

These thoughts strayed dreamily through the mind of Prince Michael, as he smiled under the stubble of his polychromatic beard. Lounging thus, clad as the poorest of mendicants in the parks, he loved to study humanity. He found in altruism more pleasure than his riches, his station, and all the grosser sweets of life had given him. It was his chief solace and satisfaction to alleviate individual distress, to confer favors upon worthy ones who had need of succor, to dazzle unfortunates by unexpected and bewildering gifts of truly royal magnificence, bestowed, however, with wisdom and judiciousness.

And as Prince Michael's eye rested upon the glowing face of the great clock in the tower, his smile, altruistic as it was, became slightly tinged with contempt. Big thoughts were the Prince's; and it was always with a shake of his head that he considered the subjugation of the world to the arbitrary measures of Time. The comings and goings of people in hurry and dread, controlled by the little metal moving hands of a clock, always made him sad.

By and by came a young man in evening clothes and sat upon the third bench from the Prince. For half an hour he smoked cigars with nervous haste, and then he fell to watching the face of the illuminated clock above the trees. His perturbation was evident, and the Prince noted, in sorrow, that its cause was connected, in some manner, with the slowly moving hands of the timepiece.

His Highness arose and went to the young man's bench.

"I beg your pardon for addressing you," he said, "but I perceive that you are disturbed in mind. If it may serve to mitigate the liberty I have taken I will add that I am Prince Michael, heir to the throne of the

Electorate of Valleluna. I appear incognito, of course, as you may gather from my appearance. It is a fancy of mine to render aid to others whom I think worthy of it. Perhaps the matter that seems to distress you is one that would more readily yield to our mutual efforts."

The young man looked up brightly at the Prince. Brightly, but the perpendicular line of perplexity between his brows was not smoothed away. He laughed, and even then it did not. But he accepted the momentary diversion.

"Glad to meet you, Prince," he said, good humoredly. "Yes, I'd say you were incog. all right. Thanks for your offer of assistance—but I don't see where your butting-in would help things any. It's a kind of private affair, you know—but thanks all the same."

Prince Michael sat at the young man's side. He was often rebuffed but never offensively. His courteous manner and words forbade that.

"Clocks," said the Prince, "are shackles on the feet of mankind. I have observed you looking persistently at that clock. Its face is that of a tyrant, its numbers are false as those on a lottery ticket; its hands are those of a bunco steerer, who makes an appointment with you to your ruin. Let me entreat you to throw off its humiliating bonds and to cease to order your affairs by that insensate monitor of brass and steel."

"I don't usually," said the young man. "I carry a watch except when I've got my radiant rags on."

"I know human nature as I do the trees and grass," said the Prince, with earnest dignity. "I am a master of philosophy, a graduate in art, and I hold the purse of a Fortunatus. There are few mortal misfortunes that I cannot alleviate or overcome. I have read your countenance, and found in it honesty and nobility as well as distress. I beg of you to accept my advice or aid. Do not belie the intelligence I see in your face by judging from my appearance of my ability to defeat your troubles."

The young man glanced at the clock again and frowned darkly. When his gaze strayed from the glowing horologue of time it rested intently upon a four-story red-brick house in the row of dwellings opposite to where he sat. The shades were drawn, and the lights in many rooms shone dimly through them.

"Ten minutes to nine!" exclaimed the young man, with an impatient gesture of despair. He turned his back upon the house and took a rapid step or two in a contrary direction.

"Remain!" commanded Prince Michael, in so potent a voice that the disturbed one wheeled around with a somewhat chagrined laugh.

"I'll give her the ten minutes and then I'm off," he muttered, and then aloud to the Prince: "I'll join you in confounding all clocks, my friend, and throw in women, too."

"Sit down," said the Prince calmly. "I do not accept your addition. Women are the natural enemies of clocks, and, therefore, the allies of those who would seek liberation from these monsters that measure our follies and limit our pleasures. If you will so far confide in me I would ask you to relate to me your story."

The young man threw himself upon the bench with a reckless laugh.

"Your Royal Highness, I will," he said, in tones of mock deference. "Do you see yonder house—the one with three upper windows lighted? Well, at six o'clock I stood in that house with the young lady I am—that is, I was—engaged to. I had been doing wrong, my dear Prince—I had been a naughty boy, and she had heard of it. I wanted to be forgiven, of course—we are always wanting women to forgive us, aren't we, Prince?

" 'I want time to think it over,' said she. 'There is one thing certain: I will either fully forgive you, or I will never see your face again. There will be no halfway business. At half-past eight,' she said, 'at exactly half-past eight you may be watching the middle upper window of the top floor. If I decide to forgive I will hang out of that window a white silk scarf. You will know by that that all is as was before, and you may come to me. If you see no scarf you may consider that everything between us is ended forever.' That," concluded the young man bitterly, "is why I have been watching that clock. The time for the signal to appear has passed twenty-three minutes ago. Do you wonder that I am a little disturbed, my Prince of Rags and Whiskers?"

"Let me repeat to you," said Prince Michael, in his even, well-modulated tones, "that women are the natural enemies of clocks. Clocks are an evil, women a blessing. The signal may yet appear."

"Never, on your principality!" exclaimed the young man, hopelessly. "You don't know Marian—of course. She's always on time, to the minute. That was the first thing about her that attracted me. I've got the mitten instead of the scarf. I ought to have known at eight thirty-one that my goose was cooked. I'll go West on the eleven forty-five tonight with Jack Milburn. The jig's up. I'll try Jack's ranch awhile and top off with the Klondike and whiskey. Good-night—er—er—Prince."

Prince Michael smiled his enigmatic, gentle, comprehending smile and caught the coat sleeve of the other. The brilliant light in the Prince's eyes was softening to a dreamier, cloudy translucence.

"Wait," he said solemnly, "till the clock strikes. I have wealth and power and knowledge above most men, but when the clock strikes I am afraid. Stay by me until then. This woman shall be yours. You have the word of the hereditary Prince of Valleluna. On the day of your marriage I will give you one hundred thousand dollars and a palace on the Hudson. But there must be no clocks in that palace—they measure our follies and limit our pleasures. Do you agree to that?"

"Of course," said the young man, cheerfully, "they're a nuisance, anyway—always ticking and striking and getting you late for dinner."

He glanced again at the clock in the tower. The hands stood at three minutes to nine.

"I think," said Prince Michael, "that I will sleep a little. The day has been fatiguing."

He stretched himself upon a bench with the manner of one who had slept thus before.

"You will find me in this park on any evening when the weather is suitable," said the Prince, sleepily. "Come to me when your marriage day is set and I will give you a check for the money."

"Thanks, Your Highness," said the young man seriously. "It doesn't look as if I would need that palace on the Hudson, but I appreciate your offer, just the same."

Prince Michael sank into deep slumber. His battered hat rolled from the bench to the ground. The young man lifted it, placed it over the frowsy face, and moved one of the grotesquely relaxed limbs into a more comfortable position. "Poor devil!" he said, as he drew the tattered clothes closer about the Prince's breast.

Sonorous and startling came the stroke of nine from the clock tower. The young man sighed again, turned his face for one last look at the house of his relinquished hopes—and cried aloud profane words of holy rapture.

From the middle upper window blossomed in the dusk a waving, snowy, fluttering, wonderful, divine emblem of forgiveness and promised joy.

By came a citizen, rotund, comfortable, home-hurrying, unknowing of the delights of waving silken scarfs on the borders of dimly lit parks.

"Will you oblige me with the time, sir?" asked the young man; and the citizen, shrewdly conjecturing his watch to be safe, dragged it out and announced:

"Twenty-nine and a half minutes past eight, sir."

And then, from habit, he glanced at the clock in the tower, and made further oration.

"By George! that clock's half an hour fast! First time in ten years I've known it to be off. This watch of mine never varies a—"

But the citizen was talking to vacancy. He turned and saw his hearer, a fast-receding black shadow, flying in the direction of a house with three lighted upper windows.

And in the morning came along two policemen on their way to the beats they owned. The park was deserted save for one dilapidated figure that sprawled, asleep, on a bench. They stopped and gazed upon it.

"It's Dopy Mike," said one. "He hits the pipe every night. Park bum for twenty years. On his last legs, I guess."

The other policeman stooped and looked at something crumpled and crisp in the hand of the sleeper.

"Gee!" he remarked. "He's doped out a fifty-dollar bill, anyway. Wish I knew the brand of hop that he smokes."

And then "Rap, rap, rap!" went the club of realism against the shoe soles of Prince Michael, of the Electorate of Valleluna.

ROADS OF DESTINY

I go to seek on many roads
What is to be.
True heart and strong, with love to light—
Will they not bear me in the fight
To order, shun or wield or mould
My Destiny?

UNPUBLISHED POEMS OF DAVID MIGNOT

THE song was over. The words were David's; the air, one of the countryside. The company about the inn table applauded heartily, for the young poet paid for the wine. Only the notary, M. Papineau, shook his head a little at the lines, for he was a man of books, and he had not drunk with the rest.

David went out into the village street, where the night air drove the wine vapor from his head. And then he remembered that he and Yvonne had quarrelled that day, and that he had resolved to leave his home that night to seek fame and honor in the great world outside.

"When my poems are on every man's tongue," he told himself, in a fine exhilaration, "she will, perhaps, think of the hard words she spoke this day."

Except the roysterers in the tavern, the village folk were abed. David crept softly into his room in the shed of his father's cottage and made a bundle of his small store of clothing. With this upon a staff, he set his face outward upon the road that ran from Vernoy.

He passed his father's herd of sheep huddled in their nightly pen—the sheep he herded daily, leaving them to scatter while he wrote verses on scraps of paper. He saw a light yet shining in Yvonne's window, and a weakness shook his purpose of a sudden. Perhaps that light meant that she rued, sleepless, her anger, and that morning might— But, no! His decision was made. Vernoy was no place for him. Not one soul there could share his thoughts. Out along that road lay his fate and his future.

Three leagues across the dim, moonlit champaign ran the road, straight as a ploughman's furrow. It was believed in the village that the road ran to Paris, at least; and this name the poet whispered often to himself as he walked. Never so far from Vernoy had David travelled before.

THE LEFT BRANCH

Three leagues, then, the road ran, and turned into a puzzle. It joined with another and a larger road at right angles. David stood, uncertain, for a while, and then took the road to the left.

Upon this more important highway were, imprinted in the dust, wheel tracks left by the recent passage of some vehicle. Some half an hour later these traces were verified by the sight of a ponderous carriage mired in a little brook at the bottom of a steep hill. The driver and postilions were shouting and tugging at the horses' bridles. On the road at one side stood a huge black-clothed man and a slender lady wrapped in a long, light cloak.

David saw the lack of skill in the efforts of the servants. He quietly assumed control of the work. He directed the outriders to cease their clamor at the horses and to exercise their strength upon the wheels. The driver alone urged the animals with his familiar voice; David himself heaved a powerful shoulder at the rear of the carriage, and with one harmonious tug the great vehicle rolled up on solid ground. The outriders climbed to their places.

David stood for a moment upon one foot. The huge gentleman waved a hand. "You will enter the carriage," he said, in a voice large, like himself, but smoothed by art and habit. Obedience belonged in the path of such a voice. Brief as was the young poet's hesitation, it was cut shorter still by a renewal of the command. David's foot went to the step. In the darkness he perceived dimly the form of the lady upon the rear seat. He was about to seat himself opposite, when the voice again swayed him to its will. "You will sit at the lady's side."

The gentleman swung his great weight to the forward seat. The carriage proceeded up the hill. The lady was shrunk, silent, into her corner. David could not estimate whether she was old or young, but a delicate, mild perfume from her clothes stirred his poet's fancy to the belief that there was loveliness beneath the mystery. Here was an adventure such as he had often imagined. But as yet he held no key to it, for no word was spoken while he sat with his impenetrable companions.

In an hour's time David perceived through the window that the vehicle traversed the street of some town. Then it stopped in front of a closed and darkened house, and a postilion alighted to hammer impatiently upon the door. A latticed window above flew wide and a night-capped head popped out.

"Who are ye that disturb honest folk at this time of night? My house is closed. 'Tis too late for profitable travellers to be abroad. Cease knocking at my door, and be off."

"Open!" spluttered the postilion, loudly; "open for Monseigneur the Marquis de Beaupertuys."

"Ah!" cried the voice above. "Ten thousand pardons, my lord. I did not know—the hour is so late—at once shall the door be opened, and the house placed at my lord's disposal."

Inside was heard the clink of chain and bar, and the door was flung open. Shivering with chill and apprehension, the landlord of the Silver Flagon stood, half clad, candle in hand, upon the threshold.

David followed the marquis out of the carriage. "Assist the lady," he was ordered. The poet obeyed. He felt her small hand tremble as he guided her descent. "Into the house," was the next command.

The room was the long dining-hall of the tavern. A great oak table ran down its length. The huge gentleman seated himself in a chair at the nearer end. The lady sank into another against the wall, with an air of great weariness. David stood, considering how best he might now take his leave and continue upon his way.

"My lord," said the landlord, bowing to the floor, "h-had I ex-expected this honor, entertainment would have been ready. T-t-there is wine and cold fowl and m-m-maybe—"

"Candles," said the marquis, spreading the fingers of one plump white hand in a gesture he had.

"Y-yes, my lord." He fetched half a dozen candles, lighted them, and set them upon the table.

"If monsieur would, perhaps, deign to taste a certain Burgundy—there is a cask—"

"Candles," said monsieur, spreading his fingers.

"Assuredly—quickly—I fly, my lord."

A dozen more lighted candles shone in the hall. The great bulk of the marquis overflowed his chair. He was dressed in fine black from head to foot save for the snowy ruffles at his wrist and throat. Even the hilt and scabbard of his sword were black. His expression was one of sneering pride. The ends of an upturned moustache reached nearly to his mocking eyes.

The lady sat motionless, and now David perceived that she was young, and possessed of pathetic and appealing beauty. He was startled from the contemplation of her forlorn loveliness by the booming voice of the marquis.

"What is your name and pursuit?"

"David Mignot. I am a poet."

The moustache of the marquis curled nearer to his eyes.

"How do you live?"

"I am also a shepherd; I guarded my father's flock," David answered, with his head high, but a flush upon his cheek.

"Then listen, master shepherd and poet, to the fortune you have blundered upon tonight. This lady is my niece, Mademoiselle Lucie de Varennes. She is of noble descent and is possessed of ten thousand francs a year in her own right. As to her charms, you have but to observe for yourself. If the inventory pleases your shepherd's heart, she becomes your wife at a word. Do not interrupt me. Tonight I conveyed her to the château of the Comte de Villemaur, to whom her hand had been promised. Guests were present; the priest was waiting; her marriage to one eligible in rank and fortune was ready to be accomplished. At the altar this demoiselle, so meek and dutiful, turned upon me like a leopardess, charged me with cruelty and crimes, and broke, before the gaping priest, the troth I had plighted for her. I swore there and then, by ten thousand devils, that she should marry the first man we met after leaving the château, be he prince, charcoal-burner, or thief. You, shepherd, are the first. Mademoiselle must be wed this night. If not you, then another. You have ten minutes in which to make your decision. Do not vex me with words or questions. Ten minutes, shepherd; and they are speeding."

The marquis drummed loudly with his white fingers upon the table. He sank into a veiled attitude of waiting. It was as if some great house had shut its doors and windows against approach. David would have spoken, but the huge man's bearing stopped his tongue. Instead, he stood by the lady's chair and bowed.

"Mademoiselle," he said, and he marvelled to find his words flowing easily before so much elegance and beauty. "You have heard me say I was a shepherd. I have also had the fancy, at times, that I am a poet. If it be the test of a poet to adore and cherish the beautiful, that fancy is now strengthened. Can I serve you in any way, mademoiselle?"

The young woman looked up at him with eyes dry and mournful. His frank, glowing face, made serious by the gravity of the adventure, his strong, straight figure and the liquid sympathy in his blue eyes, perhaps, also, her imminent need of long-denied help and kindness, thawed her to sudden tears.

"Monsieur," she said, in low tones, "you look to be true and kind. Hs is my uncle, the brother of my father, and my only relative. He loved my mother, and he hates me because I am like her. He has made my life one long terror. I am afraid of his very looks, and never before dared to disobey him. But tonight he would have married me to a man three times my age. You will forgive me for bringing this vexation upon you, monsieur. You will, of course, decline this mad act he tries to force upon you. But let me thank you for your generous words, at least. I have had none spoken to me in so long."

There was now something more than generosity in the poet's eyes. Poet he must have been, for Yvonne was forgotten; this fine, new loveliness held him with its freshness and grace. The subtle perfume from her filled him with strange emotions. His tender look fell warmly upon her. She leaned to it, thirstily.

"Ten minutes," said David, "is given me in which to do what I would devote years to achieve. I will not say I pity you, mademoiselle; it would not be true—I love you. I cannot ask love from you yet, but let me rescue you from this cruel man, and, in time, love may come. I think I have a future; I will not always be a shepherd. For the present I will cherish you with all my heart and make your life less sad. Will you trust your fate to me, mademoiselle?"

"Ah, you would sacrifice yourself from pity!"

"From love. The time is almost up, mademoiselle."

"You will regret it, and despise me."

"I will live only to make you happy, and myself worthy of you."

Her fine small hand crept into his from beneath her cloak.

"I will trust you," she breathed, "with my life. And—and love—may not be so far off as you think. Tell him. Once away from the power of his eyes I may forget."

David went and stood before the marquis. The black figure stirred, and the mocking eyes glanced at the great hall clock.

"Two minutes to spare. A shepherd requires eight minutes to decide whether he will accept a bride of beauty and income! Speak up, shepherd, do you consent to become mademoiselle's husband?"

"Mademoiselle," said David, standing proudly, "has done me the honor to yield to my request that she become my wife."

"Well said!" said the marquis. "You have yet the making of a courtier in you, master shepherd. Mademoiselle could have drawn a worse prize, after all. And now to be done with the affair as quick as the Church and the devil will allow!"

He struck the table soundly with his sword hilt. The landlord came, knee-shaking, bringing more candles in the hope of anticipating the great lord's whims. "Fetch a priest," said the marquis, "a priest; do you understand? In ten minutes have a priest here, or—"

The landlord dropped his candles and flew.

The priest came, heavy-eyed and ruffled. He made David Mignot and Lucie de Varennes man and wife, pocketed a gold piece that the marquis tossed him, and shuffled out again into the night.

"Wine," ordered the marquis, spreading his ominous fingers at the host.

"Fill glasses," he said, when it was brought. He stood up at the head of the table in the candlelight, a black mountain of venom and conceit, with something like the memory of an old love turned to poison in his eye, as it fell upon his niece.

"Monsieur Mignot," he said, raising his wineglass, "drink after I say this to you: You have taken to be your wife one who will make your life a foul and wretched thing. The blood in her is an inheritance running black lies and red ruin. She will bring you shame and anxiety. The devil that descended to her is there in her eyes and skin and mouth that stoop even to beguile a peasant. There is your promise, monsieur poet, for a happy life. Drink your wine. At last, mademoiselle, I am rid of you."

The marquis drank. A little grievous cry, as if from a sudden wound, came from the girl's lips. David, with his glass in his hand, stepped forward three paces and faced the marquis. There was little of a shepherd in his bearing.

"Just now," he said, calmly, "you did me the honor to call me 'monsieur.' May I hope, therefore, that my marriage to mademoiselle has placed me somewhat nearer to you in—let us say, reflected rank—has given me the right to stand more as an equal to monseigneur in a certain little piece of business I have in my mind?"

"You may hope, shepherd," sneered the marquis.

"Then," said David, dashing his glass of wine into the contemptuous eyes that mocked him, "perhaps you will condescend to fight me."

The fury of the great lord outbroke in one sudden curse like a blast from a horn. He tore his sword from its black sheath; he called to the hovering landlord: "A sword there, for this lout!" He turned to the lady, with a laugh that chilled her heart, and said: "You put much labor upon me, madame. It seems I must find you a husband and make you a widow in the same night."

"I know not sword-play," said David. He flushed to make the confession before his lady.

" 'I know not sword-play,' " mimicked the marquis. "Shall we fight like peasants with oaken cudgels? *Hola!* François, my pistols!"

A postilion brought two shining great pistols ornamented with carven silver from the carriage holsters. The marquis tossed one upon the table near David's hand. "To the other end of the table," he cried; "even a shepherd may pull a trigger. Few of them attain the honor to die by the weapon of a De Beaupertuys."

The shepherd and the marquis faced each other from the ends of the long table. The landlord, in an ague of terror, clutched the air and stammered: "M-M-Monseigneur, for the love of Christ! not in my house!—do not spill blood—it will ruin my custom—" The look of the marquis, threatening him, paralyzed his tongue.

"Coward," cried the lord of Beaupertuys, "cease chattering your teeth long enough to give the word for us, if you can."

Mine host's knees smote the floor. He was without a vocabulary. Even sounds were beyond him. Still, by gestures he seemed to beseech peace in the name of his house and custom.

"I will give the word," said the lady, in a clear voice. She went up to David and kissed him sweetly. Her eyes were sparkling bright, and color had come to her cheek. She stood against the wall, and the two men levelled their pistols for her count.

"Un—deux—trois!"

The two reports came so nearly together that the candles flickered but once. The marquis stood, smiling, the fingers of his left hand resting, outspread, upon the end of the table. David remained erect, and turned his head very slowly, searching for his wife with his eyes. Then, as a garment falls from where it is hung, he sank, crumpled, upon the floor.

With a little cry of terror and despair, the widowed maid ran and stooped above him. She found his wound, and then looked up with her old look of pale melancholy. "Through his heart," she whispered. "Oh, his heart!"

"Come," boomed the great voice of the marquis, "out with you to the carriage! Daybreak shall not find you on my hands. Wed you shall be again, and to a living husband, this night. The next we come upon, my lady, highwayman or peasant. If the road yields no other, then the churl that opens my gates. Out with you to the carriage!"

The marquis, implacable and huge, the lady wrapped again in the mystery of her cloak, the postilion bearing the weapons—all moved out to the waiting carriage. The sound of its ponderous wheels rolling away echoed through the slumbering village. In the hall of the Silver Flagon the distracted landlord wrung his hands above the slain poet's body, while the flames of the four and twenty candles danced and flickered on the table.

THE RIGHT BRANCH

Three leagues, then, the road ran, and turned into a puzzle. It joined with another and a larger road at right angles. David stood, uncertain, for a while, and then took the road to the right.

Whither it led he knew not, but he was resolved to leave Vernoy far behind that night. He travelled a league and then passed a large château which showed testimony of recent entertainment. Lights shone from every window; from the great stone gateway ran a tracery of wheel tracks drawn in the dust by the vehicles of the guests.

Three leagues farther and David was weary. He rested and slept for a while on a bed of pine boughs at the roadside. Then up and on again along the unknown way.

Thus for five days he travelled the great road, sleeping upon Nature's balsamic beds or in peasants' ricks, eating of their black, hospitable bread, drinking from streams or the willing cup of the goatherd.

At length he crossed a great bridge and set his foot within the smiling city that has crushed or crowned more poets than all the rest of the world. His breath came quickly as Paris sang to him in a little undertone her vital chant of greeting—the hum of voice and foot and wheel.

High up under the eaves of an old house in the Rue Conti, David paid for lodging, and set himself, in a wooden chair, to his poems. The street, once sheltering citizens of import and consequence, was now given over to those who ever follow in the wake of decline.

The houses were tall and still possessed of a ruined dignity, but many of them were empty save for dust and the spider. By night there was the clash of steel and the cries of brawlers straying restlessly from inn to inn. Where once gentility abode was now but a rancid and rude incontinence. But here David found housing commensurate to his scant purse. Daylight and candlelight found him at pen and paper.

One afternoon he was returning from a foraging trip to the lower world, with bread and curds and a bottle of thin wine. Halfway up his dark stairway he met—or rather came upon, for she rested on the stair—a young woman of a beauty that should balk even the justice of a poet's imagination. A loose, dark cloak, flung open, showed a rich gown beneath. Her eyes changed swiftly with every little shade of thought. Within one moment they would be round and artless like a child's, and long and cozening like a gypsy's. One hand raised her gown, undraping a little shoe, high-heeled, with its ribbons dangling, untied. So heavenly she was, so unfitted to stoop, so qualified to charm and command! Perhaps she had seen David coming, and had waited for his help there.

Ah, would monsieur pardon that she occupied the stairway, but the shoe!—the naughty shoe! Alas! it would not remain tied. Ah! if monsieur *would* be so gracious!

The poet's fingers trembled as he tied the contrary ribbons. Then he would have fled from the danger of her presence, but the eyes grew long and cozening, like a gypsy's, and held him. He leaned against the balustrade, clutching his bottle of sour wine.

"You have been so good," she said, smiling. "Does monsieur, perhaps, live in the house?"

"Yes, madame. I—I think so, madame."

"Perhaps in the third story, then?"

"No, madame; higher up."

The lady fluttered her fingers with the least possible gesture of impatience.

"Pardon. Certainly I am not discreet in asking. Monsieur will forgive me? It is surely not becoming that I should inquire where he lodges."

"Madame, do not say so. I live in the—"

"No, no, no; do not tell me. Now I see that I erred. But I cannot lose the interest I feel in this house and all that is in it. Once it was my home. Often I come here but to dream of those happy days again. Will you let that be my excuse?"

"Let me tell you, then, for you need no excuse," stammered the poet. "I live in the top floor—the small room where the stairs turn."

"In the front room?" asked the lady, turning her head sidewise.

"The rear, madame."

The lady sighed, as if with relief.

"I will detain you no longer, then, monsieur," she said, employing the round and artless eye. "Take good care of my house. Alas! only the memories of it are mine now. Adieu, and accept my thanks for your courtesy."

She was gone, leaving but a smile and a trace of sweet perfume.

David climbed the stairs as one in slumber. But he awoke from it, and the smile and the perfume lingered with him and never afterward did either seem quite to leave him. This lady of whom he knew nothing drove him to lyrics of eyes, chansons of swiftly conceived love, odes to curling hair, and sonnets to slippers on slender feet.

Poet he must have been, for Yvonne was forgotten; this fine, new loveliness held him with its freshness and grace. The subtle perfume about her filled him with strange emotions.

On a certain night three persons were gathered about a table in a room on the third floor of the same house. Three chairs and the table and a lighted candle upon it was all the furniture. One of the persons was a huge man, dressed in black. His expression was one of sneering pride. The ends of his upturned moustache reached nearly to his mocking eyes. Another was a lady, young and beautiful, with eyes that could be round and artless, like a child's, or long and cozening, like a gypsy's, but were now keen and ambitious, like any other conspirator's. The third was a man of action, a combatant, a bold and impatient executive, breathing fire and steel. He was addressed by the others as Captain Desrolles.

This man struck the table with his fist, and said, with controlled violence:

"Tonight. Tonight as he goes to midnight mass. I am tired of the plotting that gets nowhere. I am sick of signals and ciphers and secret meetings and such *baragouin*. Let us be honest traitors. If France is to be rid of him, let us kill in the open, and not hunt with snares and traps. Tonight, I say. I back my words. My hand will do the deed. Tonight, as he goes to mass."

The lady turned upon him a cordial look. Woman, however wedded to plots, must ever thus bow to rash courage. The big man stroked his upturned moustache.

"Dear captain," he said, in a great voice, softened by habit, "this time I agree with you. Nothing is to be gained by waiting. Enough of the palace guards belong to us to make the endeavor a safe one."

"Tonight," repeated Captain Desrolles, again striking the table. "You have heard me, marquis; my hand will do the deed."

"But now," said the huge man, softly, "comes a question. Word must be sent to our partisans in the palace, and a signal agreed upon. Our stanchest men must accompany the royal carriage. At this hour what messenger can penetrate so far as the south doorway? Ribout is stationed there; once a message is placed in his hands, all will go well."

"I will send the message," said the lady.

"You, countess?" said the marquis, raising his eyebrows. "Your devotion is great, we know, but—"

"Listen!" exclaimed the lady, rising and resting her hands upon the table; "in a garret of this house lives a youth from the provinces as guileless and tender as the lambs he tended there. I have met him twice or thrice upon the stairs. I questioned him, fearing that he might dwell too near the room in which we are accustomed to meet. He is mine, if I will. He writes poems in his garret, and I think he dreams of me. He will do what I say. He shall take the message to the palace."

The marquis rose from his chair and bowed. "You did not permit me to finish my sentence, countess," he said. "I would have said: 'Your devotion is great, but your wit and charm are infinitely greater.' "

While the conspirators were thus engaged, David was polishing some lines addressed to his *amorette d'escalier*. He heard a timorous knock at his door, and opened it, with a great throb, to behold her there, panting as one in straits, with eyes wide open and artless, like a child's.

"Monsieur," she breathed, "I come to you in distress. I believe you to be good and true, and I know of no other help. How I flew through the streets among the swaggering men! Monsieur, my mother is dying. My uncle is a captain of guards in the palace of the king. Someone must fly to bring him. May I hope—"

"Mademoiselle," interrupted David, his eyes shining with the desire to do her service, "your hopes shall be my wings. Tell me how I may reach him."

The lady thrust a sealed paper into his hand.

"Go to the south gate—the south gate, mind—and say to the guards there, 'The falcon has left his nest.' They will pass you, and you will go to the south entrance to the palace. Repeat the words, and give this letter to the man who will reply 'Let him strike when he will.' This is the password, monsieur, entrusted to me by my uncle, for now when the country is disturbed and men plot against the king's life, no one without it can gain entrance to the palace grounds after nightfall. If you will, monsieur, take him this letter so that my mother may see him before she closes her eyes."

"Give it me," said David, eagerly. "But shall I let you return home through the streets alone so late? I—"

"No, no—fly. Each moment is like a precious jewel. Some time," said the lady, with eyes long and cozening, like a gypsy's, "I will try to thank you for your goodness."

The poet thrust the letter into his breast, and bounded down the stairway. The lady, when he was gone, returned to the room below.

The eloquent eyebrows of the marquis interrogated her.

"He is gone," she said, "as fleet and stupid as one of his own sheep, to deliver it."

The table shook again from the batter of Captain Desrolles's fist.

"Sacred name!" he cried; "I have left my pistols behind! I can trust no others."

"Take this," said the marquis, drawing from beneath his cloak a shining, great weapon, ornamented with carven silver. "There are none truer. But guard it closely, for it bears my arms and crest, and already I am suspected. Me, I must put many leagues between myself and Paris this night. Tomorrow must find me in my château. After you, dear countess."

The marquis puffed out the candle. The lady, well cloaked, and the two gentlemen softly descended the stairway and flowed into the crowd that roamed along the narrow pavements of the Rue Conti.

David sped. At the south gate of the king's residence a halberd was laid to his breast, but he turned its point with the words: "The falcon has left his nest."

"Pass, brother," said the guard, "and go quickly."

On the south steps of the palace they moved to seize him, but again the *mot de passe* charmed the watchers. One among them stepped forward and began: "Let him strike—" but a flurry among the guards told of a surprise. A man of keen look and soldierly stride suddenly pressed through them and seized the letter which David held in his hand. "Come with me," he said, and led him inside the great hall.

Then he tore open the letter and read it. He beckoned to a man uniformed as an officer of musketeers, who was passing. "Captain Tetreau, you will have the guards at the south entrance and the south gate arrested and confined. Place men known to be loyal in their places." To David he said: "Come with me."

He conducted him through a corridor and an anteroom into a spacious chamber, where a melancholy man, somberly dressed, sat brooding in a great, leather-covered chair. To that man he said:

"Sire, I have told you that the palace is as full of traitors and spies as a sewer is of rats. You have thought, sire, that it was my fancy. This man penetrated to your very door by their connivance. He bore a letter which I have intercepted. I have brought him here that your majesty may no longer think my zeal excessive."

"I will question him," said the king, stirring in his chair. He looked at David with heavy eyes dulled by an opaque film. The poet bent his knee.

"From where do you come?" asked the king.

"From the village of Vernoy, in the province of Eure-et-Loir, sire."

"What do you follow in Paris?"

"I—I would be a poet, sire."

"What did you in Vernoy?"

"I minded my father's flock of sheep."

The king stirred again, and the film lifted from his eyes.

"Ah! in the fields!"

"Yes, sire."

"You lived in the fields; you went out in the cool of the morning and lay among the hedges in the grass. The flock distributed itself upon the hillside; you drank of the living stream; you ate your sweet, brown bread in the shade, and you listened, doubtless, to blackbirds piping in the grove. Is not that so, shepherd?"

"It is, sire," answered David, with a sigh; "and to the bees at the flowers, and, maybe, to the grape gatherers singing on the hill."

"Yes, yes," said the king, impatiently; "maybe to them; but surely to the blackbirds. They whistled often, in the grove, did they not?"

"Nowhere, sire, so sweetly as in Eure-et-Loir. I have endeavored to express their song in some verses that I have written."

"Can you repeat those verses?" asked the king, eagerly. "A long time ago I listened to the blackbirds. It would be something better than a kingdom if one could rightly construe their song. And at night you drove the sheep to the fold and then sat, in peace and tranquillity, to your pleasant bread. Can you repeat those verses, shepherd?"

"They run this way, sire," said David, with respectful ardor:

" '*Lazy shepherd, see your lambkins*
Skip, ecstatic, on the mead;
See the firs dance in the breezes,
Hear Pan blowing at his reed.

"*Hear us calling from the tree-tops,*
See us swoop upon your flock;
Yield us wool to make our nests warm
In the branches of the—' "

"If it please your majesty," interrupted a harsh voice, "I will ask a question or two of this rhymester. There is little time to spare. I crave pardon, sire, if my anxiety for your safety offends."

"The loyalty," said the king, "of the Duke d'Aumale is too well proven to give offence." He sank into his chair, and the film came again over his eyes.

"First," said the duke, "I will read you the letter he brought:

" 'Tonight is the anniversary of the dauphin's death. If he goes, as is his custom, to midnight mass to pray for the soul of his son, the falcon will strike, at the corner of the Rue Esplanade. If this be his intention, set a red light in the upper room at the southwest corner of the palace, that the falcon may take heed.'

"Peasant," said the duke, sternly, "you have heard these words. Who gave you this message to bring?"

"My lord duke," said David, sincerely, "I will tell you. A lady gave it me. She said her mother was ill, and that this writing would fetch her uncle to her bedside. I do not know the meaning of the letter, but I will swear that she is beautiful and good."

"Describe the woman," commanded the duke, "and how you came to be her dupe."

"Describe her!" said David with a tender smile. "You would command words to perform miracles. Well, she is made of sunshine and deep shade. She is slender, like the alders, and moves with their grace. Her eyes change while you gaze into them; now round, and then half shut as the sun peeps between two clouds. When she comes, heaven is all about her; when she leaves, there is chaos and a scent of hawthorn blossoms. She came to me in the Rue Conti, number twenty-nine."

"It is the house," said the duke, turning to the king, "that we have been watching. Thanks to the poet's tongue, we have a picture of the infamous Countess Quebedaux."

"Sire and my lord duke," said David, earnestly, "I hope my poor words have done no injustice. I have looked into that lady's eyes. I will stake my life that she is an angel, letter or no letter."

The duke looked at him steadily. "I will put you to the proof," he said, slowly. "Dressed as the king, you shall, yourself, attend mass in his carriage at midnight. Do you accept the test?"

David smiled. "I have looked into her eyes," he said. "I had my proof there. Take yours how you will."

Half an hour before twelve the Duke d'Aumale, with his own hands, set a red lamp in a southwest window of the palace. At ten minutes to the hour, David, leaning on his arm, dressed as the king, from top to toe, with his head bowed in his cloak, walked slowly from the royal apartments to the waiting carriage. The duke assisted him inside and closed the door. The carriage whirled away along its route to the cathedral.

On the *qui vive* in a house at the corner of the Rue Esplanade was Captain Tetreau with twenty men, ready to pounce upon the conspirators when they should appear.

But it seemed that, for some reason, the plotters had slightly altered their plans. When the royal carriage had reached the Rue Christopher, one square nearer than the Rue Esplanade, forth from it burst Captain Desrolles, with his band of would-be regicides, and assailed the equipage. The guards upon the carriage, though surprised at the premature attack, descended and fought valiantly. The noise of conflict attracted the force of Captain Tetreau, and they came pelting down the street to the rescue. But, in the meantime, the desperate Desrolles had torn open the door of the king's carriage, thrust his weapon against the body of the dark figure inside, and fired.

Now, with loyal reinforcements at hand, the street rang with cries and the rasp of steel, but the frightened horses had dashed away. Upon the cushions lay the dead body of the poor mock king and poet, slain by a ball from the pistol of Monseigneur, the Marquis de Beaupertuys.

THE MAIN ROAD

Three leagues, then, the road ran, and turned into a puzzle. It joined with another and a larger road at right angles. David stood, uncertain, for a while, and then sat himself to rest upon its side.

Whither those roads led he knew not. Either way there seemed to lie a great world full of chance and peril. And then, sitting there, his eye fell upon a bright star, one that he and Yvonne had named for theirs. That set him thinking of Yvonne, and he wondered if he had not been too hasty. Why should he leave her and his home because a few hot words had come between them? Was love so brittle a thing that jealousy, the very proof of it, could break it? Mornings always brought a cure for the little heartaches of evening. There was yet time for him to return home without anyone in the sweetly sleeping village of Vernoy being the wiser. His heart was Yvonne's; there where he had lived always he could write his poems and find his happiness.

David rose, and shook off his unrest and the wild mood that had tempted him. He set his face steadfastly back along the road he had come. By the time he had retravelled the road to Vernoy, his desire to rove was gone. He passed the sheepfold, and the sheep scurried, with a drumming flutter, at his late footsteps, warming his heart by the homely sound. He crept without noise into his little room and lay there, thankful that his feet had escaped the distress of new roads that night.

How well he knew woman's heart! The next evening Yvonne was at the well in the road where the young congregated in order that the *curé* might have business. The corner of her eye was engaged in a search for David, albeit her set mouth seemed unrelenting. He saw the look; braved the mouth, drew from it a recantation and, later, a kiss as they walked homeward together.

Three months afterward they were married. David's father was shrewd and prosperous. He gave them a wedding that was heard of three leagues away. Both the young people were favorites in the village. There was a procession in the streets, a dance on the green; they had the marionettes and a tumbler out from Dreux to delight the guests.

Then a year, and David's father died. The sheep and the cottage descended to him. He already had the seemliest wife in the village. Yvonne's milk pails and her brass kettles were bright—*ouf*! they blinded you in the sun when you passed that way. But you must keep your eyes upon her yard, for her flower beds were so neat and gay they restored to you your sight. And you might hear her sing, aye, as far as the double chestnut tree above Père Gruneau's blacksmith forge.

But a day came when David drew out paper from a long-shut drawer, and began to bite the end of a pencil. Spring had come again and touched his heart. Poet he must have been, for now Yvonne was well-nigh forgotten. This fine new loveliness of earth held him with its witchery and grace. The perfume from her woods and meadows stirred him strangely. Daily had he gone forth with his flock, and brought it safe at night. But now he stretched himself under the hedge and pieced words together on his bits of paper. The sheep strayed, and the wolves, perceiving that difficult poems make easy mutton, ventured from the woods and stole his lambs.

David's stock of poems grew larger and his flock smaller. Yvonne's nose and temper waxed sharp and her talk blunt. Her pans and kettles grew dull, but her eyes had caught their flash. She pointed out to the poet that his neglect was reducing the flock and bringing woe upon the household. David hired a boy to guard the sheep, locked himself in the little room in the top of the cottage, and wrote more poems. The boy, being a poet by nature, but not furnished with an outlet in the way of writing, spent his time in slumber. The wolves lost no time in discovering that poetry and sleep are practically the same; so the flock steadily grew smaller. Yvonne's ill temper increased at an equal rate. Sometimes she would stand in the yard and rail at David through his high window. Then you could hear her as far as the double chestnut tree above Père Gruneau's blacksmith forge.

M. Papineau, the kind, wise, meddling old notary, saw this, as he saw everything at which his nose pointed. He went to David, fortified himself with a great pinch of snuff, and said:

"Friend Mignot, I affixed the seal upon the marriage certificate of your father. It would distress me to be obliged to attest a paper signifying the bankruptcy of his son. But that is what you are coming to. I speak as an old friend. Now, listen to what I have to say. You have your heart set, I perceive, upon poetry. At Dreux, I have a friend, one Monsieur Bril—Georges Bril. He lives in a little cleared space in a houseful of books. He is a learned man; he visits Paris each year; he himself has written books. He will tell you when the catacombs were made, how they found out the names of the stars, and why the plover has a long bill. The meaning and the form of poetry is to him as intelligent as the baa of a sheep is to you. I will give you a letter to him, and you shall take him your poems and let him read them. Then you will know if you shall write more, or give your attention to your wife and business."

"Write the letter," said David, "I am sorry you did not speak of this sooner."

At sunrise the next morning he was on the road to Dreux with the precious roll of poems under his arm. At noon he wiped the dust from his feet at the door of Monsieur Bril. That learned man broke the seal of M. Papineau's letter, and sucked up its contents through his gleaming spectacles as the sun draws water. He took David inside to his study and sat him down upon a little island beat upon by a sea of books.

Monsieur Bril had a conscience. He flinched not even at a mass of manuscript the thickness of a finger length and rolled to an incorrigible curve. He broke the back of the roll against his knee and began to read. He slighted nothing; he bored into the lump as a worm into a nut, seeking for a kernel.

Meanwhile, David sat, marooned, trembling in the spray of so much literature. It roared in his ears. He held no chart or compass for voyaging in that sea. Half the world, he thought, must be writing books.

Monsieur Bril bored to the last page of the poems. Then he took off his spectacles and wiped them with his handkerchief.

"My old friend, Papineau, is well?" he asked.

"In the best of health," said David.

"How many sheep have you, Monsieur Mignot?"

"Three hundred and nine, when I counted them yesterday. The flock has had ill fortune. To that number it has decreased from eight hundred and fifty."

"You have a wife and a home, and lived in comfort. The sheep brought you plenty. You went into the fields with them and lived in the keen air and ate the sweet bread of contentment. You had but to be vigilant and recline there upon nature's breast, listening to the whistle of the blackbirds in the grove. Am I right thus far?"

"It was so," said David.

"I have read all your verses," continued Monsieur Bril, his eyes wandering about his sea of books as if he conned the horizon for a sail. "Look yonder, through that window, Monsieur Mignot; tell me what you see in that tree."

"I see a crow," said David, looking.

"There is a bird," said Monsieur Bril, "that shall assist me where I am disposed to shirk a duty. You know that bird, Monsieur Mignot; he is the philosopher of the air. He is happy through submission to his lot. None so merry or full-crawed as he with his whimsical eye and rollicking step. The fields yield him what he desires. He never grieves that his plumage is not gay, like the oriole's. And you have heard, Monsieur Mignot, the notes that nature has given him? Is the nightingale any happier, do you think?"

David rose to his feet. The crow cawed harshly from his tree.

"I thank you, Monsieur Bril," he said, slowly. "There was not, then, one nightingale note among all those croaks?"

"I could not have missed it," said Monsieur Bril, with a sigh. "I read every word. Live your poetry, man; do not try to write it anymore."

"I thank you," said David, again. "And now I will be going back to my sheep."

"If you would dine with me," said the man of books, "and overlook the smart of it, I will give you reasons at length."

"No," said the poet, "I must be back in the fields cawing at my sheep."

Back along the road to Vernoy he trudged with his poems under his arm. When he reached his village he turned into the shop of one

Zeigler, a Jew out of Armenia, who sold anything that came to his hand.

"Friend," said David, "wolves from the forest harass my sheep on the hills. I must purchase firearms to protect them. What have you?"

"A bad day, this, for me, friend Mignot," said Zeigler, spreading his hands, "for I perceive that I must sell you a weapon that will not fetch a tenth of its value. Only last week I bought from a peddler a wagon full of goods that he procured at a sale by a *commissionaire* of the crown. The sale was of the château and belongings of a great lord—I know not his title—who has been banished for conspiracy against the king. There are some choice firearms in the lot. This pistol—oh, a weapon fit for a prince!—it shall be only forty francs to you, friend Mignot—if I lose ten by the sale. But perhaps an arquebuse—"

"This will do," said David, throwing the money on the counter. "Is it charged?"

"I will charge it," said Zeigler. "And, for ten francs more, add a store of powder and ball."

David laid his pistol under his coat and walked to his cottage. Yvonne was not there. Of late she had taken to gadding much among the neighbors. But a fire was glowing in the kitchen stove. David opened the door of it and thrust his poems in upon the coals. As they blazed up they made a singing, harsh sound in the flue.

"The song of the crow!" said the poet.

He went up to his attic room and closed the door. So quiet was the village that a score of people heard the roar of the great pistol. They flocked thither, and up the stairs where the smoke, issuing, drew their notice.

The men laid the body of the poet upon his bed, awkwardly arranging it to conceal the torn plumage of the poor black crow. The women chattered in a luxury of zealous pity. Some of them ran to tell Yvonne.

M. Papineau, whose nose had brought him there among the first, picked up the weapon and ran his eye over its silver mountings with a mingled air of connoisseurship and grief.

"The arms," he explained, aside, to the *curé,* "and crest of Monseigneur, the Marquis de Beaupertuys."

AFTERWORD

A LINGERING AFTERGLOW

This afterword has been adapted from O. Henry: The Legendary Life of William S. Porter *by Richard O'Connor, published in 1970. A native of Ireland, O'Connor was the author of more than 60 books, including several biographies of literary figures.*

ON THE Big Board of Literature, O. Henry's stock has never been lower. It is not even listed, in fact, by the more fashionable speculators. If he were alive and practicing today, and if his style were unchanged, it is difficult to imagine where his stories would be published.

There is nothing odd, of course, about the violent fluctuations of a man's literary reputation. The Brahmins of literary criticism are constantly reassessing, revising, reviving some writers and consigning others to oblivion. The English professors and creative-writing teachers, too, dig up the usable past. But none of the resurrecters has been brave or foolish enough to attempt a restoration of O. Henry.

Both his strengths and weaknesses as a writer are held in contempt—his cleverness and his sentimentality, his mastery of technique, his facility at constructing plots, his trick endings, his hyperbolic humor. All his devices are exactly what young writers are told to shun. At best, he is regarded as an artifact of the semiliterate early-century years when the two-penny newspapers and the dime magazines were the conveyers of popular culture. At worst, perhaps, he is regarded as a hack, an opinion that O. Henry would have shared. Overpraise from the critics of his own day, such as comparisons with Poe or Maupassant, usually annoyed him; he dealt with editors, whom he depended upon to evaluate the tastes of the reading public; all others were to him merely loafers in the marketplace.

At the time of his death, in fact, O. Henry in this country, after a career of only eight productive years, was regarded as a burned-out star in comparison with Jack London, Willa Cather, Edith Wharton, Henry James, and others of more prominent reputation. In popular esteem, however, he rose higher than ever in the dozen years after his death, and his work was held up for adoration by such appraisers of contemporary culture as Christopher Morley, Alexander Woollcott and Carl Van Doren, the latter writing that "no writer in the language seems clever immediately after one has been reading O. Henry." Collected volumes of O. Henry were a staple in middle-class American homes; any library of as many as 20 books was almost certain to include his work. No other short-story writer except Rudyard Kipling sold better in hard cover than O. Henry in the decade following his death in 1910. More than 5 million copies of his books were sold in the United States. During that period he also became ever more popular abroad, particularly in England, where he was heralded by Hugh Walpole as "the father of this new American literature." And he was translated into French, German, Russian, Spanish, Swedish, Japanese, and Norwegian. He appealed particularly to the Russians, both before and after the Revolution, and was regarded as the founder of a new literary school, as a writer to be ranked with Chekhov and Turgenev.

To American readers before and just after World War I, his collected works—O. Henry must be taken in toto or not at all—constituted the body of a revealed myth, a concept of themselves they accepted and liked. His optimism about the eventual success of the American experiment, always implicit even when he described the inequities and injustices of the social system, exactly suited the national mood.

It may seem incredible to those who associate O. Henry only with literary entertainment of the more meretricious sort, but on the popular level he was a social commentator of considerable impact. In *Postscript to Yesterday,* the late Lloyd Morris discussed most perceptively O. Henry's penetration of the American scene. "He turned away from the prosperous levels of society, so popular at the time as a subject for fiction. He ignored the Four Hundred to deal with the four million. This choice was more the result of his previous misfortunes than of any interest in social reform, but its net effect was to produce an optimistic social myth. His stories mainly turned on the fortunes of humble folk, shopgirls and clerks and mechanics—a group that, on the whole, had been anonymous and inarticulate in American life, and absent from American fiction. They formed the group that a later generation was to describe as 'the little people,' and that politicians would aggregate as the 'forgotten man' and 'common man.' In the rapid urbanization and industrialization of American life, their numbers were constantly increasing. They were the vast, hard-pressed, hard-working lower middle class of the great cities, to whom the present was usually precarious and the future equivocal.

"It was O. Henry's special gift to portray them as they saw themselves. They did not consider themselves proletarians, victims of an exploiting social order, tragic subjects for rescue or salvage. Although this interpretation of their condition might be made by political radicals and social reformers, by the muckraking journalists and the young school of writers, it was not acceptable to them. Did not the old tradition of American life hold out the assurance that they might rise in the social circle? Did not the American Federation of Labor teach that every skilled worker might, in time, become a member of the bourgeoisie? However hard pressed, they were still hopeful.

O. Henry was very much a part of that lower middle class himself and an earnest subscriber to its moral view. Until the last years of his life he had never earned more than $25 a week, and it has usually been money that fixes an American's social position. It was the bank clerk speaking when Al Jennings urged him to call the lady blackmailer's bluff, and O. Henry replied, "I have much to lose. I don't look at things as you do." And it was the bank clerk, not the world-famous writer he had become, who devoted so much thought and energy to concealing the shame of having been convicted as an embezzler.

Russian Communism's approval of him as a proletarian writer is, of course, a misapprehension. (Russian publishing figures are not readily obtainable, but the state printing presses turned out 94 printings of his works between 1920 and 1945, for a total of 1,403,500 copies. In 1953, for instance, the Soviet Union published 900,000 copies of American writers' books, and of these, 225,000 were O. Henry's, exactly one-fourth of the total output. Deming Brown, the American expert on such matters, has written that "one may speculate on the motivation of the Communist Party" in keeping O. Henry alive in Russia, but "it is clear that, despite years of constant indoctrination, Russian readers still like to seek release in a good yarn.") He did attack the abuses of capitalism, but that was hardly a radical social or political stance to assume. Nevertheless, as Lloyd Morris has written, "his indictment, though it indicated general social sympathies which recommended him to the reformers, implied no such social skepticism as other young writers were beginning to express. The workers of his stories had confidence in their future, and he appeared to share it. He gave the old dogmas a new sanction in terms of the commonplace. His myth was the one which most Americans lived by, and wanted to believe. In an age of wealth for the few and poverty for the many, it asserted that all things were still possible to the common man, and that most of them would turn out to be good."

There was, in fact, something for everyone in O. Henry's stories about the urban masses. "Social reformers," Morris continues, "counted him sympathetic to their aims. Apologists for an expanding capitalism found their complacency reinforced by his optimism; and, because he seemed to be a conservative, they were quite willing to praise him for being a democrat. The class about whom he wrote liked him for shedding on their existence a light of romance."

The range of his admiring readership was indicated by an incident that occurred in the fall of 1906 outside a bookshop in Cambridge, Massachusetts, just off the Harvard Yard. In the window was a display of O. Henry's recent works. A Harvard freshman and an elderly bearded gentleman, though strangers, began excitedly discussing the author and his stories. It developed that both considered O. Henry their favorite writer. The older man was William James, the famed psychologist and philosopher. The freshman was John Reed, who was to become a radical prophet, author of *Ten Days That Shook the World,* and one of the few Americans buried under the Kremlin wall.

Shortly after his death, a commentator, writing in the New York *Times,* rather neatly defined O. Henry as "the Bret Harte of the City," adding that "his style was perfect; it was the man himself: nervous, picturesque, quick, supple, with easy, inevitable metaphors." There was something of Bret Harte in the humanism, the gallant humor, the technique of the surprise twists, the mechanism of his plotting. As Bret Harte was the literary discoverer of the West for the ordinary reader,

O. Henry was the explorer of the cityscape. He pictured New York as the outlanders wanted to see it, the thundering metropolis of "four million mysterious strangers," the magical place they would see from the upper deck of a rubberneck bus or more likely through someone else's imagination. To Van Wyck Brooks he "shared Dickens's vision of a happy domesticity, sharing as well his feeling for the city streets, for the crowds and the lights of the metropolis, the night-blooming cereus unfolding its dead-white heavy-odoured petals." Brooks considered him "too hard or too soft in the wrong way," but conceded that "O. Henry was occasionally an artist, nevertheless, who escaped from the mechanical formulas of the cheap magazines, the last to vindicate William Dean Howells's belief that the 'more smiling aspects of life' were the most characteristic of America, as no doubt they had been."

A definite slippage in O. Henry's standing was to be noted in the early 1920's with writers such as Sherwood Anderson and James Branch Cabell, with their greater subtlety, already on the scene, along with the young Scott Fitzgerald and Ernest Hemingway just around the corner. In his *Prejudices: Second Series* (1920), H. L. Mencken charged O. Henry with a "smoke-room and variety show smartness" and declared that "in the whole canon of O. Henry's work you will not find a single recognizable human character; he makes Mexican brigands, Texas cowmen and New York cracksmen talk the same highly ornate Broadwayese."

A few years later the task of dismantling O. Henry as a popular idol, and perhaps more particularly as a writer to be taken seriously (as he was) in high school and college English studies, was taken up by F. L. Pattee, the literary historian. In *The Development of the American Short Story* (1923), Professor Pattee declared, "The elements of his art were not many. He knew precisely how much of the sugar of sentimentality the great average reading public must have, and how much of the pepper of sensation, and the salad dressing of romance.... But brilliant as were the possibilities of his powers, and distinctive as was his technique, his final place can never be high even among the writers of short stories. He did not take literature seriously; he was a victim of the swiftly ephemeral press. His undoubted powers were completely debauched by it. He became exclusively an entertainer, with no thought but of the moment, and no art save that which brought instant effect upon his reader. To accomplish that he would sacrifice everything, even the truth."

To much of this criticism, Prof. Eugene Current-Garcia, in his study *O. Henry* (1965), has succinctly replied that "to condemn O. Henry's stories in toto for not being realistic and serious, for depending too heavily on coincidence, and for playing to the gallery is an evasion of the critic's responsibility—unless it can be shown that these characteristics invariably result in badly written stories. This, O. Henry's severest critics have seldom been willing to do. His intention rather than his achievement has been the object of their censure."

All this scholarly and literary and academic discussion of O. Henry's work is, of course, beside the point and beyond the notice of the ordinary reader, for whom O. Henry labored. Judging by the publishing history of his collected stories—including a 1,692-page, one-volume leviathan, *The Complete Works of O. Henry*—he continues to be read for pleasure by considerable numbers of people. In this manner he is still a "live" author, as Stephen Crane and Jack London are, regardless of the changes in literary fashion.

One way of measuring his literary importance is to examine the gap that would be left in popular literature if he had been content to compound prescriptions for the rest of his life in a Greensboro drugstore. Certainly he encouraged Americans to take a gentler view of the unorganized, nonviolent criminal in such stories as "A Retrieved Reformation" and "The Cop and the Anthem." In many of his Western tales he modified the dime-novel view that the West was settled exclusively by good guys with guns and bad guys with more guns. In the collection of stories entitled *Cabbages and Kings* he provided a brilliantly lit picture of Central America in its banana-republic heyday, and of the "culture shock" provided by an American colony consisting of two murderers, an army paymaster afflicted by a shortage in his accounts, two bank presidents with similar problems, and a mysterious widow. But it was in the 140 stories with a New York background that he passed along a storyteller's heritage of continuing value to his readers. With them one can reconstruct a fairly accurate panorama of the nation's first city during those years when it was being packed by hundreds of thousands of immigrants, both from the American hinterland and from Europe.

A Lingering Afterglow

He was New York's biographer. In his stories one can grasp exactly how people lived, struggled, survived, and eventually bettered themselves in the pre-welfare state. If the city had a soul, O. Henry was the man who understood it.

Himself an outlander, he was able to merge with the ordinary people. Even better, he was able to observe the city with a fresh and sustained curiosity, illuminated by an unflagging imagination. Who but O. Henry could have conceived a conversation, as he did in one tale, between the revolving statue of the naked Diana atop Madison Square Garden and the Statue of Liberty a few miles down the bay? Or conveyed so much of the city's essence in a few sentences that preceded that lofty conversation: "Three hundred and sixty-five feet above the heated asphalt the tip-toeing symbolic deity on Manhattan pointed her vacillating arrow straight, for the time, in the direction of her exalted sister on Liberty Island. The lights of the great Garden were out; the benches in the Square were filled with sleepers.... The statue of Diana on the tower of the Garden—its constancy shown by its weathercock ways, its innocence by the coating of gold that it had acquired, its devotion to style by its single, flying scarf, its candor and artlessness by its habit of ever drawing the long bow, its metropolitanism by its posture of swift flight to catch a Harlem train—remained poised with its arrow pointed across the upper bay. Had the arrow sped truly and horizontally it would have passed fifty feet above the head of the heroic matron whose duty it is to offer a cast-ironical welcome to the oppressed of other lands."

One cannot help but wonder how much better O. Henry would have done if he had not turned out his stories in hot haste under the constant prod of creditors and obligations; if he had been able to rewrite and reconsider instead of sending off the first draft to impatient editors. But that has been the fate of many writers. O. Henry, such is his enduring charm, is as lovable for his artistic failings as he was admirable for his successes. The afterglow of that hectic eight-year career will continue to linger in the global village whose beginnings he glimpsed in brownstone New York, in a more innocent and hopeful age.